DISMANTLED HEARTS

Through it all, will love prevail?

J. HENRY

ISBN: **979-8-218-11585-2**
Printed in the United States of America
Printing 2, 2023

This book is dedicated to my family and friends who always support me. Also, want to acknowledge one of my prior employees, Ms. Janel for pushing me to finish writing my manuscript and had me make a promise to publish one day. It's been years in the making but here I am, sticking to my commitment. Likely, the first of many!

IS IT REAL?

"God, I know I messed up, but I desperately need your help right now. I'm so ashamed and this guilt is weighing me down day by day. Lord, please step in because I need some direction on what to do."

These were the words of desperation uttered from Shaniece Brown's mouth as she sobbed on her way driving home from the gym. At thirty-six years old, Shaniece felt she had everything together but at the same time her life was falling apart. She thought that once she made it to the next level in life that it would be less problematic.

She was a college graduate, now working in a career that she loved as a thriving entrepreneur.

She met the man of her dreams and had recently gotten engaged.

She was a great person all-around: a loving single mother, a dedicated Christian, a genuine friend, and an inspiration to others.

She knew there were some problems she had brought on herself, but some things she felt she just didn't deserve.

* * * * * *

"Hey, babe, I'm going to be late again tonight."

Shaniece was used to hearing those very words from Derek, her fiancé, so she stuck to her same reply.

"Okay, babe. Do you want me to wait up for you?" she asked while rolling her eyes and shaking her head like she had done many times before.

"No, you don't have to. I have an important deadline to meet by tomorrow afternoon and still have a lot of work to do here at the office," Derek told her.

"Okay, I'll see you in the morning," she replied in a disappointing voice that only she was aware of.

"Alright, I love you. I'll be home later."

Shaniece met Derek, a thirty-seven-year-old entrepreneur, a year ago at a business networking event. He had seen her from across the room, laughing and conversing with a group of women. Derek, like most of the other men at the event, was immediately mesmerized by how her summer-bronzed caramel skin lit up the room. Her skin was offset by her dark blue pantsuit that indicated she was dressed to impress, but from Derek's view she didn't have to put in much effort. Her personality also drew him in, much like it had attracted others to hear what she had to say. She appeared she was in her element and had this quiet confidence about her that he noticed without even speaking to her. However, Shaniece never noticed Derek's attempts to get her attention. He would walk by and stand idle and close to whatever space she was in, but every time he tried to approach her, someone else would walk up and lose his opportunity.

Eventually, Shaniece went into the lobby to regroup and nurse a migraine before discussing business for the millionth time. She wanted to leave, but the networking opportunities were just too good to pass up. After waiting for a while, Derek noticed that Shaniece was sitting in the lobby alone. He finally had her to himself, so he walked over and cleared his throat as he began to speak.

"Hello, my name is Derek," he stated as he stuck out his hand. Shaniece looked up from where she was seated. She thought the coast was clear but mustered up a partial smile. She tucked her long chestnut brown locks behind her ears, put on her game face, jumped into business mode, and greeted him with a firm handshake in return.

"Hello, my name is Shaniece," she stated as the two released hands. She stood up to continue the conversation, asking him about what he did for a career. Derek chuckled and smiled because he picked up on her switch to what seemed to be her networking routine. He saw her from across the room and noticed her beauty but now that they were face-to-face, he was intrigued by how naturally stunning she was. Her deep brown slanted eyes, infectious smile and plump lips glossed with a soft pink tint were an instant attraction to him. He observed earlier how her fitted pantsuit complimented her slender waist and it was quite obvious she was racking squats up at the gym faithfully. He didn't want to seduce her with his eyes and wanted to be a real gentleman, but he couldn't help but notice. He smiled gradually without giving it away.

"I own a consulting firm. Pretty much what my team does is serve as the liaison between organizations and external parties. We write, negotiate, and monitor business agreements and make sure all parties follow and fulfill contractual obligations," he answered. Shaniece smiled and nodded her head. She was quite impressed with his business and how he represented himself at this point.

"Oh, okay -- that's great!" Shaniece wanted to focus solely on being a professional, and she typically would ask more questions about someone's business at these kinds of events. However, she was a little nervous talking to Derek. She couldn't help but admire how good-looking he was. The entire time Derek was speaking, Shaniece noticed his pearly white teeth and gorgeous smile. She took note of his cocoa complected skin tone, close-cut waves, well-trimmed beard, athletic stature, and suit game. She was five foot six with stiletto heels on and had to look up at him, so she predicted he was maybe six foot three or six four. This man was the true definition of tall, dark, and handsome.

"What about yourself?" he asked in return, taking advantage of the silent moment, picking up on Shaniece checking him out.

"Oh, I own a recruitment agency. Basically, I assist employers with hiring the right talent to fill vacant positions within their organizations."

After several minutes, they both exchanged more details about their businesses. Derek was in awe of Shaniece's exuded confidence, professionalism, and beauty, while Shaniece was stunned by his intellect, looks, and genuine interest in what she had to say. Shaniece had met several men with white collar professions, and many tried pursuing her, but she always kept it strictly professional and let them down gently. What she liked about Derek was that he wasn't coming on too strong and listened without gawking at her. At least that's how he made her feel and she respected that.

"Maybe we could help each other out business-wise. How about we exchange cards and catch up sometime next week?" Derek asked.

Shaniece agreed. They both knew there wasn't much of a business connection but went along with the charade. Derek called a few days later and asked Shaniece out for lunch, and the two became inseparable.

* * * * * *

Derek's parents had been married for forty plus years, so he respected his father's point of view on love and relationships. His dad showed him how a man should treat a woman by treating his mom like the queen she was. His older brother, Jeffrey, followed his father footsteps and married Morgan, his college sweetheart. However, Derek fell off track somewhere. Derek wanted to do things on his own terms, so he overlooked marriage and focused more on his career. Derek figured that when he was ready to settle down, the right woman would come along. Every woman he dated he always found something that turned him off and didn't stick around. When he met Shaniece, something overcame him that he had never felt before. He didn't hide his feelings and couldn't see life without her. She was different from any other woman he dated in the past. Part of the reason was that she was already working on her own career and excelling in it. The women he was used to were just pretty faces with no real-life goals other than modeling. At first, none of Derek's friends or family believed that he would go all the way and end up marrying Shaniece. His family loved her and saw her as the perfect woman for him but knew enough about Derek's past to know that he would always be a bachelor. Derek knew he didn't have to prove anything to anyone but still wanted to prove that he was serious this time around.

* * * * * *

After six months of dating, Shaniece and Derek were engaged. Derek's father played a big part in him proposing to Shaniece early on. Just about every Sunday, Derek would go out fishing or golfing for one to two hours with his father. Somehow, the conversation each week always led to his father saying that Derek needed to overcome his commitment issues and truly settle down. His father would tell him:

"I'm proud that you made the first step with committing. Now I just want to see you take the leap and marry that girl." Eventually, Derek acted on impulse, went out bought a ring, and proposed.

When he did, Shaniece was surprised by the timing. Still, the proposal didn't seem too out of the ordinary considering how quickly their relationship progressed. By their second week of dating, Derek introduced her to his family. Within two months, he had confessed his love for her. The third month, they went away to a tropical island together for one of his college buddies' weddings and met his friends. He started talking about babies four months in, and right after the engagement, he moved in.

Shaniece was so caught up in the hype that she failed to ignore some red flags. Derek told her early on that he hadn't been in a committed relationship for years, and he was really stepping out on a limb with her. He was finally ready to settle down and start a family but with the right woman. He showed Shaniece through his actions that he wanted to make it work and was serious about her. She was big on people proving themselves, and Derek was definitely doing so. Regardless, she was so blinded by his efforts that she was willing to become involved with someone who had become unfamiliar with commitment. On top of that, Derek was a charmer and essentially the type of man that every woman would want: he was good-looking, highly educated, and financially secure with a promising start-up. Because of Derek's attributes, she always felt like she needed to be in competition with other women when it came to dating Derek even though she was highly self-confident. She made sure to work out four to five times during the week and started wearing eyeliner and lipstick so that he would continue to find her appealing and sexy. She ultimately became obsessed with keeping herself perfect just to keep him interested.

Beyond the red flags, Shaniece felt things were moving a little fast but agreed to marry Derek because she did love him. However, she wasn't in love with him yet; she just figured that by the time they got married, she would be. Another six months passed, and she was starting to get concerned because her feelings didn't change. He was the perfect gentleman, and she could very well see her future with him, but she was disappointed in herself at the same time. After her last major heartbreak and the minor relationships that came after it, she wanted to do things differently the next time she got into a real relationship. She didn't want to shack up and wanted to wait until marriage for sex. Yet, when Derek entered the picture, she broke those vows to herself and to God. She looked back on her past relationships and realized she was repeating the same trend. Her love for Derek was there but not in the way she wanted -- all because she didn't follow her standards from the start.

I NEED HELP

"Mom, are you on your way home? It's nothing here to eat, and I'm starving," Justin, Shaniece's fifteen-year-old son, asked over the phone. It seemed like Justin called every day at the same time asking what was for dinner. Shaniece was on her way back from the gym. She loved when she got a good workout in after work. She could relieve a lot of stress that way, but her son was about to stress her out all over again.

"Justin, there's leftover chicken stir fry from last night. Why can't you eat that?"

"Mom, seriously? Leftovers? You know I don't eat leftovers. Can I just DoorDash a pizza or something before you get home?" Shaniece sighed.

"I really have you spoiled. Go ahead and order something; I'll see you when I get there."

* * * * * *

After being stuck in traffic for what seemed like forever, Shaniece pulled up forty minutes later. She grabbed her gym bag out the trunk and entered the house.

"Hey, I'm home, son," she yelled out. Justin walked down the steps chomping down on a slice of pepperoni pizza.

"Hey, Mom…the pizza man just left. Good looking out. You the best!" he stated with his mouth full.

"Justin, what I tell you about eating with food in your mouth? It's so disgusting." She walked past him to go up the stairs to her room. Nothing frustrated her more than when Justin didn't use his manners.

Shaniece recently enrolled Justin at a prestigious private school, where he was currently a freshman. Justin was what Shaniece called a "triple threat" when it came to academics and extracurricular activities. She noticed how gifted he was when he was just a child, in and outside of school. When he was in elementary school, teachers would always tell her how bright he was. She thought that was something that they told all parents, especially since she paid tuition. She quickly found out what they meant when she realized he needed minimal homework help and would consistently make honor roll. *When he was just five, she noticed he had a talent for drawing. She would place objects in front of him to draw and the final results were astonishing. At the age of ten, he revealed his amazing singing voice in a school play and Shaniece nearly cried.*

Shaniece wanted Justin to pursue both of these talents, but he always told her they weren't his passion: skateboarding was. Once or twice a month, he participated in different skate competitions and repeatedly placed first or second. Although she wasn't thrilled about his passion for skateboarding, she still stood by him and didn't mind investing her time and money into the sport. After all, she realized it was an outlet for him.

Shaniece had been through some things, but she was most heartbroken when Justin started experiencing major behavioral issues between ages eleven and fourteen. She noticed his behavior change a few weeks after attending an open house at his school. *All his friends had both parents sitting with them and for Justin it was just him and Shaniece as always. Shaniece knew the root cause was due to his father's absence. She knew she couldn't change the situation and make his father come back around. He walked away from them both when Justin was nine and because Shaniece refused to be with him, he took his feelings out on their son and now he's suffering because of his selfishness.*

Justin became angrier as the years went by, and Shaniece didn't know how to handle Justin's erratic behavior. After dealing with years of multiple suspensions, an expulsion, anger, and violent outbursts,

Shaniece needed a quick fix to escape her reality and turned to alcohol for comfort. It got to the point where she would drink a glass or two for breakfast before heading out to work. *She kept this facade up like everything was all good in her life when on the inside she was drowning.* Over time, she fell into a state of depression, and it took over her life for a while. She would lock herself in the house for entire weekends and wouldn't answer anyone. Her mother really became concerned when she didn't answer her phone or show up for planned family dinners. She was a trooper who overcame many battles, but when it came to her son hurting, there was nothing left for her to do but break. In an attempt to pull herself together, she took handling Justin's behavior into her own hands. She tried old-fashioned whippings, timeouts, taking away electronics, and even therapy, but none of those methods worked. She received advice from doctors who tried telling her to put him on medication, but she didn't want to follow that option without at least exploring every other option possible. As a last resort, she went to the House of the Lord for help.

At the time, Shaniece was attending a church that she had been going to for quite a while but wasn't officially a member. She believed in God and the power of prayer but felt like her prayers weren't being answered. One Sunday, the preacher did an altar call, and both she and Justin walked up without hesitation. An older woman dressed in all black with a voluminous hat approached them with her hands outstretched and went into immediate prayer. It was like the woman could sense the desperation and exhaustion on Shaniece's face and felt bad for her or maybe could've related to her situation as a single mother. During the prayer, Shaniece and Justin began crying and saying, "Amen! Amen! Yes, Lord!" repeating after the woman. When they were tired out, the woman in black kept going and wouldn't let them go. After several minutes, the lady finally released them both and handed Shaniece some tissues. Shaniece remembered just about every word the woman uttered and felt like a big burden had been lifted off of her. As she was walking out the church doors, Shaniece grabbed Justin and held him tight until she felt the same burden lift off of him too. Thereafter, when Justin was fourteen, he was given a diagnosis of attention-deficit hyperactivity disorder and intermittent explosive disorder, Shaniece finally gave in and went along with the medications the therapists recommended for him years ago. She ran out of options and changing schools each year had become too exhausting. Still, she gained relief from all of the turmoil caused by Justin's behavior, and life began to get better again.

"Can you sign these papers for school?" Justin asked.

"Just leave them on the table, and I'll get to them," she told him from the top of the stairs.

Shaniece had a difficult day at work and wanted nothing more than to take a shower and go to bed. She knew Derek wasn't going to be home anytime soon, so she was looking forward to an early night. Even with her feelings of exhaustion, she still wanted to make time for her son. She read in an article that even if you lead a busy life that your children would appreciate at least ten minutes of your time each day. No matter how hectic her days were she still made time for her son even if some days it was only for ten minutes. "Knock, knock!" Shaniece said as she barely cracked his door open to enter his room.

"Come in!" he blurted over his Beethoven music that was playing from the laptop on his desk. Justin learned through therapy that music was his true escape; it had helped him a lot over the years. He could feel his mother's eyes burning through his back, so he turned around in his computer chair and gave Shaniece his undivided attention after turning his music down.

"I went downstairs and signed those papers. They'll be on the table when you're ready to get them."

"Thanks, Mom." Justin picked up his math book and started thumbing through a few of the pages.

"Also…how do you think you did on your math test?" Shaniece asked as she laid across his bed. Justin knew his mom was going to start talking about school at some point. He had no choice but to do well because his mom was obsessed about him getting a good education, especially after the setbacks he encountered during the last few years.

"I know I passed it. It was one question that I struggled with so I may get some points off for that." She saw the look on his face that he wasn't feeling the conversation, so she decided to change course.

"That's good. You're such a smart kid."

"Mom, would you please stop calling me a kid?" he expressed, rolling his eyes and planting his face in his book. She couldn't do anything but laugh because he looked like he was about to die.

"I'm sorry. Geesh." She shook her head.

"Is Derek working late again?" Justin didn't want to look his mom in the eyes when he asked because last time he mentioned it, she put her head down, almost ashamed to answer. Justin was well aware of how Derek hadn't been coming home at a decent time. He would run into Derek in the mornings when he went out to catch the bus, but most evenings, Derek wasn't there to eat dinner with them. The most Justin ever saw him was on weekends. Justin knew Derek was working on a big project at work, but his concern was more for his mom. She was either in his room harassing him about school or on her laptop working after she had already put in a ten-to-twelve-hour shift. She was lonely and didn't have much of a social life without Derek around. She was like a lost puppy. In the past, Shaniece and Derek would go out for dinner sometimes, play board games together, and occasionally go out to business networking events. However, whenever Derek was gone, Justin noticed his mom would step out every now and then after work but not much to declare as having a life.

Justin liked Derek, and their relationship started off great but became even better as time progressed. He admired Derek because he looked successful when he first got to know him. Justin was impressed by his status as well as his determination and respected him for that. Derek also treated Justin as if he was his son, and he spoiled him every chance he got. There was even a time Shaniece had to stop Derek from buying Justin what he wanted because she taught her son that he had to work and that nothing came easy. As a result, Justin ended up working for most of the expensive things he had in some way, but when

Derek came into his life, he had become comfortable with getting something for nothing.

"Yes, he will be late and won't be here for dinner again tonight. You know Derek's a hard worker." She moved to get off his bed and started making her way to the door. Justin just shook his head and agreed with whatever his mother believed. He changed the direction of the conversation to focus on himself.

"Soooo, Moooommmm, if I get at least a ninety-five on my test, can I get the new Jordans?" he asked with a big smile on his face.

"We'll see," she told him as she was walking out the door. She was beginning to feel down about Justin mentioning Derek, but she didn't want him to see her start tearing up.

"But Mom...," Justin repeated over and over as he put down his book and made his way toward the door following behind her. Shaniece slammed his door, almost hitting his foot and rushed into the hallway to get away from him. The tears were streaming out of her eyes now, but Justin was right on her heels following her foot to foot. She managed to get into the bathroom in her bedroom and close the door.

"Leave me alone, Justin. I said we'll see. If you keep harassing me, then 'we'll see' will turn into 'no,'" Shaniece snapped. He finally called it quits and walked back into his room. Shaniece knew he was gone when she heard the Beethoven music return to its former higher volume.

"Lord, it's me again. Please help! I fell into the trap of doing things my way, and I regret it. This burden is starting to take a toll on me and I need your guidance on how to handle this situation." Shaniece pleaded as she looked into the bathroom mirror. While wiping her eyes with the backs of her hands, she began pacing the floor back and forth awaiting any type of whisper from God on what to do next. She sat in the bathroom for close to twenty minutes desperately crying out. She knew she had messed up, and the guilt from her mistake was violating her conscience. She didn't want to lose her man, her business, or even her reputation, and she knew all of it was on the line. She started questioning if her success had changed her as a person and hoped that

11

wasn't the case. She had morals and values, and no amount of money was worth jeopardizing that. She exited the bathroom frustrated because she didn't get a revelation. She decided to go to bed and seek him again in the morning. She wasn't going to stop because she had shame in her heart that needed to be released and knew God would be the only one to help her on what to do.

CAN'T RESIST

At 4 a.m., the streetlights were glaring through the blinds in the bedroom. Shaniece was sleeping soundly when she heard a familiar deep voice speaking to her.

"Good morning, beautiful," Derek whispered to Shaniece as she was turning over.

"Did my alarm go off? What time is it?" She sat up quickly with her eyes half-way opened.

"No, it's four in the morning; you're good," he said quietly as he chuckled.

"Why are you up this early?" she asked in a raspy voice, laying her head back down.

"I'm getting in the bed now. Had to do a few things to prepare for this meeting," he told her. Derek had a meeting later with one of the largest corporations in the country. He had met with large players before but gaining this contract would give his business the break it needed to place him at the next level.

"Okay…I love you. I'm going…" Shaniece placed the pillow over her head and fell back into a deep sleep before she could finish her sentence. Her tight abs and perky breasts turned Derek on in every way. She looked completely flawless sleeping next to him in nothing but her panties on. It had been a while since he last made love to her, but after hearing the heavy snoring resume from when he entered the room, he decided to let her be.

* * * * * *

"Aww, maaaannnn…it's time to get up already," Shaniece complained as she stretched her arms above her head and yawned one final time before waking completely up. Dawn had finally come around, and the streetlights had turned into rays of sun shining through the windows.

"Good morning again, beautiful!" Derek greeted her with a smile as he walked over to the bed from the computer desk.

"Mmmm…good morning," Shaniece answered.

"I missed you so much," he uttered as he laid down next to her with just his boxers on. "I know these last few months have been hectic with work and all. I know that I haven't been home, but after a few weeks' things will finally go back to normal. I promise."

Shaniece never told Derek how she felt about him coming in late nights, so she dealt with it. She didn't want to contradict herself because if she ever ran into a similar situation with her business, she wouldn't want to seem like a hypocrite.

"I missed you too…I can't wait until we can spend more time together," she told him as she drew back the sheets from her lower body and got up to go into the bathroom.

Derek went to his desk to wrap up his presentation and laid back across the bed in his boxers and durag with his hands behind his head. He turned his head and stared at Shaniece through the doorway of the bathroom while she brushed her teeth and washed her face. He licked his lips slowly as he watched the side view of her tight abs and firm butt in her hot pink panties. He felt like the luckiest guy in the world to have a woman who was successful, smart, understanding, committed, and beautiful. He knew that she had been dealing with him and his late hours and didn't want to lose her. For the first time in his life, he was willing to trade it all just to be with her. He loved his work but wanted to start making sacrifices for his relationship the same way he did with his business. Shaniece walked out the bathroom, now having put on a satin robe that tightly gripped her body and entered the closet.

"Blue or tan today?" she asked as she held up two suits in front of him.

"Definitely blue," Derek stated as he got off the bed, walked up to her, and took both of them from her hands. Shaniece scoffed as he hung them back into the closet. He picked her up, carried her over to the bed, and set her down. Her bobby pinned bun unraveled and her chestnut brown locks flowed to her shoulders.

"Babe, don't you have to be to work soon?" she inquired playfully as she tried to place her hair back into a bun.

"I'm not worrying about work right now. I'm more concerned about what's under this robe." Shaniece laughed and stopped with the questions because she knew what time it was. Derek untied the belt of her robe and, for a few seconds, admired her body underneath. He undraped the sheer satin robe and climbed on top as he slowly caressed her with his robust hands. He gently combed his fingers through her well-trimmed locks while staring into her dark brown eyes. Shaniece loved it whenever his cocoa coated body dripped over hers. She never could resist him because he looked too damn good. He bit her juicy lips as he kissed her passionately. She let out a moan as she scratched and plunged her manicured nails into his firm back leaving imprints into his dark skin as he found his way inside her. He sucked and nibbled on her tasty nipples, like he wanted to devour them for his morning breakfast. She grabbed his muscled buttocks pulling him in more, hoping the penetration would give her the orgasm she wanted and knew she deserved. He stroked up, down, and in circles, making her feel it from every angle within her bulging walls. He could feel she was enjoying herself and was happy to be included in on the experience.

"Aaahh, baby, I'm ready to cum!" Shaniece warned him. Her legs began to buckle, and her body shook uncontrollably. She began yelling out whatever came to mind. Derek wanted the finale to be well-remembered, so he hopped off her body and pulled up downtown. He used his tongue to clean up the mess and reached for her clitoris to massage it. He flicked his tongue up and down to get the reaction he was expecting: Shaniece losing control over her whole body.

"Baby, why are you doing this to me?" she pleaded, not really expecting a response. The more moans and groans he heard from Shaniece, the more into their lovemaking he was. The overdue orgasm was more than what Shaniece had bargained for. She couldn't take it and backed her body away from his head to finish off her orgasm alone. Once she got herself reacquainted with her body again after a few minutes, Shaniece took care of Derek the same way he took care of her. Following twenty minutes of much needed seductive pleasure, they both were satisfied and ready to conquer the day.

When Shaniece made love to her man, it excited her, but she couldn't get over the guilt she had and felt unworthy of such a good man. Despite those feelings, she didn't know if he was cheating or not and kept her guard up. She didn't want to end up like the women who bragged about how great of a man they had while that same man was making a fool out of them, but everyone knew except for them. She had been in that position before and didn't want to be that woman again. Derek got dressed and was out the door first, but Shaniece was home alone for another ten minutes before it was time for her to leave out. She went into Derek's closet and checked the pockets of his jackets, shirts, pants, and anything else suggesting that he may have been with another woman. She found nothing.

She used to feel bad, but these investigations had become her everyday routine for the last few months. She was trying to catch Derek in the wrong for anything, but there was never any evidence. She occasionally checked his phone and never found inappropriate text messages or unknown phone numbers. The majority of the time when she called him at work, he answered. She never found anything at home either. The only thing she had to go off of was the changes in their sex life. They used to make love at least four to five days. Derek was addicted to her body and couldn't keep his hands off her. Lately when she tried seducing him, he was always tired, and their sex life diminished greatly. For that alone, she was certain that he was cheating because she knew him and how he operated when it came to getting off. Shaniece just couldn't let her brain believe that Derek was at the office late almost every night for the past four months and staying faithful.

CHOICES & REGRETS

Shaniece arrived at work, and everyone in the office was happy to see her as usual. Her employees loved working for her. She was the ideal, well-respected boss. Her business was well known throughout the Jersey area, and just about every billboard in town had her company name, Top Notch Recruitment LLC, on it.

"Come in--it's open." Shaniece told whoever had just knocked on the other side of her office door. Julian, her office manager, walked in with a bag of breakfast and placed it on her desk. He got comfortable and sat down in the chair in front of her with one leg bent across the other, cradling a tablet in his lap.

Shaniece hired Julian over a year ago as the office manager. He was smart, had an impressive professional background, and ended up being the best fit out of everyone she interviewed over a two-month period. He was also noticeably attractive. He was six three, jet black waves, pecan complexion, pearly white teeth and a body made of steel per his well-fitted suits. Shaniece figured that his looks would be another asset that could help with closing business deals.

"Ahem." He cleared his throat as he sat there patiently waiting for Shaniece to acknowledge him.

"Good morning, Julian," she responded as she quickly glanced away from her papers. When she looked up, she saw the bag from her favorite breakfast spot. "Julian, you didn't have to, but thanks anyway," she stated with a slight smile.

"Everything exactly how you like it is in there," he told her showing off his white teeth in a wide smile.

"Okay, thanks again," she uttered as she dug into the bag. After a few moments of dead silence except for the rattling of the bag as Shaniece was going back and forth grabbing her sandwich and home fries, Shaniece paused from eating and looked at Julian.

"I'm not trying to be rude, but I have a lot of work to do this morning," she told him as she looked back down at her papers in front of her.

"Well, I guess I'll be on my way." Julian stated as he started walking towards the door, holding the tablet in the crease of his elbow. Halfway to the door, he stopped in his tracks and turned back around.

"How long are you going to ignore what happened between us?" he asked as he closed the office door behind him. "I know you want to forget about us because you're engaged, but you act like it wasn't nothing. You're really going to marry someone that you're not in love with?"

Shaniece continued reviewing her papers, but this time around she was pretending. She was glad they were there because she had an excuse not to look up at him. He tossed the tablet on the chair and slammed his hands down on her desk.

"Man, say something. This is crazy. One minute, we're on your office desk making love and then the next minute, you're giving me the cold shoulder," he yelled with aggravation. Shaniece knew at that point she had to say something because she didn't want the office to know what was going on behind closed doors.

"Look, I was confused. I'm sorry. I know we have to see each other at work, but please, let's just stay professional like it was before and act like what we had never happened. You're engaged yourself so it should be easy for you to forget about us too," she pleaded with him. She sat back in her chair with tears in her eyes and turned away from Julian because she felt bad that she even made the mistake of having an affair with him in the first place.

With Derek working so many late nights the last few months and never having time for her anymore, she was sure that he was cheating, but she never thought that she would be the one being unfaithful. Around two months ago, she stayed after work to catch up on some paperwork, and that same evening, Julian just so happened to stay after himself. Shaniece had an argument with Derek about something minor that she overreacted about. Julian overheard her crying and walked into her office to see if she was okay. They began talking, and she asked his opinion about Derek staying after work the last few months and took it as far as sharing their lack of sex. Julian gave his honest opinion and told Shaniece that Derek was most likely not being faithful. Shaniece had had the same conclusion in mind but wanted to hear it from a man's perspective.

"I won't say he doesn't love you but any man who goes more than three days with you in the bed next to him and nothing not happening, something not right." Julian reminded her once again.

"I guess you might be right…" Shaniece responded quietly. After they discussed her situation, Julian opened up about his girlfriend. "What do you think about my girlfriend? I feel she's unappreciative and using me. I do everything for that woman and nothing I do seem to be enough. I love her but I'm not sure if she is right for me."

"Seems to me that she became comfortable with you and if you're going to keep giving then she's going to keep taking. After a while you're going to get tired and could end up resenting her."

After hours of more talking and less working, they both were emotional wrecks. They continued talking about their relationships and then about next steps for the business, but when there was nothing left to talk about, sex became the topic of discussion but not in conversation, more so with their bodies.

They ended up on top of Shaniece's desk. She had always fantasized about having sex on an office desk but never would've imagined it would have been with Julian. Neither one of them held back, going all the way like they were already used to each other's bodies. It was like they were craving it all along and finally got what they wanted. After a few body slams and heavy tongue kissing, Shaniece came to her senses and made Julian put on a condom. She always kept some in her handbag for when she would forget to take her birth control, and she was relieved she had them for that night. After an hour of guiltless sex, they both looked each other in the eyes but didn't say a word afterwards. Even though they both got dressed in silence, their minds were racing. Shaniece immediately started thinking about her business and how she could lose it all by being involved with someone who worked for her. Julian immediately started thinking that he just jeopardized his job. Still, their thoughts didn't stop them from meeting up again and again after that night.

Julian and Shaniece kept it going for weeks. They would meet up at hotel rooms on lunch breaks or stay after hours at work and have sex in one of their offices and sometimes in each other's cars, which excited them the most. After a month, the guilt started to really get to Shaniece, and she shut everything down immediately. Julian knew Shaniece would eventually call it quits because she had too much going for herself and knew she wasn't going to let him ruin what she had. He stayed with his girlfriend and proposed to her one week before everything ended. Shaniece had made the decision in part because of her guilt but also in part because she was upset about Julian's proposal. She didn't want him and his new fiancée to live happily ever after; she wanted him to struggle with his relationship like she had been with hers.

Julian stood in front of Shaniece's desk for a few seconds in silence with his arms folded, looking out the window. Shaniece sat at her desk staring at the floor with tears still rolling down her face with nothing left to say. She couldn't stop crying because she was unhappy with herself. She tried fixing her makeup so as not to ruin her white silk shirt. Julian saw how distraught she was. He unfolded his arms and walked around to Shaniece's side of the desk to try consoling her, grabbing some nearby tissues on his way and kneeling on one knee next to her desk.

"Look, I'm sorry for putting the pressure on you. Maybe it wasn't the best time to bring this up, but no time is ever the right time anymore. I know you wanted to call it quits, and I get that, but don't dismiss me and completely ignore me whenever I come around. That's all I'm asking." Shaniece grabbed the tissues from Julian's hand and started fixing the rest of her makeup. After she got herself together, she finally spoke.

"I'm not going to lie and say I didn't enjoy what we had. I ended it and left you in the dark, so I understand where you're coming from.

You're right; me ignoring you is cruel, and I'm sorry. Right now, Derek and I are in a good place, and I just want to focus on getting married. I definitely want you and me to go back to how things were before and keep it strictly professional. It will take some time, but we need to let go of what we had and focus on the relationships we're in." Julian nodded in agreement. He had no other choice but to respect Shaniece's wishes. He did want closure, so he had to settle for this. Julian stood up and returned to his seat across from his boss.

"Okay, now that we've addressed the elephant in the room, we can move on to business. I'm not sure if you checked your calendar yet, but tomorrow we have a meeting with our biggest client at 9 a.m. They want to place a big order and want us to be on board."

"Yes, Karen called and emailed the invitation. I'm accepting it now." The conversation continued as Julian scrolled through his calendar on his tablet to make sure he had updated Shaniece about the upcoming meetings.

* * * * * *

"Alright, that's all I have," Julian stated as he walked to the door.

"Thank you, Julian -- for everything!" Shaniece stated with a smile and a sense of relief. Julian returned the same smile that had a meaning to just the two of them before walking out the office and shutting her door. Shaniece swiveled her chair around and gazed outside at the city view. "Thank you Lord for getting me through that awkward yet necessary conversation!" she whispered to herself. That was the moment that she'd been avoiding for weeks and God stepped in once again helping her through and still showing grace and mercy. She was satisfied that they had discussed their issues and could get back to work. She felt better because she didn't want to keep ignoring him or being distant. She valued him as an employee and knew her business could have been jeopardized, but she was grateful that they had come to a resolution.

After five minutes of peace, her assistant, Karen, called her line.

"Ms. Brown, I have Derek on line two."

Shaniece's face lit up. "Go ahead and send him through, Karen.

Thank you." She picked up the phone to hear an excited voice on the other end.

"Guess who's celebrating tonight?" Derek yelled through the phone. Shaniece gasped with excitement.

"You got the contract?" Her heart was racing waiting on his response.

"And you know it!"

"Babbbyy, I'm so proud of you. You worked your butt off to make this happen."

"Yeah! But I'm really thankful for having a wonderful fiancée who's been understanding and patient. I love you so much."

The more she talked to him, the guiltier she started to feel. She never had hardcore proof that he was cheating, but she was the one who cheated for sure. She was starting to think maybe he really was working.

"Aww babe. I love you too. When are you getting home? I can meet you there so we can go out and celebrate."

"Most likely I'll be home around four. For all that hard work we put in, I'm getting out of here early today. I invited my staff and their partners to join in on the celebration."

"Okay, I'll leave here at three-thirty and meet you at the house."

"Alright, babe. I love you! See you then."

* * * * * *

After a long yet successful day, Shaniece pulled up to the house and sat in her black-on-black Mercedes with dark tint for a few minutes to get herself together. The conversation that she had with Julian earlier crept in her mind, and she wanted to steer clear of thinking about him when she came into Derek's presence.

"Okay, I can do this," she whispered to herself. She got out of the car, approached the house, and turned the key into the front door.

"Hi, honey, I'm home," she yelled out while placing her Coach work bag on the ivory-colored kitchen island.

"Hey babe, I'm upstairs. I'm in the bathroom – just now getting out the shower," Derek yelled from the second-floor bathroom. Shaniece flopped on the off-white loveseat in the living room and rested her eyes for a good five minutes. She was always working that she never had time to get a good eight hours of sleep in.

"Hey, babe, what you doing?" Derek's voice caused Shaniece to awake abruptly. Shaniece jumped up, grabbed her bag, and headed up the steps. Derek was at the top of the stairwell looking down with a towel wrapped around his waist, a toothbrush in his mouth, and water beads still rolling down his chest. Shaniece walked up to him and kissed him on his cheek. Derek walked into the bathroom to finish brushing his teeth while Shaniece laid on the bed. He walked out and saw Shaniece stretched out.

"What are you doing? Why you not getting ready?" he asked, this time with annoyance.

"I'm sorry. I'm just more tired than I was aware of. Did you decide on where we're going?" she asked while getting off the bed and getting undressed. Derek was in the closet checking out his shoe collection.

"Yes, we're going to that new steakhouse off of Main Street. We need to be there by six o'clock. I reserved half of the restaurant."

"Okay, sounds good." She finished getting dressed, and when they were both ready, the two of them got into Derek's car to head over to the restaurant. Shaniece was drained from a long day, and the guilt about Julian was starting to drag her down. She was frustrated because she thought she had put everything with Julian behind her, but the situation with him was starting to overwhelm her like a flood.

LET'S CELEBRATE

"Babe, this restaurant is gorgeous -- definitely my type of place," Shaniece mentioned while sitting in the lobby waiting for the rest of the party to arrive. While looking around at the glittering chandeliers that hung in the restaurant, Shaniece remembered how it had been a while since she and Derek had last dressed up and went out. With his schedule and late nights, they barely had time to do much of anything, and on weekends, he was always in chill mode due to his hectic schedule during the week. Shaniece was happy that she finally had gotten some time with her man back.

"I know; a few of the guys came here for the grand opening and suggested it," he told her. He watched Shaniece in awe as she walked around checking out the restaurant. She was in a knee-length black Vera Wang leather dress with a slit on the side that complimented her body and cheetah-print, red-bottom stilettos with a touch of leather around the bottom lining. Her hair was pinned up in a bun with a few curls in the front, and her lips were dipped in a shade of dull red lipstick. She looked incredible, and he wanted to tell her again but decided not to because he had mentioned it nearly three times already before they arrived. He just smiled and admired her as they sat and waited for their guests to arrive.

Shaniece gave him his props once more. "Baby, I'm so proud of you. You've had your eye on this client since we started dating and finally you got what you wanted." Derek was smiling as he recalled the first day he told his firm that they were going to start bringing on the heavy hitters. Some believed in him, while others believed he was just selling them another dream. Either way, he had proven to everyone that he meant business.

"Thanks, babe. Especially for being so patient," Derek stated as he pecked her on the forehead. Minutes later, the guests started to arrive one by one.

"Hello, Mr. Reeler." Josh, one of his interns, spoke to him at the lobby entrance.

"Tonight, my man, just call me Derek." He patted the twenty-two-year-old on his back. Derek was surprised to see him with such a hot date. The guy was always quirky, but his tech skills were a big reason why they landed the contract.

"Mr. Reeler, I mean, Derek, thank you so much for the opportunity to work with you and the team. I feel like I'm starting my career off on the right foot working with so many talented individuals and contributing to landing a big client like this. Thanks again!"

Derek couldn't stop smiling. He even felt himself getting emotional because when he started his company, he didn't want to just be successful but wanted to inspire and help the next generation. He was living out his dream right before his eyes. He didn't have many words left to say after what Josh told him. He patted the young intern on his shoulder before turning to greet others who were just arriving as well.

Derek invited his entire team and their significant others, but he had also invited his brother Jeffrey and Morgan. Derek and his brother were very close and supported each other full force. They were both successful and wanted to see the best for each other. Jeffrey was an architect and Morgan owned a Charter school in Philadelphia. When Derek initially told Shaniece about his brother and sister-in-law, she automatically assumed they would be uptight, but they were down to earth. Shaniece didn't understand at the time, but they were ecstatic that Derek had dumped his last fling he brought around. She was so bad that Morgan referred to her as a "self-centered bitch." The couple was glad that Derek finally settled down, and they sensed that he was serious about Shaniece so they were willing to welcome her with open arms. Shaniece and Derek didn't get to see them too much, but when they did it was all love.

Once all the guests were present, Derek and the restaurant host led everyone to the back. Shaniece was impressed with her future husband and how he handled himself. He had everything under control and demonstrated himself as a leader from taking charge of planning the night and securing reservations at a popular spot on such short notice; his poise and professionalism when he greeted his team and how he interacted with the restaurant staff turned her on in every way. Shaniece was happy to be there standing right by his side.

After a two-hour evening of tasty food, drinks, and mingling, Derek called everyone to the deck of the restaurant for his speech and asked his team, including Josh, to come up next to him. He went on to state how appreciative he was of their dedication and hard work and how he wouldn't have been able to pull it off without them. After a few minutes of giving accolades, he asked Shaniece to pass him his briefcase. She walked up, handed it over to him, and returned to her previous spot on the deck. He pulled some envelopes out of the briefcase and started handing them out.

"I hope you all enjoy what these envelopes hold; you definitely deserve it." Everyone on his team was shocked – they did not come expecting to receive a bonus. Once he was done, he then called Shaniece to come forward. She was caught off guard, not anticipating that she would be put on the spot. She had pretty much been under his wing for the night, and she was cool with that. Shaniece walked up with a warm smile and stood next to her man. Derek grabbed her by the waist to pull her closer to him. He then began to publicly express his feelings and gratitude.

"This woman right here...not only is she beautiful and smart, but she is also a good woman. She stood by my side without nagging about me putting in long hours, and I didn't hear one complaint. She's been patient and I'm lucky to have her in my life. Most of the nights at the office, I wanted to leave just to be home with her, but she understood how badly I wanted this day to happen and pushed me to finish what I started. I love you so much. Here's a bonus for you, too. Treat yourself!" Derek handed her an envelope, and Shaniece was smiling ear to ear while everyone else chanted.

Though she smiled, she glanced at everyone around the deck hoping no one could see through her facade. She was feeling so awful that she believed it was noticeable to everyone there. To mask things even more, she grabbed Derek's face and kissed him passionately for a moment in front of the crowd. She whispered in his ear, "You mean everything to me!" After another two hours of sharing work stories and endless drinking, Derek and Shaniece decided to call it a night. Everyone caught on to the cue and started heading to the door as well. Derek and Shaniece held hands at the restaurant entrance as they wished everyone safe travels home. After the final person exited, they made their way to the car to head home themselves.

* * * * * *

"I had a wonderful time! We need to go out more often. By the way, you look good as hell tonight." Derek said, looking over at Shaniece briefly as they were riding back to the house.

"Thank you, babe. It's been a while since we've been out…it felt good." She leaned her head back against the headrest and looked in Derek's direction, smiling at him. "I am so proud of you," she told him once again.

"Couldn't have done it without you," he reminded her, returning the smile. Once he returned his gaze to the road, Shaniece glanced down at her engagement ring and grazed her right index finger over it. The ring, dazzling with three carats of diamonds, seemed to glitter a lot brighter as they passed by streetlights that swept over it. Still, her smile slowly went away, and she then turned her head to look out of the passenger window.

Shaniece was starting to become annoyed because the more Derek thanked her, the more she wanted to crawl under a rock. In an attempt to shake off the feeling, she placed her hand behind his neck and fiddled with his left earlobe, trying to get an arousal out of him. Derek picked up on what she was doing and was instantly turned on. He decided to pull over on the side of the road. Shaniece looked back at the dark empty road from the passenger side mirror, slightly alarmed by his sudden decision to pull over.

"Come here," he requested. Shaniece was thinking to herself, *I know this man is not wanting what I think he wants.* He unzipped his pants and nodded his head, hoping she'd get the point. Shaniece started laughing.

"Are you serious, right here? Right now?" She loved when he was spontaneous but felt this was a bit much. She decided to go along with his desires because she wanted to please her man. If she didn't, she felt another woman would be glad to, so she got down to work. After a while, Derek turned out to be quite happy with his roadside assistance.

SHE'S A FREAK

"I'm sorry I couldn't make it to the dinner last night. Oh wait, I wasn't invited," Danita stated with much sarcasm.

"Uh, you were invited but you decided not to come because my fiancée was going to be there, remember that?" Derek retorted.

Danita was Derek's temporary employee until his assistant, Melanie, returned from maternity leave. Shaniece hired Danita for Derek's firm, as she was new in town and in desperate need of a job. She had an impressive resume as a result of having worked for some of the largest firms in her home state of North Carolina. She had also graduated at the top of her class with a degree in accounting. Derek needed someone with Danita's particular skillset especially when it came to calculating numbers. Shaniece had completed reference checks to follow up on Danita's skills, work ethic, and education. However, Derek wished that Shaniece had also done some personality reference checks on this woman.

Danita was a single woman of average height and an hourglass build with smooth, double mocha chocolate skin. She also wore a short, pixy haircut that was styled on point every day. Danita made sure to wear the latest fashions too; in the office, she kept her outfits professional, but on her own time, she was always in sexy diva mode. Because she was single, Danita focused on clawing her nails into men who were already taken. She always felt that she didn't have to be Halle Berry as long as she was shaped like Nicki Minaj. With her banging body, she would be able to get her hands on any man she wanted. It had only been a few weeks since Danita's arrival, and Derek was ready for her to be gone already so things could get back to normal as quickly as possible.

Derek figured out that Danita was thirsty for him from day one. On her first day, he saw how she looked at him. He was used to women throwing themselves at him and having to turn them down, so he was quite familiar with the thirsty look. Week three in the office, he noticed she started wearing more skirts and dresses opposed to pantsuits when she first took on the job; at one point, she dropped a pen and bent down in front of him hoping he would enjoy the view, which he did. Each week, her thirsty behavior was on full display, and he continued to ignore it. However, he gave in to Danita one night when he was stuck in the office and frustrated after hours of crunching numbers. Danita came in and helped him with his report, figuring out where he went wrong. After that night, she expected a favor. He didn't give in immediately, but after days of persistence on Danita's part, he fell into her trap. He didn't really find her attractive and never had any real intentions of sleeping with her. It just happened, and he went along with it. After the first time, though, he was hooked.

Danita had rocked his world like never before. She pulled out all the tricks and didn't hold back. He had dealt with freaks before, but Danita was on a different level. He was barely getting any at home because of his long work hours, but he needed to get a temporary fix, so he gave in every time she came around. He was happy that she wouldn't be working for him for very long so he would eventually be able to break away from her. He knew if she continued working for him, he wouldn't stop what he was doing.

"So, when you going to tell her?" Danita crossed her arms and tilted her head to the side.

"Tell her what? There's nothing to tell as far as I'm concerned," Derek replied sarcastically. He walked past her to get to his cup of coffee that had just got done brewing.

"Okay, so what you're saying is that us sleeping together is nothing?" she scoffed, placing her hands on her hips. He wanted cream and sugar for his coffee, but at this point, he just wanted to leave the room.

"Yes, that's exactly what I'm saying. It's only been a few times so get over it. I love my fiancée and we're getting married soon."

Danita ignored Derek whenever he talked about his fiancée. According to her, she didn't even exist, especially with Derek spending his late-night hours at the office with her instead of his woman.

"Yeah, yeah, yeah. Keep telling yourself that same lie. Love don't cheat," she told him as she sashayed past him to grab his mail and handed it to him. Derek didn't want to keep going back and forth, so he snatched his mail out of her hand, headed to his office, and closed the door behind him. He knew that he messed up but also knew he only needed to ride the situation out just a few more weeks.

Danita had been attracted to Derek from the first day she laid eyes on him. She had freaky tendencies, but she surprised herself with how she handled Derek. She figured the pornos she watched had finally taught her something after all. Derek was one of her many victims, and she was determined to get his fiancée out the picture. She didn't have a plan yet but knew eventually Derek would be wrapped around her finger. Her last victim lost everything: his wife, his job, and the custody of his children. That was Danita's moment to disappear. In all honesty, she didn't feel bad about interrupting happy homes. Her motto was "If a man is gonna cheat, then home wasn't that happy after all." She knew one day her actions would catch up to her but was willing to keep playing with fire until she got burned. "Knock, knock!" Danita stood outside Derek's office. He cracked the door slightly when he heard her voice.

"Yeah, what is it?" he asked. Danita pushed the door back and gently slid into his office with a devious smile, slightly closing the door behind her.

"Well, I wanted to know what you wanted. You forgot to put in your lunch order."

Derek rolled his eyes. "Really, you couldn't call me?"

Danita didn't pay attention to when Derek was mad because he always fell under her spell. He was always short-tempered with her, so she completely ignored his rudeness. She didn't get that it wasn't an act and that he wanted her to be gone more than anything.

"Okay, I get it. You had a bad night. I'll just order your favorite," she stated as she licked her lips and bit the bottom one when she was done. He knew what she was implying.

"I doubt if you even know what that would be." Danita chuckled.

"Well, I can take a guess."

Derek gave her a look of disgust. "Look, just order me the chicken parmesan from Rotto's." Danita wrote down his order with her pen and pad. Before she could get another word in, he was waiting at the door for her to leave. He needed to start his day and could tell she was not going anywhere any time soon. She got his drift and walked back to her desk, hearing the door shut hard behind her. While she updated her calendar, she thought about how she was starting to lose her touch, and Derek was really done with her once and for all. She logged into her Facebook account and pulled up Derek's page. He never mentioned his fiancée's name to her, so she wanted to find it out for herself. His page was private, but she could view some of his profile pictures. She saw pictures of Shaniece and was surprised that the woman who interviewed her for the job was his fiancée. She didn't put two and two together that she belonged to Derek. "So, she's the future Mrs. Reeler?" she whispered to herself. Danita believed that by stalking his page, she would feel better. Instead, it made her bitter. She wasn't expecting Shaniece to be the love of his life. She was threatened because Shaniece was stunning and heavy competition. Danita knew she was putting her job on the line but was willing to take the risk. She logged out and sat in her chair staring at the wall. *What can I do?*, she thought to herself. A devious smile appeared across her face when she came up with the perfect plan.

BACK TO NORMAL

"Hey, Mom, what you cooking?" Justin asked as he was skimming the fridge.

"I'm cooking your favorite dinner. Don't you smell the wonderful aroma?" she replied. Justin started moonwalking and sliding across the kitchen floor in his socks with a big smile on his face.

"What's the special occasion? You haven't cooked in a minute. Lately, it's been takeout and restaurants."

Shaniece smiled. "Wellllll, it's not really a special occasion, but I figured since Derek comes home at a regular time now, and you're done with your skating competitions, we can start spending some family time together."

Even though he asked, Justin didn't really care about the reason. He was more concerned about when he was going to eat. "Okay, cool, Mom. Just hurry up please. I'm starving," he begged as he walked away biting into an apple.

Shaniece was in a happy mood – a Freddie Jackson and Luther Vandross kind of mood. She liked old school music, so she danced all around the kitchen sipping on a glass of Merlot. She wasn't expecting Derek for another hour, so she decided to go upstairs and freshen up while the food was simmering.

While she was in the shower lathering soap all over her body, Shaniece was smiling to herself as she mused about how life suddenly gotten better for her. She was glad things were finally going back to the way they were. She was almost done with her shower when she heard a familiar "Hey!" She squealed with excitement.

Derek laughed as he peeped in the shower at Shaniece's soapy body.

"Babbbbyyy, what are you doing here? I wasn't expecting you for another hour," she stated in a high-pitched voice.

"I know. I decided I can push some stuff off until tomorrow. I wanted to be home." Shaniece was even more happy that he was back to making their relationship a priority.

"Dinner is smelling good…damn, I miss this," he stated as he sniffed the air. Shaniece missed him being home and spending time with family just as much as he did. She was ecstatic that she could cook for him now. Even more, Derek couldn't wait to get home to see his future wife and the only thing on his mind was making love to her. He had been thinking about her dark brown seductive eyes, soft cherry-balm-flavored lips, and contagious smile all day.

"What you do with my towel? It was on the toilet seat," she asked as she stood at the foot of the tub with her arms wrapped around her wet body.

"It's right here, but I don't want you to dry off yet," he told her. She chuckled as she was shivering.

"So, what do you want to see me do then?" she asked in a clueless tone. She knew what he wanted, but she also didn't want to end up burning the food. Derek looked at her seductively, and all she could do was laugh.

"Look, I know what you want. You should already know that it's going down tonight so you don't have to worry about that. So how about you give me my towel to dry off and then in about an hour you can take whatever you want from me."

Derek couldn't do anything but comply. "Here's your towel...and it's definitely one of those nights," he agreed.

Shaniece just looked at him, smiled, and pecked him on his forehead. "I got you, babe," she told him as she walked out of the steamy bathroom.

* * * * * *

"Mom, you snapped with this dinner," Justin stated with food still in his mouth.

"Thank you but close your mouth when talking."

"Yeah, babe -- this is really good," Derek added.

"Thank you, guys; I know it's been a while, so I had to make it extra special." Shaniece made a combo meal that she knew would satisfy both of the men in her life. For Justin, she made a T-bone steak, and for Derek, she cooked steamed shrimp and lobster. She added diced potatoes, asparagus, and buttered rolls to the mix, just to keep things fancy. Apparently, the meal was so good that Justin volunteered to do the dishes, much to Shaniece's surprise. This was her opportunity to get to Derek.

"Okay, now that dinner is done, I'm in need of dessert," Shaniece hinted quietly in a naughty voice. She and Derek left Justin downstairs to dish duty while they walked upstairs to the bedroom. Derek loved that about her because she was straight up. When she wanted a piece of him, she didn't hesitate or beat around the bush. She was a boss all around, in and out of the bedroom.

Once the door was shut, Shaniece didn't waste any time and immediately began taking off her garments one by one until she was in her birthday suit. Derek picked her up and placed her on top of the dresser; she sat up like a porcelain doll. She gently grabbed both sides of his face and kissed him from the top of his head to his collar bone. After a few minutes of exchanged kisses, she wanted him inside of her and didn't want to wait any longer. She unbuttoned each button on his shirt, but she had gotten so aroused that she popped the last of his buttons off by pulling his shirt out of his pants. She unhooked his belt buckle, and his pants and boxers dropped. He was finally in the perfect position to enter in.

"Ahh, baby, yes, right there," Shaniece directed. He went in and out of her slowly. He took his time while positioning his hands underneath her dimpled butt cheeks, lifting her halfway off the dresser. While still inside, he moved her from the dresser to the bed. Her legs were wrapped around his waist and her arms around his neck. She was ready for whatever he had in mind next. He placed her on her back and climbed on top, still managing to stay connected. He grabbed the back of her neck and kissed her face, earlobes, neck, and breasts while grinding back and forth. He chilled on the foreplay and grabbed her buttocks, pulling her closer to get deeper. Shaniece wanted to orgasm so bad but didn't want to ruin the moment so she hung in there as long as she could.

"Damn babe, this feels so good," she repeated more than once. Derek was usually the talkative one in the bedroom, but he was concentrating on putting in as much effort as possible. He treated sex like a sport: either he was the crazy fan looking for that win, or the athlete focused on not losing. After thirty minutes of amazing sex, Derek finally cried out.

"I'm there, babe!"

33

"Go ahead, baby -- I'm there too!" Shaniece instructed. After about six more pumps, they both screamed like they were on a rollercoaster at Six Flags. Shaniece climaxed to a place where she had never been before. She felt like her body was an ocean that she had just drowned in.

"Wow, what was that all about?" she asked as they laid back on the bed looking up at the ceiling trying to catch their breath.

"I missed everything about you, let alone your body. We haven't really been getting down like that and I needed you like never before," he confessed. Shaniece looked at him with small tears in the crack of her eyes and climbed on top of him with a sheet in between her thighs and rested on his chest.

"I can't wait to be your wife. I love you so much." This was the moment Shaniece had been waiting for all this time. She had finally fallen in love with Derek.

CATCHING UP

"Hey, girl, what you doing? Want to go to lunch?" Karina asked over the phone.

"Hey, sissy, I thought you weren't going to be in town until Friday -- not today," Shaniece replied.

"Yeah, girl, I came earlier to handle some business. So, what's up? You want to do lunch this afternoon or what?"

"Yes, of course. I'll be done here in the office at four." Karina laughed.

"Uhhhhh, I said lunch, that's dinner time. How about tomorrow? I'll only be in town for two more days before I hit the road again for my next book signing."

Shaniece looked at her calendar. "You are so demanding. I will change my schedule around and make myself available." Karina always got her way with Shaniece.

Karina was Shaniece's best friend, but she considered Karina more of a sister. They had met each other when they were both ten years old and had grown up together since. Karina was tall but slender with a butter pecan complexion and long, light brown hair. If she had been any taller, she could have passed as Tyra Banks. She was super skinny up until senior year of high school. When she left for college and returned on spring break during freshman year, she had practically blossomed into a woman. Shaniece learned that Karina had a college boyfriend and lost her virginity. As a result, her hips ended up spreading for getting it on the regular. Karina's confidence boosted after she gained some weight, and no one could tell her anything. She knew she was blessed in the looks department. On top of all of that, she was now a successful book writer and well-known in the Atlanta area. She has done numerous book signings and even made it on the best-seller list a few times. The only downfall of this success was that Karina still didn't have a personal life of her own. Shaniece knew she didn't want to be like that and was happy that her success came after. She was able to see some of the mistakes Karina made along the way and was able to avoid some pitfalls while on her own journey.

"Okay, darling. See you tomorrow at one. I'll text you the location details later." Shaniece shook her head and smiled.

"Okay, that's cool. See you then." She knew that when she met with Karina, she needed to be ready to spill the beans. She knew Karina would be all in her love life, career life, and anything else. She didn't mind though because out of twenty-five years of friendship, she had never had issues with Karina sharing her personal business.

* * * * * *

"Ugghh, I hate when she wants to meet up at these uppity places. She could have picked someplace a little less upscale," Shaniece whispered to herself as she walked into the five-star restaurant. She immediately noticed that not one person of color was there. She was appropriately dressed because she was in her work attire but didn't feel like being on that type of time -- being bougie, proper, and intact. She wanted to let her hair down a bit and be in a setting where they could cut up like old times and not worry about who was around or who they may offend. Karina was always in upscale mode because she had been living like that for years.

Shaniece approached the host station, looking for Karina as she spoke to the man standing there.

"Hi, sir. My name is Shaniece Brown, and I'm here for a 1 p.m. reservation under Karina Scott."

The well-dressed host looked at the reservation list and checked off her name. "Yes, please follow me to your table. Your party has already arrived."

Shaniece walked past six other tables on the way to hers and noticed older white men with younger women at just about every table. She thought to herself, *This must be the rich people creep spot.* The host pulled out Shaniece's chair and handed her a menu. She thanked him as Karina stood up.

"Hi, darling, thank you for joining me! You look beautiful." Karina leaned over the small table and pecked Shaniece on both cheeks. Shaniece saw how great Karina looked. She thought to herself, *Life is definitely treating her right.* Karina was dressed to impress, and her diamond earrings and watch nearly blinded Shaniece. Shaniece grinned as she briefly took in her surroundings.

"Thank you. You look amazing as always. It's so nice to finally see my best friend."

Two drinks in, Karina tried to start with her round of questions. Shaniece was prepared to talk but wanted to know about Karina's personal life first because she noticed a glow on her sister's face. She cut to the chase and asked her question quickly.

"Sooooo, Karina…do you have a man yet?" She thought after she opened her mouth that it came out in a very condescending tone.

"Well, yes, I do, to answer your question," Karina told her with a huge smile on her face.

"Wow, you're smiling ear to ear. You were able to find a man that could really tame you?"

"Well, yes, and I would say 'tame' is an understatement. He got this thing on lock." Shaniece was shocked because she was expecting the usual response of "I don't need a man in my life right now because I'm building my career and can't afford any distractions." Shaniece knew she didn't have a problem getting a man but was curious about why her sister always stayed single for the most part.

"So, what do he do? Where did you two meet? How long has this been going on? Annnnd, why am I just finding out about it?" Karina tried answering each question as fast as she could to keep up.

"Welllll, he's a CEO at a marketing firm in New York…we met at a dinner party…we've been seeing each other for six months…no, seven months now, and made it official a month ago…aaannndd I didn't tell you about it because we were just dating, and I didn't know where it was going until we sat down and established that we were officially together."

Shaniece was excited for Karina and knew she was happy with this man because of the way her face lit up when she talked about him. She didn't want to tell Karina about her issues because she didn't want to spoil the moment.

"So, now that you know about me, spill it, honey. What's going on with the wedding? No…better yet, how's my godson?" Karina asked as she sipped on her last swig of Cabernet.

"Girl, Justin thinks he's a man now. He hasn't been giving me problems too much. He's on honor roll, and he's taking this skateboarding sport all the way. He's actually good. I'm proud of him."

"I see your pics on Facebook, and he's soooo handsome. I sent him an IG request, but I guess I'm too old to be in his mix because he never accepted." Shaniece laughed as she sipped her sparkling water.

"Girl, don't feel bad. He won't even accept me."

Karina and Shaniece talked, laughed, ate, sipped, and shared as much as they could with each other for nearly two hours. In conversation, Shaniece did complain about Derek and his late hours, but Karina brushed it off as paranoia. She was in a long-distance relationship, so it was not unfamiliar territory for her. She figured that she would rather her man work late living in the same state as her than see her man just a few times a month, but she knew in a matter of time things would eventually change. Shaniece wanted to tell her best friend about Julian so bad but didn't want to be judged. She knew she could trust her with the information but didn't feel like opening that can of worms. She had ended things with Julian, and he understood there wouldn't be anything between them and agreed to keep it strictly professional. Eventually, she felt there was no need to bring up something that didn't matter anymore.

"So, when you coming back home? I miss hanging out with you," Shaniece said with a sigh.

"Well, you know I'll be here for the wedding of course, but until then I will be spending most of my time between New York and Atlanta," Karina told her.

"Okay, well maybe we can hang out again before then."

"You know what…that would be nice. I haven't had a night out in some time so let me check my schedule and get back to you," Karina stated as she passed the tab and her credit card over to the waiter. Shaniece had wanted to cover at least the tip for their meals, but Karina insisted.

"Don't worry about today. You can treat me some other time! And I can't wait until the wedding. I'm so excited!

"I know! I can't either. You know we're going to turn up like the old days. I told the DJ I want nothing but eighties and nineties music."

"Well, you know how I'm going to act!" Karina started doing the Wop as they exited the restaurant and Shaniece joined in. They both started laughing as the uptight customers and staff stared with their noses up in the air.

WHEN? WHAT? WHERE?

Shaniece and Derek went back and forth about when they wanted to get married. They had been engaged for over a year, but they disagreed about almost everything when it came to the wedding and needed to compromise for it to take place. Their original date had already been pushed back. The new date was now four months away, and they had nothing planned. Their entire wedding party wasn't in order, and they didn't even have a location yet. Derek was ready to tie the knot as soon as possible, while Shaniece wanted to wait at least another year. Shaniece wanted a destination wedding, but Derek wanted a wedding at home. Shaniece wanted a small intimate wedding; Derek wanted to invite everyone and their mamas.

"So, babe, what we doing? We really need to get the wedding details in order. I'm hiring a wedding planner because I don't know how we would pull it off with our schedules," Shaniece asked and told him at the same time.

"I think we may need to push the date back again because we don't have nothing together except for the darn DJ. We don't even have a reception hall so where is he going to play?" Derek asked.

"How about we call the wedding planner now? I have a referral for a guy who I heard was very good and knows how to make things happen. Let's give him a call and see what he can do for us. If he can get us a hall, fine, and if not then we will have to change the date again."

Derek was willing to go to the courthouse at this point. Having a big wedding was a tradition in his family, and it was more for his mother than himself. His brother, cousin, and godbrother all had large weddings. He wanted to keep up the tradition and not let his mom down because she would be furious. His family had to always do things on a larger scale, but he always had the feeling that his mom used weddings as a family reunion. She didn't get to see the extended family too often so she would look forward to big family events.

Derek decided to follow Shaniece's flow and let her contact the wedding planner for assistance. They both felt like the other person was dragging their feet on one of the most important days of their life when, in actuality, they both wanted it more than anything. They both felt guilt in their heart but also felt that once they tied the knot, their marriage would bring them closer together, and all their past mistakes would stay in the past.

* * * * * *

"Hello, may I speak to Bobby?" Shaniece asked.

"Hi, this is Bobby. How may I help you?"

"Hi, yes my name is Shaniece. I was referred to you by Lauren Tilley, and I was told that you were the man to call for help with a wedding….I'm in desperate need of your help."

Bobby chuckled. "Well, yes, I am the man. Tell me your dilemma and I'll see if I can be of assistance."

"Well, are you sitting down?" Shaniece warned him.

Bobby chuckled again. "Trust me sweetheart, I heard it all, carry on."

"Okay, I'm supposed to be getting married in four months. I originally had June of last year as the wedding date, which was six months from our engagement. We cut it too close, so we had to postpone that date to April of this year. Both my fiancé and I have very demanding jobs and are guilty of putting the wedding off. It's now four months away, and we have no church, no hall, an incomplete wedding list, no flowers, and somewhat of a wedding party. My fiancé wants to have a large wedding, but I want to have a destination wedding. We don't seem to agree on anything. The only thing I do have is a wedding dress, which I probably can't fit anymore, and a confirmed DJ with no place to play." Shaniece laid everything out without taking a breath. She felt good getting everything off her chest and venting but saying everything out loud made their situation sound even worse than she thought.

Bobby paused for a moment before he spoke. "Okay, so I heard everything you said. Not the worst I have heard but definitely a lot to do in such little time. I can tell you now that a destination wedding is your best bet. You can have a small intimate wedding and enjoy your honeymoon in the same place and then come back to the states and have a reception. Also, finding a hall within four months would be challenging. Depending on how much you're willing to spend, I may be able to pull some strings. I would have to sit down and meet with you to discuss a budget and cover other aspects. Once we meet, I can start the process for you."

Shaniece liked Bobby's recommendations because that's what she originally wanted. If he could help them get their wedding plans in place, she saw no reason to put the wedding off another day.

PUSHING BUTTONS

"Hello. Hi, Danita. This is Shaniece. Is Derek available?"

Shaniece had called into his office to chat with him briefly about some wedding details. She usually called Derek's cell, but he didn't pick up.

Danita wasn't too happy that the wedding was finally happening. She put Shaniece on hold without even a "Just a second" or a "Let me check for you" -- nothing. Shaniece was annoyed, but she let it go and just remained on hold. If she hadn't heard the hold music, she would've thought Danita hung up on her. Danita came back to the phone after what Shaniece felt was the longest three minutes.

"He's not available right now," Danita communicated.

"Okaaaay...is he in a meeting?" Shaniece inquired, wondering why she had an attitude.

"No, he's just not available right now."

"Okay, well I'll just call him on his cell again."

"Okay, but he's not going to answer," Danita boldly and defensively replied.

"Well, how do you know that?" Shaniece was fuming now.

"I don't know for sure, but his lunch is coming up and a lot of times he's not available to talk on his lunch break." At that point, Shaniece went from annoyed to pissed off.

"Okay Danita, how about I come up there? I'm sure he'll be available for me then." Danita started to comment back, but Shaniece had already disconnected the call. Shaniece told Karen to send her calls to voicemail. She got in her car and didn't turn on any music. All types of thoughts were going through her head. Her first thought was to was to find out what Danita's problem was. The next thought was to walk up to Danita's desk and fire her ass or tell Derek to fire her on the spot. The one after that was to beat her ass and ask questions later. Whatever way Shaniece decided to handle the situation, she just knew she needed to correct the disrespect.

She pulled up to the parking lot, checked her hair, fixed her makeup, and headed straight to Derek's office. Danita was on the phone as she walked past and barely could speak when she saw Shaniece strutting by, flashing her a fake smile. She didn't think Shaniece was really going to come to his office. She thought she was all talk. After hanging up the phone, Danita started packing her stuff up because she was sure it was her last day on the job.

Derek's door was closed, and Shaniece barged in without warning. Derek was sitting in his chair with his feet propped up on the desk while on the phone. When he saw Shaniece, he was caught completely off guard. He almost fell out of his chair while trying to put the phone on mute.

"What's going on babe? Is everything okay?" he asked in a very concerned voice.

"Yes, but I'll wait 'til you get done. I'll just sit here," she told him with the same fake smile she gave Danita when she arrived. Derek's heart was pounding; his entire life flashed before his eyes. He wanted to know how Shaniece had found out about him and Danita. He tuned out the voice on the other line and tried to think of how he was going to handle the situation.

Danita walked into the office shortly after and handed Derek a note and walked out with a smirk on her face. Shaniece beat Derek to the punch and quickly snatched the sticky note out of his hand. It read, *Meeting in an hour at 1 p.m.*, accompanied by a smiley face at the bottom. Derek saw what was on the note, but because he was on a conference call and it was his turn to speak, he couldn't say what he wanted to say to Shaniece or Danita. Shaniece wanted to go into the lobby and put Danita and her belongings out on the street, but she remembered Danita was an employee, and it would be bad for Derek's business. As she sat there tapping her leg and patiently waiting for Derek to get done with his phone call, she realized she was jeopardizing her own business by being there. After several minutes, she came to her senses, grabbed her Birkin bag off the chair, and walked out of his office. She blew him a kiss before she walked out and whispered for him to call her when he was done. He wanted to chase after her to find out what was going on but couldn't get off the call, so he just complied by nodding his head. Shaniece hurried past Danita's desk and told her to have a lovely day as professionally as she could. Danita wondered what had happened behind closed doors. She thought to herself that it was a rather brief conversation and not too much could've been said. She was expecting a shouting match but got nothing.

Shaniece drove back to her building and waited for Derek to call as she sat at her desk. After fifteen minutes passed, Derek was yelling through the phone.

"What the hell was that all about? You insult my worker and then snatch my message out my hand?!" he went on and on. She walked out then practically ran out of her office down to the first floor and into the parking garage to her car where she could really get out what she wanted to say.

"What the fuck you mean I insulted your worker?" was her first question. That was all she heard and lost it. Shaniece rarely cursed so for her to do so she had to be livid.

"Yes, insult my worker! Danita said that you were rude on the phone and then threatened her!"

"I did not insult that bitch! It was actually the other way around, and no, I didn't threaten her!"

"So, why did you come up here then?!"

"Because she was disrespectful and I wanted to know what her problem was face to face, but when I got there, I realized I would be wrong for addressing her so I wanted to address you about it. Like what type of business are you running by having your staff handle phone calls the way that she did?!"

"Oh, please! Don't get me started on how unprofessional your…" Derek stopped in his tracks. He didn't want to go back and forth with her about the situation.

Shaniece was so mad at this point. She had to look at her phone to make sure it was Derek's number. He had never talked to her like that before, and she didn't understand why he was defending Danita and not willing to hear her out.

"The bottom line is as a CEO and a professional, you were wrong, and you should've thought of that before you even came to my place of business," Derek argued once more before he ended the call.

Shaniece hung up pissed because now he questioned her professionalism. Before walking back into her office, she wiped the tears from her eyes. She waited a few minutes because when she wiped her eyes, it seemed like one more tear would roll down her face as soon as the previous one was gone. When she finally got herself together, she took a deep breath, held her head high, and walked back into her building in an attempt to get back to her own business.

THE TRUTH HURTS

"Man, I don't know what I'm going to do. I messed up really bad with Danita. I wish I would've turned her down, but she came on so damn hard. How do I get out this mess without Shaniece finding out about it?"

Derek was venting to his friend, Marcus, while they were sitting at The Jersey Bar. Derek wasn't a huge fan of bar drinking, but whenever he was in a tight bind, that's where he went to be around other men who were down and out just like him. Sometimes, he listened to their issues, and that was all he needed to make himself feel better about his own situation.

"Listen, man, stop beating yourself up. You messed up. Right now, forgive yourself for it and move on. You said Danita will be out of there in another week or so, right?" Marcus questioned.

Marcus had been Derek's friend for ten years; the two met while completing the same master's program. His light brown eyes, bald head, sandy brown goatee, and bulging muscles had gotten him into a lot of trouble over the years, which is why he knew so much about handling relationship issues with women. Back in high school, he was the quiet, nice guy and didn't date much, but college had turned him into a wilder, more outgoing person. Marcus' confidence skyrocketed during his undergraduate years of college because he caught a lot of attention from women. He somewhat settled down with Natalie, his long-term girlfriend of fourteen years. They started dating during their junior year of undergrad and had gone through a lot, including infidelity. The most shocking thing was that Natalie still stood by Marcus' side and accepted the fact that she might not ever become his wife.

Marcus belief was that he needed to work on himself and fix his own issues before he makes her his wife which is the reason why he hasn't popped the question in close to fourteen years.

Derek didn't agree with Marcus' belief, because it can take a lifetime to fix your entire self, but he appreciated the fact that Marcus would tell him what was right and not what he wanted to hear in a crisis.

"Yeah, but her and Shaniece got into it the other day. With her leaving, she doesn't have anything to lose at this point. That's the problem!" Derek stated with frustration while throwing back a glass of whiskey.

"Look, if she tells Shaniece, whatever you do just tell the truth and face the consequences. If you deny it, all you're doing is breaking the trust even more and making things worse for yourself. If Shaniece truly loves you, she'll eventually forgive you. You have to be willing to take it head on and deal with it." Derek heard what Marcus was telling him, but the thought of seeing Shaniece hurt made him sick.

"I don't know if I can go through with it, man. I love Shaniece more than anything. She's the first woman I felt guilty about cheating on. Honestly, I never felt this guilty about anything in my life."

After several rounds of drinks, they decided to call it quits and head home for the night. Derek walked away knowing that if the truth

45

surfaced, he needed to be a man about it, face it head on, and deal with whatever consequences came about. It wasn't what he wanted to hear, but he had to respect it.

MAKE-UP SEX

"Hey, babe. What you doing?" Derek asked as he walked into the bedroom.

"Catching up on some office work." Shaniece was sitting on the bed working on her laptop and never looked away from the screen but continued typing away.

Derek and Shaniece had been very distant from each other since their big argument. Shaniece was more disappointed because her ethics had been questioned and Derek had somewhat exposed her. Even if she was out of character, she didn't want him to point it out to her. She thought that, as her man, Derek should have had her back more.

"Can we talk please?" He had a few days to think about the entire situation and was tired of the little interaction they had been experiencing. When Derek sat down beside her, Shaniece stopped typing briefly then put her hands in her lap and cut her eyes at him.

"About what? You said what you needed to say the other day. I got it so let's move past it." She rolled her eyes and resumed working on the laptop.

"So, you ignoring me and walking around with an attitude for a week is your version of moving past it?" he asked, raising his eyebrows. Shaniece sucked her teeth and sat up on the bed with her arms folded. She turned to look at him.

"Okay, go head. You have my attention." Derek smirked about the attitude he was getting but quickly made a straight face and decided to take the floor.

"Alright, let me start by saying I apologize about what I said when we had it out. I know how serious you are about your work, and I was wrong. In another week, Danita will be gone, and trust me, she's been addressed about the other day. You won't have the problem of the disrespect from anyone again, and, if it does happen, let me take care of it and believe me when I say it'll be handled. My only concern is that you took things into your own hands based off emotions, and I just can't have that at my place of business."

He was surprised that Shaniece agreed with him and apologized as well. He was even more surprised that she didn't question him about Danita. What he didn't know was that the thought of him sleeping with Danita had crossed her mind, but she just couldn't get herself to believe it. She knew Danita was nowhere near his type. She had seen pics of his exes in the past, and Danita didn't even measure up. Shaniece led herself to believe that Danita just had a bad day and took it out on her.

After fifteen minutes of discussion, they both decided to bury the argument and leave it in the past.

"I'm so glad I got my baby back," Derek joked as he tackled Shaniece down onto the bed. Shaniece was all smiles as she gazed into his eyes, immediately losing the attitude.

"I miss you, babe," she whispered, wrapping her arms around his neck.

"I miss you more," he uttered as he kissed on her full, soft lips. He eased out of her arms to come up out of his jacket then gently closed her laptop and placed it on the nightstand. Shaniece was so in tune to the moment that she didn't even check to see if her work saved. She didn't want to fight, ignore, or resist him any longer.

He climbed on top, looking in her eyes, and kissed her passionately like it was the last time he would see her. He stopped kissing her for a moment to undo the buttons of his shirt. As his shirt started to come off, Shaniece kissed his masculine arms and chest one peck at a time. He massaged his fingers through her silky chestnut brown hair while kissing on her neck. He pulled her tank top off, then she started working on undoing his belt buckle. After a few minutes of passionate foreplay, Shaniece pulled his pants and boxers off and started to massage his third wheel. Derek instantly became aroused, and somehow, Shaniece managed to make it on top. She sat in position with her back arched, and they both stared into each other's eyes without

47

saying a word while their hands intertwined. After the stare down, she proceeded to go down and do what he liked most. After a few minutes, she knew he was about to bust because he nearly pulled her hair out of her head. She let up, even though she enjoyed making him go crazy, but wanted him to experience more pleasure before he released. She wrapped her hands around his manhood and yanked on it gently until it became rock hard. She peeked up to see if he was still breathing because he was so quiet. She smirked when she saw his eyes squinted grabbing ahold of the sheets trying to hold his composure. His excitement turned her on in every way possible.

She went back to finishing what she started. Once she sensed that he had reached his peak, she tapped his leg for him to release. She used to dread giving oral sex, but with Derek, she didn't mind it anymore. She actually liked it--maybe more than he did. She was in a genuine relationship with a man whom she loved and who loved her unconditionally, so she was willing to do just about anything for him behind closed doors. After Derek got himself together, he returned the favor by laying her back on the bed. He started from the top of Shaniece's body and twirled his tongue around the tips of her perky breasts attempting to get an arousal, which didn't take long.

"Turn over," he demanded, and Shaniece was quick to do exactly as he requested. While Shaniece laid on her front side, Derek kissed her on the back of her neck, which always drove Shaniece crazy. He gave her a short back massage before his mouth graced her plump buttocks. He became aggressive and sucked her backside, placing hickey marks all over it. He was like an animal that was starving for food and had finally found his prey. She bent her legs onto the bed, poking her buttocks up in the air. He slid in between her thighs, placing a pillow down as a head rest. He stuck his tongue out and licked the tip of her clitoris. He opened his mouth wide to catch the juices that dripped from her walls. It was like ice cream on a cone that was melting from the scorching summer sun. Shaniece was almost embarrassed because her body wouldn't let up. Derek made her comfortable in every way because he saw that she enjoyed it. He wanted more so he kept hitting the areas that she loved the most. He sucked her walls dry until she had nothing left. She finally broke, and her body shook into convulsions. She couldn't stay on her knees any longer and buckled onto his face. He flipped her over on the bed and climbed on top, sliding his lower man into her well-cleaned walls. He finally got to his peak and pumped fifteen to twenty times before they both released for the second time.

"Baaaabbbby, this feels sooo goood," Shaniece yelled out.

"Yes, this is good -- damn…" he had to agree. Shaniece was still shaking while Derek was laying on the bed trying to gain his composure. They both started laughing after they were done.

"Damn, damn, damn…we have the best sex," Derek breathed as he laid with his hands behind his head.

"Damn right we do. We need to fight more often because that was bananas," Shaniece agreed. Derek pulled Shaniece close and kissed her forehead. She laid on his shoulder, resting her hand on his chest, and they cuddled one another in the sheets, falling asleep soon after.

NO MORE DRINKS

Derek was relieved that he had gotten his life back to normal. Melanie returned from maternity leave, and Danita was finally out the picture. He broke away from her with no issues and was rather surprised how she left without any drama. Both he and Shaniece were tending to each other more and having amazing sex at least four times a week. With the big day approaching, they were both nervous but excited to be united as one.

* * * * * *

Shaniece and Julian met in her office three days before the wedding day. She decided to put him on the guest list to make it not look suspicious. After all they did work together, and it would have been questioned by some as to why he wasn't in attendance and others were. They were both past what they had, and Shaniece was pleased with how their professional relationship had gotten back on track.

"Okay, so let's discuss the wedding rules," she told Julian as she sat on the edge of her desk.

"I can't believe I'm agreeing to this, but, okay, whatever you want, boss lady," he replied sarcastically.

"Okay, there's a two-drink limit for you, and after that you have to call it quits. The last thing I need is for you to get drunk and start blurting out accusations that will ruin my day. For some reason, I had a dream that you were drunk at my wedding and was yelling out to everyone that we slept together, and you were thrown out so I'm just making sure this dream doesn't become a reality."

Julian couldn't do anything but laugh. "I know you almost shit your pants when you woke up from that dream, but, no, I get it. I wouldn't ruin your day like that." Shaniece looked at him with a serious face.

"Thank you for understanding." Julian looked into her eyes.

"So, are you excited about the big day?" Shaniece was kind of hesitant to talk with him about it but thought, *What the heck.*

"Actually, I am. I can't wait until we make it official!" Julian nodded his head as he got up from the chair he was sitting in.

"Well, that's good. I'm really happy for you too." He walked out and shut her door behind him.

* * * * * *

The day of the wedding was perfect. Bobby was able to pull things off so that Shaniece and Derek could have a big local wedding. They were rather impressed with how everything came together at the last minute. The wedding day was everything they had imagined and more, from the church to the reception venue. On top of that, practically all of their family, friends and associates came to the ceremony and reception; the couple ended up having two hundred and ten people in attendance.

At the reception, so many people were having a fun time laughing, conversing, drinking, taking selfies or group pics, and dancing. While she sat next to Derek at the couple's table taking it all in, Shaniece felt like a weight had been lifted once she jumped the broom. She felt like the past mistakes she made no longer existed, and she had a clean slate. The feeling she felt that day was something she knew she wouldn't get again so she enjoyed every moment of it.

Shaniece eventually noticed Julian standing alone in a corner with a drink in his hand watching everyone else having an enjoyable time. She had a chance to break free from the crowd and walked over to him. Julian noticed her approaching and took in all her beauty as she walked up to him in her white mermaid sequined wedding dress.

"Hey, no dancing for you?" she inquired while attempting to fix her crystal jeweled tiara that was starting to tilt off the side of her head.

"Well, yes, but I'm more in the mood for drinking," he told her as he took a big gulp of his brown drink. Shaniece looked at him with the biggest eyes but then squinted briefly.

"Oh, so you're in the drinking mood? How many so far?"

"Oh, I don't know. I think I lost count," he told her.

At this point, Shaniece was pissed. She assumed he had a trick up his sleeve and wanted to beat him to the punch.

"Well, let's find your date and get you home. Don't want you getting too drunk that you embarrass yourself." She was secretly praying he would comply.

"Oh, my date…I don't have a date. Yeah, my fiancée and I called it off…and do you mean embarrass you?" Julian was outspoken, and he obviously had too much to drink. Shaniece was even more concerned because she knew he didn't have anything to lose. She had no idea he and his fiancée weren't together anymore. She thought, *Well maybe he cares about his job.* She wanted him to at least think about that.

"Well, you don't want to make a fool out of yourself drinking in front of the employees. You don't want them to look at you in a different light come Monday." Julian knew what she was trying to do, but at this point he couldn't care less. He was in love with Shaniece and kept his feelings sealed deep down for the sake of his job. Once his engagement was off, he didn't even bother pursuing his fiancée to get her back because he really wanted Shaniece. He knew publicly embarrassing her at her own wedding wasn't the best approach, so he thought he'd give her an ultimatum.

"So, I heard what you said weeks back, and it got me to thinking. I want you, and I never stopped wanting you. I understand that you're a married woman now, but the only way you'll stay happily married is if you give me your time at least twice a month. It doesn't necessarily have to be sex, but I want some personal one-on-one time with you outside of the office. If you don't agree, I will ruin your marriage before it even starts."

Shaniece laughed hysterically. She didn't mean to but that was her response. She kept the laughing going more so because she didn't want anyone to think anything was out of the ordinary talking with Julian as long as she was while her reception was still in progress. Before she could retort, Karina popped up and stopped their conversation.

"Shaniece, come on. People want you to take some pictures. Excuse me, sir." Karina whisked Shaniece away by her arm as Julian stood there alone. All night, Derek and Shaniece greeted folks, took pictures, danced, laughed, and cried. Shaniece wasn't too concerned about Julian but was concerned about trusting him with her business. She felt bad because she was more willing to risk her marriage than her business. She was confident that she would be able to get her husband back if he ever found out, but it would be hard to build her business back up if Julian intentionally tried to destroy it -- or her for that matter.

I'M SORRY

"Babe, I have a headache," Shaniece complained as they woke up toward the middle of the day. After the discussion with Julian at the wedding, she drank the rest of the night away. She then passed out in the room, and no wedding night sex took place. Derek wasn't upset because they had made love two days ago, so he wasn't too much in need. Still, he felt it would've been nice to make love to his wife the night of their wedding.

"I know you do. I lost count of how many glasses you had," Derek reminded her. Shaniece blew his comment off and looked at the clock. It showed that it was a little past noon.

"Oh my gosh, we slept that long?"

"Yeah, don't worry we're good. We have enough time to sleep in before we need to pack."

"I know. I'm just saying I don't remember the last time I slept in until noon."

Derek smiled briefly but heard his stomach rumble. They hadn't eaten since the reception, and he was starting to feel a little famished. "You hungry? I'm ready to order some room service."

Shaniece was surprised how tired and sick she was, so she passed on the food and went back to sleep.

* * * * * *

A few hours later, Shaniece woke up to Derek talking in her ear.

"Babe get up, your phone is ringing." She thought she was in a dream because she kept hearing repeatedly, "Babe, wake up, it's the phone." She wasn't fully awake but sat up on the bed on one elbow and took the phone from Derek without questioning who was on the other line.

"Helllooo?" Her voice was groggy from her abrupt awakening.

"Hi Shaniece, it's Julian. Look, I'm at the office, and I can't find the Krosher file. I have that big meeting Monday morning. Do you think you can come down and help me find it?" Shaniece looked at her screen to make sure it was actually Julian on the line. She cleared her throat before she spoke again.

"Well did you try checking with Karen before calling me? She has access to everything I have access to. I'm sure she can help you." She waited for a response, but instead she heard silence. "Hello?! Did you hear me?"

"Yes, I heard you but I didn't want to call Karen, I wanted to call you. Today is our first meet up, and I want to see you before you leave for your honeymoon, so I should be expecting you within an hour or two, correct?" Shaniece sat up on the bed in an upright posture then looked at Derek as he focused on packing up his clothes.

"Okay, I'll be there. Give me an hour. I'll help you find it." Shaniece hung up the phone, and she was angry to the point she wanted to punch a wall. So many thoughts went through her head as she sat on the bed. She contemplated for a few minutes whether she should tell Derek about what happened and Julian now blackmailing her. She knew the day after their wedding and the day before their honeymoon wasn't the best time, but she also knew she wouldn't be able to think straight on their trip knowing Julian was handling things back at the office. He was filling in for her on Monday, and she knew she couldn't be there to attend. The thought of him trying to sabotage her business raced through her mind. She just didn't trust him at this point.

"Hey, what's wrong? You have to leave to go to the office?" Derek asked while sorting through his clothes.

"Yeah, I have to go find this file that Julian needs for Monday's meeting with one of our big clients. He'll be filling in for me and needs it to prep." Shaniece slowly swung her legs over the side of the bed, praying Derek didn't ask any other questions because she didn't want to start lying.

"Mmm. Oh, what happened to Julian's fiancée? I don't recall seeing him with a date at the wedding."

"Yeah, I'm not sure."

"I saw you chatting with him at the reception; you never asked?" At this point, Shaniece chest started tightening because she wasn't sure what Derek knew or what he didn't know. She was ready to come clean and let him know what was going on because she didn't want to go through with Julian blackmailing her. If she told him what was going on, Julian wouldn't be able to hold anything over her head. Despite this, she held back on what she wanted to say.

"No, I'm not too concerned with his personal life."

Anxiety began to take over as Shaniece was stooped on the edge of the bed in a daze, wondering what to do next. She finally got off the bed and went into the bathroom to brush her teeth, wash her face, and take a shower with Derek. She instantly thought that by giving him what he liked the most, she would get an advantage regarding the situation and Derek wouldn't flip out on her if she did decide to come clean. So, she rocked his world in the shower. Derek was a very pleased man afterwards and wouldn't stop chanting about how he was a lucky man. After the steamy shower session, Shaniece sat back on the bed with her towel wrapped around her body. Derek was chest down on the bed while Shaniece climbed up on his back to massage him down with lotion. She kept going back and forth in her mind whether she should have this conversation right here, right now. Every time she opened her mouth, nothing would come out. She just didn't have the words. Finally, she struck up the nerve. She knew the timing wasn't right but had to come clean. *If not now, then when?* she asked herself. She closed her eyes and whispered a quick prayer to herself before taking a deep breath.

"Babe, we need to talk," she mentioned as she slowly moved from being on top of his body. She instantly felt numb. It was like the words came out without any final warning or permission from her. Immediately, Derek turned over on the bed with his towel wrapped around his waist, staring into her eyes with his hands tucked behind his head.

"Talk about what?" he asked in a concerned voice.

"You know I love you, right?" Derek wasn't for the games, so he sat up and leapt from the bed to start putting on his boxers, t-shirt, and socks. He used that same line many times so he knew something was up.

"Look, go head and say what you have to say." Tears started to stream from Shaniece's eyes, and she could barely speak but struck up the nerve once again.

"I'm just going to come out and say it. Okay, some time back when you were working on your first big deal, you were never home. Honestly, I thought you were cheating on me. I thought you had somebody else, so I stepped out on our relationship and had an affair with Julian and now he's blackmailing me. He wants to ruin our marriage and I don't know what to do." Shaniece spoke so fast she didn't realize what she was saying and wasn't sure if she got out all that she wanted to say. She sat and stared at Derek for ten seconds straight without blinking.

Derek now had his head down on the dresser and was shaking his head. Shaniece was scared because she didn't know how he was going to react. She finally blinked then jumped while clutching her towel when he finally did speak.

"So, you mean to tell me I've been cool with this dude and had conversations with him about business and sometimes you, and he had you. I can't believe you're telling me this, especially now."

For the first time in his life, he felt betrayed by a woman. He was used to being the player and the one stepping out, not it being the other way around. Shaniece wanted him to focus solely on the blackmailing part instead of the affair.

"I'm sorry…it happened a while back. I called it quits before it got to anything really serious. We've been business professionals since, but the problem is I want to terminate him, and I want to do it today, but I need you by my side because he's blackmailing me and I'm not sure how to handle this situation." Shaniece was mad at herself because she thought maybe this wasn't the best moment, but she also didn't want to go along with the blackmailing plot and dig herself into a deeper hole.

Derek lifted his head from the dresser and turned away from Shaniece. "If I see this dude…I might kill him so I don't think it's a good idea for me to go to that office. It won't be good for business," he warned her. Shaniece understood because if it was the other way around, she would've felt the same way.

"Okay…I will…handle it on my own. I'll be back in a few. I have to get rid of this guy."

Shaniece put on her clothes and walked out the hotel suite. Derek walked over to the bed and sat on the edge in disbelief. He was hurt to the core and even though he wanted to react irrationally in the moment his heart was too broken. He never imagined Shaniece would cheat on him. He knew he hadn't been faithful himself but never thought that he would be on the receiving end of infidelity.

SOMEBODY CALL 911

"Julian, where are you?" Shaniece yelled out while walking through the office. She thought maybe he left because she didn't see his car, and there wasn't a sign that anyone was in the building. She called his cell and didn't get an answer. She walked into her office and looked through her desk and immediately found the file. She walked out into the lobby and called Julian's phone again. After no response a second time, she decided to text him: *I'm here, where are you? I have the file.* She kept her phone in hand and decided to leave the file out on the front desk after no reply back. As she approached the front lobby, Shaniece got ready to dial Derek's number to tell him she was on her way back, but Julian bumped into her while walking in through the front door.

"Oh my goodness, you scared me! Where were you?" she asked in a startled tone. Julian looked at her with a smile, but he didn't say a word. Shaniece crossed her arms and squinted at him. "What's up with the big Kool-Aid smile?" Julian started chuckling and then suddenly went on a rant.

"Actually, I'm just happy you're here…but why did you marry him?! You know it was supposed to be me and you, and you just messed it up. Why? Why?!" he demanded. She was taken aback with the sudden change in tone. She stared at him for a moment with a confused look but was starting to become alarmed.

"Look, Julian…I'm not sure where all this is coming from, but you have to stop it…I never did and never will want you as my man. That's the honest truth," she said, hoping he hadn't heard her voice crack. Julian was running on his emotions and didn't seem to be in his right frame of mind. Shaniece realized that what she said may have come off a little strong, so she started moving toward the front door and tried to switch up her approach. "But maybe we can go out somewhere and get some coffee and talk. How about that? Let me look up a place. I hear there's a new one just right up the road."

She started backing out of Derek's phone number, trying to dial nine-one-one but also make it look like she was doing a search. She touched the screen one last time, but by the time she thought she had pressed the call button, Julian was right in front of her. He grabbed and pinned her against the lobby area chairs, making her drop the phone to the floor.

"Julian, stop it! What are you doing?!" She prayed her phone had connected to the police and that someone could hear what was going on in the background. She tried to fight him off, but he was physically stronger than her, and she couldn't get away from him. She screamed to the top of her lungs even though she knew it probably wouldn't help. There was no one else in the building but the two of them that she was aware of, and they were on the third floor. It didn't take her long to realize how dangerous of a situation she was in.

"Okay, Julian! You're right -- I admit marrying Derek was stupid of me! I know he don't deserve me, and I was stupid to stay with him after all the late nights! You were there for me all along, and I had to be stupid not to realize you were the man for me..." she went on and on telling him what she thought he wanted to hear, trying to use reverse psychology. That tactic only made the situation worse, as he started to kiss and grope on her even more.

"I knew you wanted me all along. Let's make love here on the floor like we did back then. I know you remember how we use to do it." She cried and cried until she couldn't anymore, trying to make him let her go, but Julian had full control. He grabbed her arms and knocked her down to the carpet floor. In an attempt to get away, she kicked him in his shin, which stunned him for a moment. She picked up the phone and ran toward her office as fast as she could, trying to knock over anything she could in the process to slow him down. Julian recovered from her kick quickly and somehow dodged all of her obstacles. He caught up to her before she could slam her office door in his face. He shoved her to the floor again, and her phone went bouncing about two feet away from her grasp. In the rush to her office, she hadn't paid attention to whether there was an active call and couldn't hear if anyone was talking because the volume was turned down low. Still, if the call had been connected, she needed someone to know what Julian was about to do to her.

"So, you really going to do this, rape me on the floor in my own office? Are you really going to do this?" she screamed and pleaded at the same time, trying to crawl away backwards toward the direction of where she thought her phone had gone.

"It's not rape if you once agreed to it," he boldly told her. He grabbed her foot and dragged her back to him. He then stood up, putting a foot on her stomach to keep her pinned while taking off his pants. He quickly got down on top of her and started kissing her lips and neck. Shaniece pulled away and turned her head from side to side. "Keep still!" he yelled. Shaniece tried pushing him, but he wouldn't budge. Julian grabbed her t-shirt and ripped it off. He stroked his fingers through her hair while looking into her eyes. Shaniece looked at him with rage, but all he saw was a feisty woman who wanted the same thing he did. He pulled his boxers off then yanked her sweats and panties down to her knees and entered in. Once he was fully straddled, he let out a loud "Aaaaahhhh...I remember how this used to feel."

Tears flowed continuously from the corners of Shaniece's closed eyes. She couldn't believe a huge mistake she had made so long ago would end up like this. She tried to think of anything that would keep her from being in the moment, but nothing came through except thoughts of guilt, anger, and fear. She eventually passed out and didn't come to again until Julian was close to being done. Julian pumped harder and harder until he was ready to release. He kept ahold of her arms while on the floor and wouldn't let her go until he got it all out. When he was done, he stood up and said, "Damn, didn't that feel good?!" Shaniece opened her eyes partially but didn't and couldn't respond. She felt him get off her and passed out again.

* * * * * *

Julian was almost done getting dressed when Derek burst through the door and saw Shaniece laid out on the floor, practically naked but unresponsive to his arrival.

"What the fuck is going on here?!" he yelled.

"Hey, man! I'm sorry you had to find out like this. Look, we didn't mean to sleep together. It kinda just hap---" Before Julian could get his last word out Derek swung on him and threw him on Shaniece's desk. All the rage he had since Shaniece left the suite came out when he saw Julian.

"What the fuck is wrong with you man?" Derek blurted several times as he punched Julian repeatedly in his head and face. Suddenly, Derek snapped out of it, and his life and future flashed before his eyes. He realized he was about to kill this man, so he let him go. He grabbed Julian by his neck and threw him out the office after kicking him in his back. Julian didn't dare challenge Derek physically or verbally, so he kept it moving, getting up and hobbling toward the office exit. Once Derek saw that Julian was gone, he hurried back over to Shaniece and kneeled by her helpless body.

"Babe, get up!" he repeated more than once. He checked to see if she was still breathing then got down on both knees and tried to hold her up in his arms. She opened her eyes slightly but still seemed to be in a daze. Derek started tapping her on her left cheek until she finally came to, but as soon as she did, she jumped out of fear and tried to fight her way out of his embrace. In that moment, all she could think about was fighting for her life. "Shaniece! Shaniece! It's me, babe!" Derek yelled while blocking her hits. He finally grasped her wrists so she could stop, and she realized it was her husband and not Julian. Shaniece couldn't do anything but sob.

"Derek, he...he— "She couldn't get any other words out of her mouth. More tears began to flow, and she fell into Derek's chest, crying hysterically at this point. Derek was confused at first then realized what had happened. He patted all his pockets to find his phone and dialed nine-one-one.

"Yes, I need to report a rape. I need to report a rape!" Derek yelled out to the operator several times. "Yes, my wife was assaulted, and the rapist's name is Julian; he's an employee of hers…what's his last name babe? What's his last name?!" Shaniece couldn't speak instead just cried even more. Derek was frustrated but scared at the same time. He continued giving as many details to the operator as he could without losing his cool. "Yes, we're at the Carter Building on Max Barnes Avenue! Please send help ASAP!" he yelled through the phone before hanging up and tossing it to the floor. Derek cried hard tears as he held Shaniece in his arms rocking back and forth as he repeated over and over, "I'm sorry, Shaniece…I'm so so sorry…"

SLOWLY BUT SHORTLY

Julian was convicted of rape and sentenced to six years in prison. Shaniece wasn't upset with the sentencing because she understood how the system worked. She just wanted him out of her life for good.

Shaniece felt like Julian had won because she lived life totally different now. Whenever she went out, she would always be on alert and tried not to be alone when she did leave home. She basically spent each day in a bubble and felt like she was no longer free. Her intimacy with Derek had been affected the most and hadn't allowed him to touch her since. She never forgot what Julian told her the night of her wedding: *I will ruin your marriage before it even starts*. That's exactly what he did, even after being put behind bars.

The only good thing was she had been able to keep everything under wraps with the help of her attorneys about what really happened at the office that day. She decided not to disclose the truth to anyone because she didn't want to jeopardize her character or her company brand. As far as everyone knew, Julian decided to leave and find work in another state. Not too many questions were asked because Shaniece didn't have much to say. She had a brief meeting with her staff about the changes taking place in the office and moved on the best way she could.

* * * * * *

As the months went by, Derek tried everything to make things more comfortable for Shaniece because he knew she been through a lot. The image of her on the floor that day had never left his mind, and he cried almost every day, blaming himself for letting her go to the office alone. After the trial was over, Derek and Shaniece decided to finally take the honeymoon that they had missed. Shaniece needed a getaway because she consumed herself with work so much to block out what had happened.

"Babe, you happy about our vacation?" Derek asked excitedly.

"Yes, just me and you and no distractions…oh, how I'm looking forward to that…" Shaniece responded, smiling. Derek was looking forward to the vacation too, but he wanted even more to get his wife back again and thought maybe a tropical island would do just that.

The day before their flight, they decided to spend a full day with Justin. He was getting older and had been participating heavily in various skateboarding competitions, so they barely had a chance to hang out with him anymore. On top of that, they had also been dealing with court proceedings. After the rape happened, Derek talked with Justin about his mom. He didn't tell him the full story because he didn't want Justin to have that image in his head for the rest of his life. He just told him that his mother was assaulted in her office by an intruder and left it at that. He also knew that if Justin found out the truth, he might be in jail as well, and he didn't want to see that happen to him. The assault alone took a toll on Justin because he wasn't there to protect his mom, which was the same feeling Derek had. To help diminish those feelings, Shaniece and Derek both wanted to make up for missed time with their son.

"So, Justin…what's the plans for today? Derek asked.

"The mall!" Justin said with a smirk on his face. Shaniece laughed.

"How did we know you were going to say that?" They all chuckled on the way out to the car.

They rode in silence for a few minutes, beyond having some old school music playing softly, until Shaniece spoke up.

"You know, Justin, I'm really proud of you. I know I haven't been fully connected like I should be as a mom lately. I just want to thank you for being a great ki--...son and for your support." Shaniece was trying to hold back her emotions. Justin wasn't the emotional type now, but he knew his mom been through a lot the last few months.

He showed another side of himself that she and Derek didn't see much of often when he responded. "Mom, you've always been there since I was young. You don't know, but you were still there for me the last few months. I'm just happy that you're okay and feeling better. I love you so much, mom!"

"Aww, that is so sweet. My baby being emotional," Shaniece joked.

After a few more minutes, they arrived at the mall, and Justin took off toward his favorite shoe store. Derek and Shaniece looked at each other, smiling and shaking their heads, as they followed him. A few hours and a fifteen-hundred-dollar bill later, the family finally decided to call it quits and went home.

* * * * * *

Shaniece and Derek were beyond ecstatic waiting to leave for their honeymoon. The flight was scheduled for 8 p.m. so they had a full day to get everything in order. This was the first big vacation they were having together. They had been on local vacations but hadn't been out of the country except for when they attended his college buddy wedding in Jamaica. Hawaii was their original honeymoon destination, but they didn't want the stigma of those vacation plans to haunt them. Instead, they ended up planning a trip to Punta Cana. They read great reviews about Punta Cana before and had planned to go while engaged. However, they never got around to it; their schedules and careers wouldn't allow them to.

"We're going to Punta Canaaaa. We're going to Punta Canaaa," Shaniece started singing while dancing in the middle of the bedroom floor. Derek couldn't do anything but laugh. After hearing it so many times, he finally decided to join in on the foolishness.

"We're, we're going to Pun-ta, Pun-ta Canaaaa!" Derek started beatboxing while trying to portray LL Cool J in the bedroom mirror. Shaniece joined in and folded her arms like a tough girl, bouncing side to side and bobbing her head. They both looked at each other and fell out laughing. "I swear I love you," Derek stated as he kissed Shaniece on her forehead.

* * * * * *

"First class is sooo nice. I'm loving it," Shaniece whispered to Derek as they exchanged a toast of champagne.

"I know. This is just the beginning! Wait until you see our resort. The pics online are ridiculous. It's five stars so we should be in for a treat," Derek stated excitedly.

On the flight, they sipped champagne, nibbled on appetizers, and played footsies under their blanket; they were like two kids on Christmas Eve. Both were tired but very anxious to get to their destination to the point that they couldn't fall asleep. To occupy themselves for the remainder of the trip, they shared ear plugs and listened to an Spotify download of their wedding playlist. The more songs they listened to, the gushier they became on the inside.

"We're here, we're here, we're here," Shaniece said repeatedly while looking out the window onto the runway. Everyone else around them was sleeping, reading, or listening to music. They were the only two, at least within their eyesight, who were fully alert and excited. After the flight attendants gave instructions, they finally exited the plane.

"Okay, we need to go to pick up our luggage and then we will meet our driver, Herberto outside," Derek instructed. Shaniece had always loved that Derek was always organized and in control. That was her biggest turn-on because she shared the same qualities. She thought that they would clash because of it, but having the same characteristics worked in their favor for their businesses and in their relationship.

After grabbing their luggage, they made their way outside through the crowd where they spotted Herberto holding a sign with their last name on it. They greeted him, and he welcomed them to the island while taking their luggage and placing it in the back of a black-on-black Yukon. As they pulled up to the resort, they couldn't believe their eyes. They were so taken aback by their surroundings that they didn't bother to take pictures; they just enjoyed the moment. Shaniece hadn't felt this good deep down in a long time. Derek saw that his wife was ecstatic, and that made him even happier.

"Babe, I love you so much. I can't believe how beautiful this is. It's like paradise," Shaniece expressed as she held Derek's hand. After thanking and tipping Herberto, they exited the vehicle and were greeted by bell boys to grab their luggage. They checked in at the front lobby and then were directed to a secluded area that belonged to just the two of them.

"Damn, this place is fly," Derek stated as they both walked around the suite. They were both speechless about the view. The ocean in the early morning was to die for, and they couldn't believe this is where they would be alone for the next six days.

PARADISE

"Aaaaahhhh babe, stay right there, aaaaaahhhhh, don't stop, don't stop, yesssssssss!" Shaniece yelled out to the top of her lungs while Derek was on top giving it all he had.

Shaniece and Derek decided to spend their entire first day in Punta Cana behind closed doors. They didn't feel guilty about not going out to enjoy the scenery because they led such busy lives back at home. Relaxation and uninterrupted time together were exactly what they both needed. Somehow, Shaniece knew the change of scenery would get her to open up and allow her husband to be intimate with her again.

She looked into his eyes and saw that he was all into their moment together. She loved when he went into another world while making love to her because she was certainly going to experience the orgasm of a lifetime. It was the first time they had connected as one since the rape. Shaniece had almost forgotten how Derek used to make her feel. She was finally at a point where she could happily enjoy him all over again.

They had tried having sex many times before, but she would always freak out and push him off her. This time around, though, she was ready.

"Baabbbyyyy, it feels soooo good." One minute, she was whispering into his ear, and the next, she was as loud as she could be. She finally got to the point where she was prepared to release, and she knew Derek was too. "Baaabbyyyy I'm bout to c---" Before she could get out the last of her words, Derek released all he had into her.

"Ohhhh, ohhh, ohhh!" was all Shaniece heard from Derek. After minutes of leg shaking, hair pulling, and yelling out obscenities to each other, both of their bodies came to a complete halt. They laid on the bed staring up at the ceiling in complete silence, taking in the moment of what had just happened. They then spent the rest of their first day and the second day making love, sleeping in, and ordering around-the-clock room service. On the third day of their vacation, they decided to finally come out for air and enjoy the rest of their vacation outdoors.

* * * * * *

"Hi, honey -- good morning," Shaniece greeted Derek with a beautiful smile on her face as she kissed his cheek. Derek was so happy and in love with his wife and loved that she was getting back to her normal self. As a husband, nothing satisfied him more. He sat and stared at her for a moment before saying anything. "Earth to Derek...Earth to Derek!" Shaniece snapped her fingers in his face.

"I'm sorry, babe. I'm just admiring you for a minute," he answered, smirking. Shaniece blushed and cracked a smile. She remembered when she would dream of a man doing that and, now that she had experienced it, she realized it was a feeling like no other.

"Well, I'll just sit right here and won't say a word and let you admire every detail of me from head to toe," Shaniece chuckled as she did different poses in front of him.

"I swear I love you. You always know what to do and say. So, what's on our agenda today?" Derek asked. He knew Shaniece had come up with a list of ideas.

"Well, there's a beach party tonight at seven so we can do that. But until then we can go horseback riding or maybe snorkeling. I'm not too keen on the snorkeling idea, but I'm willing to compromise and do something you want to do." Derek didn't care what activities they did as long as they were together.

"I mean it's up to you. I'm down for whatever."

"Okay, let's do horseback riding. The shuttle leaves in two hours so we have to hurry up." They both showered, got dressed, and were out the door within ninety minutes. The staff waved to them as they came out of the room with courteous smiles on their faces.

"They're probably saying, 'Dag, they finally made it out after three days'," Shaniece whispered to Derek as they were walking to the shuttle location.

"Yeah, I know. They're probably going to burn our sheets," Derek joked. They both laughed and held hands while waiting for the shuttle to arrive.

* * * * * *

A few hours later, Derek and Shaniece returned from horseback riding and decided to take a nap before heading out to the beach party later that evening. They had been enjoying each other's company for the last few days and wanted to spend the rest of their time turning up before heading home. After an hour and a half, the alarm on Shaniece's phone started blaring.

"Babe, wake up," Shaniece said in a raspy voice while attempting to stop the alarm. Once she got it to stop, she sat up and stretched, then got out of bed to get dressed.

"I'm up, I'm up," Derek repeated until his eyes were fully adjusted. He sat up on the edge of the bed rolling his neck around trying to get out the kinks. When he did get up, he walked over to the dresser.

"Should I wear these khaki shorts or the jean shorts?" Derek asked. Shaniece peeked out the bathroom with a makeup brush in her hand.

"Well, it's a beach party so maybe you should wear your swimming trunks. I mean it's up to you. I'm not planning on getting wet, but I am wearing my two-piece under my dress," she told him, retreating back into the bathroom to finish doing her makeup in the mirror. Derek looked in the dresser drawer at his selections.

"I'm just going to do the khakis, this white polo, and flip flops and call it a day."

Derek lightly ironed over his clothes and waited on the bed for Shaniece to get out the bathroom. When she finished, Shaniece walked out looking completely flawless. She sat on the chaise lounge close to their bed.

"Your hair and makeup look nice," he complimented her. He went over and kissed her on her forehead on his way to the bathroom.

"Aww, thanks, babe." She found herself blushing as she covered her hands, arms, legs, and feet in the body butter Derek had gotten for her before they left for Punta Cana. She really couldn't believe that this was the man she had married, but she was more than happy having him in her life. *He's such a blessing,* she thought to herself.

* * * * * *

They made their way outside to the beach and were highly impressed with the setup. When they arrived, they were surprised by how many other couples were there already.

"You wanna make it over to the bar and get a cocktail?" Shaniece yelled over the loud Latin music. Derek didn't bother competing with the music. He just nodded his head "yes" as they headed over to the bar. After standing for nearly twenty minutes and listening to people yelling out orders, they were finally able to get their drinks. They left the deck and walked onto the beach where the main party was taking place. While sipping on their cocktails, a couple standing next to them introduced themselves.

"Hi, my name is Esqueza, and this is my husband, Carlos." Derek and Shaniece were a little caught off guard.

"Well, hello. My name is Shaniece, and this is my husband, Derek," Shaniece stated with a fake smile while holding her straw close to her mouth.

"You guys are in the same area as us. We saw you earlier so wanted to say hello. Beautiful couple you are." Before Shaniece and Derek could respond, several other couples had come over, and everyone introduced themselves and exchanged handshakes. The music was jumping and Shaniece was certainly feeling it, so she grabbed Derek and started backing it up on him. Everyone was dancing and having a good time. Once Derek and Shaniece exited the dance area, Esqueza had found her way to them again.

"Any plans after this?" the woman asked. Shaniece was starting to become annoyed because she didn't know or hadn't seen this lady before tonight. She wanted Esqueza to let them be and just enjoy the party.

Shaniece looked at Derek, and he replied, "We're going to our room and to bed." The woman shook her head and was about to open her mouth and reply to Derek's response, but Shaniece interjected.

"Why?" she said, clearly aggravated now. Esqueza looked at them with googly eyes.

"Well, my husband and I are having a private party back at our suite and thought maybe you guys would want to join us."

Shaniece immediately knew what that was code for. She whispered in Derek's ear, "They're swingers. Come on, let's go." Shaniece smiled at the woman. "We'll pass. I'm sure some couple will take you up on your request, but you got the wrong one here." The woman knew that Shaniece had read her.

Esqueza politely replied, "I get it. You're not into that type of party. Point taken."

Shaniece and Derek turned their backs on the woman and laughed off and on about what just took place as they danced some more. Shaniece wanted to laugh in the woman's face because she looked completely pathetic searching for a desperate horny couple like her and her husband. Esqueza looked to be in her early fifties, and her husband looked much older. After looking at her husband Shaniece saw why their sex life needed a boost and wanted a younger couple to bring it back to life. Shaniece nor Derek was into that type of party and were not flattered.

* * * * * *

"Hey, I want to go skinny dipping," Shaniece suggested after an hour of dancing and more drinks. She looked into Derek's eyes with an innocent look and smiled, hoping he would take up on her idea and be spontaneous. The multiple cocktails were starting to make her feel a little frisky.

"How we going to do that?" he asked.

"I don't know...maybe we can walk down the beach some to get away from the crowd." Derek thought about Shaniece's suggestion and agreed. It had been over three months since he's been able to enjoy his wife, and he didn't want to turn her down.

It was beautiful out, and the moon was brightly lit. The ocean water was crystal clear, even with the moonlight gleaming down. Shaniece and Derek walked the white sandy beach holding hands while laughing and joking again about the desperate couple until they were far enough where they didn't see a soul in sight.

"Let's stop here," Derek instructed as he looked around at their surroundings. However, Shaniece was beginning to become somewhat concerned: if something happened to them, no one would ever know.

"Babe, I'm starting to have second thoughts about this. It's not as nice down here like it is up by the resort," Shaniece stated as she glanced over the abundance of weeds and bushes behind them. She feared that some sort of animal would be behind the bushes. Derek agreed, but he had to keep up his macho appearance and dismissed the idea of going back. He wrapped his arms around her waist and pulled her in tightly as he squeezed her bottom to comfort her. She laid her head on his chest and then looked up at him and gazed into his eyes. They didn't say anything to each other, but their eyes said all they wanted to say. Derek scrounged up the bottom of her gold, fitted dress and pulled it from over her head. He then pulled the string to her bikini top, and she put her arms down so it would fall completely off. All that was left was the bottom of her bikini set, and she decided to help him out, sliding it down to her ankles and kicking it toward her dress.

"Lay down," Derek demanded lightly as his eyes shifted down to the sand. Shaniece laid on her back, using her garments as a pillow. While looking up at Derek standing over top of her, she watched him strip down to his birthday suit. He got down on top and kissed her all over. Shaniece usually kept her eyes closed whenever they made love, but she wanted to be more alert to her surroundings. After a little foreplay, they decided to walk down to the water and pick up where they left off. They walked into the ocean, and Shaniece jumped up on his back and wrapped her legs around his lower waist. Derek walked deeper into the water until it covered at least his middle area. Shaniece kept her arms wrapped around his neck as she looked ahead at the rest of the ocean view. After a few minutes of looking over the water and taking in the beautiful view, Derek walked back to the forefront, still holding her up by the bottom of her thighs. When they reached the shore, Shaniece hopped down, and after checking her surroundings again, she instructed Derek to lay down this time around.

He did as she commanded, and Shaniece straddled his wet body and climbed on top. She loved the fact that the beach waves were engaged in their sexual encounter, as it made things feel even sexier. She bounced up and down on his manhood. He grabbed her breasts and started playing with her nipples. That turned her on the most. The ocean waves pounced up against her backside and splashed against her caramel cheeks. She thought about the horseback ride from earlier and started to remember the movements as she rode him. She felt his manhood ready to explode because she could feel him bulging within the barriers of her vaginal walls. She didn't want him to release just yet because she wasn't quite ready, so she hopped off.

"What are you doing?" he yelled out with his hands up in the air. "I was about there!" Shaniece pulled her body up and sat on his face to quiet him down.

"You know I got you. Don't trip," she told him.

71

As she sat on his face, he licked the juices that dripped from her walls. It was one of his favorite things to do. Her hands were planted in the sand, and she thought she was going to tip over from the way he was lifting her lower body. The water was coming up more as she felt splashes up against her thighs. Between his mouth and the ocean water, she was at her peak for sure. He interlocked his arms around her legs, and every time she tried to pull up, he wouldn't loosen his grip.

"Babe, let me hop back on." Derek heard her, but he was enjoying the entrée all too well. After a few more minutes, he pulled his face out of her cookie and released the grip from her legs. Shaniece slid her wet pelvis across his chin then down his chest and straddled his manhood once again. She began riding him like a madwoman, and all Derek could do was moan and groan like a madman. She saw him losing his mind and knew he was ready to go any minute now. She was there herself, so any moment was good for her.

"Oh oh, Babe I'm there, Ohhh," Derek managed to say. He breathed heavily for a few more minutes then yelled, "I'm cuuuumming!" At that point, Shaniece knew her work was done.

They both discharged at the same time, and Shaniece loved every bit of it. Shortly after they were done, she slid off of him slowly. Before she could look down at the mess they made, a big wave came and washed it all away. Derek laid in the sand for another two to three minutes, allowing the waves to continue washing up on him. She kissed him passionately on his lips before getting up and hurrying to put her clothes back on. She grabbed Derek's clothes, balled up her swimsuit bottoms, and placed them in his pockets.

"Here, get up," she told him as she threw him his clothes. Derek was ready to get out of dodge himself. They practically ran back to the resort. They heard slow music playing and saw a few couples still on the beach dancing. They started dancing too, trying to blend back into the crowd as if they had never left.

"Babe, look," Shaniece tapped Derek on his arm. Derek looked over and saw Esqueza conversing with another young couple. They watched as the young woman grabbed her possible husband while she was shaking her head "no" and walking away. She appeared very disgusted.

"Do you think she ran all these people off?" Derek asked, laughing at his own question. Shaniece chuckled at the possibility of Esqueza being the reason why everyone else called it a night.

"I'm pretty sure she did. Poor lady. She needs to give it up for sure." They spent the last few days of their vacation snorkeling, ziplining, sightseeing, and making more love than they ever thought possible. Derek made up for all the missed time when Shaniece wasn't feeling up to it. He felt like he could finally enjoy his life as a married man.

WELCOME BACK

"Hello, Mr. Reeler. Welcome back from your vacation," Melanie stated with a smile as she handed Derek his missed notes and agenda for the week. It had been almost seven months since Melanie had returned from maternity leave, and he was thrilled every time he walked past her desk. He didn't realize how great of an assistant she was until she was out.

"Thank you, Melanie. Give me a few, and I'll call you in so you can brief me," he told her as he walked into his hot, stuffy office. He listened to his old voicemails, and one after another it was the same voice.

Derek, it's me, Danita. Call me when you get a chance.
Derek, it's Danita. Why are you ignoring me? Call me back ASAP.
Derek, I'm getting really upset. Seriously, I need to talk to you.

Derek deleted every message and completely disregarded whatever it was that she wanted. He was confused because he hadn't heard from her in months, almost close to a year, and wondered why she would be calling him now. It didn't matter to him because he wasn't going to call her back to see what she wanted. He figured it was nothing serious she would want to speak with him about; she just wanted more of him. He blocked her number from his cell months ago, so he was in the clear there. He was in a good place in his life and didn't want any other interruptions. He opened his briefcase and pulled out his work files, completely unbothered. He pulled his wedding photo out that he had framed and placed it on his desk along with other pictures of his wife. After looking at the photos for a moment, Derek then called Melanie into his office. Within thirty seconds, she was standing in front of him with a pen and pad in her hand and sat down in her usual seat. Derek loved how quirky Melanie was. She had a librarian look to her. She probably would be sexy under her old-fashioned attire, but his mind wouldn't even let him go there.

"Okay, sir. Before we get started, Danita---"

Derek immediately cut her off. "Look, you don't have to worry about her. Send all her calls to voicemail," he told her. Melanie didn't question his demand. She had an idea of what could possibly be wrong, but she wanted to focus on her job.

"Okay, no problem, sir. Let's move onto the next thing. Your meeting that I filled in for last week went well, and the client is still on board." Melanie talked for ten minutes straight about how everything was on track. That was exactly what Derrick wanted to hear because it was usually the opposite. They talked briefly about his vacation before the meeting concluded.

"Alright, Melanie. Thanks again for the updates and remember: voicemail," he reminded her as he got up and escorted her to the door.

* * * * * *

Danita began to call Derek's office every day non-stop for almost a month. Melanie did as Derek requested and sent her to voicemail. However, she was becoming a distraction, and Melanie just couldn't take it anymore.

"Sir, can I talk to you please?" Melanie asked as she tapped on Derek's door. He had just hung up from a conference call, and his next meeting wasn't scheduled until another hour, so he waved his hand for her to come in. Melanie closed the door behind herself and sat down.

Derek didn't see a pen and pad, so he knew it was more of an informal conversation. He sat back with his arms folded behind his head and asked for her to speak.

"Okay, I'm saying this to you respectfully because I have a lot of respect for you, but this Danita lady is getting way out of hand. She calls non-stop. I can't concentrate on my work, and she's just not letting up."

Derek didn't quite understand because he was annoyed with the voicemails as well, but it didn't prevent him from doing his job. He hadn't thought of how it was a burden on Melanie. He sat up in his chair and clasped his hands on his desk, debating whether he should confide in her.

"Look, I'm going to be honest with you. You'll probably think I'm a real jerk after this, but I need your help." He went on to tell her about everything from beginning to end. Melanie respected him enough that he was willing to share something so personal. She immediately put her thinking cap on of how she could get rid of Danita once and for all.

"I have a plan," she told him. Derek looked at her and nodded his head.

"I knew I could count on you."

THE PLAN

"Hey, Danita. What's up? How can I help you?" Danita was completely caught off guard because she was used to leaving voicemails and never expected to be patched through to Derek.

"Well, well, well...so I'm finally able to get pass the gatekeeper. How surprising," Danita replied.

"Look, Danita what is it? You're ringing my phone non-stop so what do you want?" he asked in a direct tone. Danita was happy to hear his voice. She wished she could rock his world, just for old times' sake, but knew that would be a stretch so didn't bother bringing it up.

"I know I no longer work for you, but it doesn't mean we need to be complete strangers."

"Well, it was strictly business, and now that business is over, we both move on. That's pretty normal, you know?" he replied sarcastically. Danita didn't hold back.

"Look, I really need to see you to talk about some things. Just give me an hour that's all I ask." Derek laughed as he spoke.

"What would you possibly need to talk to me about? Whatever trick you have up your sleeve won't work this time around. In case you haven't heard, I'm a married man now." Danita had heard it through the grapevine that he finally got married. She also checked his Facebook page and saw pictures for confirmation.

"Well, congratulations, so can we talk or what?" Derek rolled his eyes. He didn't want to but needed to find out what she wanted so he could get rid of her once and for all.

"How about I meet you somewhere, let's say around eight tonight?" Danita thought to herself, *This was way too easy.*

"I will be available for sure. How about we meet at my place?"

"No, no, no, how about we meet at The Regal–that restaurant down on Terrell Street?"

"Wait, that place is not there no more. We can--"

"Just meet me there," he stated as he quickly hung up the phone.

A few minutes later, he walked to Melanie's desk and handed her a sticky note with a message on it. Melanie read the message to herself, nodded her head at him, and slid it into the shredder next to her desk.

* * * * * *

"Where is she?" Derek uttered to himself while sitting in his dark-tinted, burgundy Tahoe waiting for Danita to pull up. Danita noticed Derek's truck right away as she pulled across the street and turned off her lights. She sat for a few minutes to check her makeup and push up her bra. She then grabbed her handbag and headed over to his truck. She knocked on his window because she couldn't see through the tint. Derek rolled down the window halfway. "Hop in," he instructed. Danita walked around to the passenger side and did as he requested.

"I told you it wasn't here no more," she told him as she got comfortable in the passenger seat.

"Yeah, I see but I already ate so I'm good," he told her. Danita didn't understand why he wanted to meet at a restaurant if he already ate. "Hand me your bag." he instructed in a demanding tone.

"What?! I am not handing over my bag." Derek then asked for her phone. "For what?" she asked. He looked at her with agitation.

"Because I'm not going to have you recording me. If you want me to stay, hand over your phone." Danita looked at his face and saw that he was serious. She rolled her eyes and dug into her handbag to find her phone and then handed it over to him. He pressed the power button to turn it off and placed it up on the dashboard.

"Okay, so do you want to do it here or want to get a room?" Danita joked. Derek looked at her with disgust.

"Neither. I thought you wanted to talk." Danita laughed.

"Calm down; it was just a joke." Derek didn't think it was funny. He wanted to cut to the chase so he could get home to his wife.

"Look, I have a deal that I want to make with you," he told her as he pulled out a briefcase and sat it on his lap. Danita sat waiting to hear what he was about to offer her. She was a little taken aback because she thought the meet up was for her to get out what she wanted to talk about, not the other way around. He opened the briefcase and inside was a stack of money with some papers on top. "This here is twenty-thousand dollars. I'm willing to give this as a sign-off bonus, and you walk away and leave my life forever." Danita got angry.

"I don't want your freaking money!" Derek was frustrated at this point. For the next few minutes, he tried talking Danita into her senses.

"Twenty thousand dollars. You need it. I did my research and you're one paycheck from eviction. Take the money." Reality kicked in, and her current financial status started to creep into her head. She needed the money more than anything, and the timing was perfect so she would be a fool to walk away from that much money. It would definitely solve many of her problems. Still, she couldn't forget what she was there for. She shook her head.

"Twenty-thousand dollars to walk away, huh? Did you do your research and see that I have a one-month-old son too?" Derek noticed she was more filled out when she walked up to his truck but never guessed she just had a baby; he thought she just let herself go. He laughed in her face.

"So, your son doesn't have nothing to do with me. I'm sure you had other victims, being the freak that you are, and I'm sure you had enough men to practice with. Just take the money." He picked up a stack and put it in her face to get the hint. Danita sat there in silence with tears. She reached in her bag, pulled out a picture, and tossed it on top of the briefcase.

"Look at it closely...he looks just like you, Derek, and don't you deny it...I'm not lying to you. He is your son! I found out I was eight weeks once I left the job..." Derek picked up the picture and looked at it briefly.

"Congrats, but I be damned if I let you come into my life and mess up everything I worked hard for. I don't love you. I never loved you. You were a cheap thrill, and I just want you out of my got damn life," he yelled, banging his hands against the steering wheel when he uttered the last of his words. Danita saw that this conversation was going nowhere, so she gave in.

"You want me to take the money and raise your kid by myself, then I'll do just that, but the guilt will haunt you, trust me...what do I need to sign?" she asked as she looked into her handbag for a pen. He took a deep breath and opened the briefcase back up to hand over the gag order. He went over the important details and told her where to sign, initial and date. She signed every page and then went to reach for the briefcase. Derek held on to it and gave her one last demand.

"If you talk and I mean to anyone about the money, contract, or even what went on today, you *will* come up missing." Danita blew him off and took him as a joke.

"Just give me the money so I can get on with my life." Derek grabbed her by her arm and made things even clearer.

"I'm not playing. I have enough money to ruin you. Don't play with me Danita. I promise you'll regret it." At that point, Danita took him very seriously.

"I got it. I got it," she stated in a groggy voice once he released his grip. He told her to open her handbag, and he placed the stacks of money in her bag until it filled the top. The remaining stacks he had her stuff in her coat pockets. Danita checked to make sure she was secure before she opened the door. Derek waited as she started her car and pulled off. He looked up on the dashboard and realized she left her phone. He wiped it down with the bottom of his shirt and tossed it out the window. When he pulled off, he heard something crack and realized he may have run it over. *Ooops...my bad,* he thought to himself as he smirked. He looked at the baby picture one last time before tearing it into little pieces. When he hit the freeway, he threw the pieces out the window to get lost in the wind. "She's out of my life for good!" he yelled out the window as he sped home.

GUILT

"So, she took the money? That's great! I knew it would work. Women like that are desperate, but when you throw money into the mix, they always choose the money," Melanie stated as she sat in Derek's office behind closed doors. He mentally questioned how she would know, but he left it alone and was grateful that she had helped him out even though it cost him. Derek went back and forth as to whether he should tell her about Danita's baby claim, but he thought, *What the heck, it's over so there's no point.* He and Melanie discussed the agenda for the remainder of the day and the upcoming week. When it was over, Melanie got up and left the office. She went to close his door, but then she stopped and turned back toward him.

"Oh, I forgot you do have some mail. One piece is from an unknown sender. I'll bring it back in." She went back to her desk and shortly returned to place the mail on Derek's desk.

"Thanks again, Melanie…for everything," Derek stated as she left his office. Melanie walked back to her desk and chuckled to herself as she sat down. She had a flashback and thought about her past experience where she had to deal with a side chick and make her disappear too.

Melanie found out about her husband Jason's affair by accident. One night, his phone rang, but he was drunk and didn't answer. Melanie didn't answer it either, but when she saw a text come through, she grabbed his phone to see who it was. It was some woman named "Asia" in her husband's phone. She replied back to the text as if she was Jason, then started looking through their message history. She was horrified and distraught to find out about the messages and the pictures that had been sent between them. After several flirtatious texts back and forth, she agreed to meet the other woman at a hotel a few hours later. Melanie gave her specific instructions and advised her to wait in the bed under the sheets with the lights off once she checked into the room. She checked in twenty minutes after Asia arrived, dressed in a long black trench coat, an auburn short wig, and a pair of dark tinted shades. She grabbed the room key from the front desk and took the elevator to the tenth floor. Once she entered the room, she took off her coat and climbed into the bed. Asia had no idea it was Melanie, but once she felt her body, she knew it wasn't Jason.

Melanie grabbed her by her hair and placed a knife to her throat. The homewrecker tried screaming, but Melanie pulled her to the bed post and put the knife to her mouth. "You scream, you die." She interrogated Asia for almost an hour, asking as many questions as she wanted to know the answers to, then gave her an ultimatum. She lied and told her that she knew everything about her, and if she continued seeing her husband or even contacted him then she would kill not only her but her entire family. Asia knew Melanie had to be serious because no wife would go through this extreme measure to keep their husband away from another woman. Melanie didn't mean what she said, but she wanted her to believe it. After that night and to this day, Jason had no idea why Asia stopped calling him. She thought back to that night and happened to laugh out loud as a tall and handsome young man walked up to her desk.

"Hi, I'm here to see Mr. Reeler. Glad to see you're having a good morning," the well-dressed gentlemen said, acknowledging Melanie's loud laughter and smile that followed. Embarrassed, she immediately snapped out of it, covering her mouth and clearing her throat before she spoke.

"Oh, yes sir. I am actually. Please have a seat. I will call him for you now."

* * * * * *

Derek looked at the pieces of mail and picked out the large yellow envelope with no return address to view first. He shook it to listen for what was inside and finally opened it up. Once he laid his eyes on it, his heart dropped. He was furious and wanted to make a phone call to shut everything down once and for all.

"Melanie, when did this mail come in?" he asked as he called her extension directly.

"This morning, sir. Is everything okay?" she asked in a concerned voice.

"Yes, everything is cool, thanks," he assured her as he hung up the phone. Melanie tried getting out that he had a client in the lobby before he hung up. She walked to his office and knocked on the door before cracking it open to pop her head in.

"Mr. Reeler. I'm sorry to interrupt but you have Mr. Stevenson here to see you," she advised him. Derek had the meeting on his schedule, but after speaking with Melanie about Danita and now getting this envelope, his mind had gone completely off track.

"Okay, Melanie. Let him know I'll be out in a few." Melanie was surprised he didn't request for her to bring him back as usual but did as he stated.

"Okay sir, will do." She backed out and closed the door.

Derek pulled out the same baby picture Danita showed him at the meet up. It read, *Congrats, you're a daddy* as the caption. He wanted to

81

tear it up or pull out his scissors and cut it into a million pieces once again, but this time his heart just wouldn't let him do it. He realized the postmark was from two days ago, so Danita had to send it prior to meeting up. In his opinion the baby didn't resemble him at all, but it didn't mean it wasn't his.

"Damn, how about this is my baby?" he whispered to himself. "I would have to be lower than low to walk away from my own flesh and blood." He tried to recall how many times they had sex. He felt stupid and guilty at the same time because majority of the times, they didn't use protection, but he did recall pulling out. He then thought about the one last time he slipped a few weeks before she left. He stayed behind in the office and had a few drinks after hours because he was stressed about the new project he just landed. He had so much to do in so little time, and the pressure was on. Danita stayed after to help him with a few things, and without her, he wouldn't have been able to pull it off. He had a glass of whiskey to calm his nerves, and Danita somehow convinced him to keep going so he drank another. After that second glass, Danita took full control of him. He tried his hardest to resist her because he was in a good place with Shaniece at the time, but Danita was persistent, and she won after pulling out all the tricks on him once again.

"Get it together, man. Get it together," he said to himself quietly as he patted his bulge through his pants. He got hard thinking about that night but came to his senses right away because he didn't want to go back down that road anymore. He took the picture and locked it in his top drawer. He shook off his issues, put his game face on, and walked into the lobby to greet his client.

* * * * * *

Throughout the remainder of the day, the image haunted him, and Derek was unable to concentrate. He remembered what Danita said to him the night before about how not claiming her baby would haunt him for the rest of his life. He did feel guilty after seeing the second baby picture --- not only about the baby but for cheating on Shaniece too. He knew he had to confess. He thought about the day after his wedding.

If Shaniece was brave enough to tell me she cheated the day after we got married, then I need to be man enough to confess my sins before it drives me crazy, he told himself. The thought of telling Shaniece everything came to mind, but he just couldn't do it. They were in a better place, and he just didn't want to bring any negative energy to a good space. He thought of all that they had been through up to this point, and he knew that adding another obstacle to their journey would nearly break her into pieces.

SURPRISE

"Babe, guess what?" Shaniece stated as she walked past Derek, who was sitting on the couch with his feet propped up watching old episodes of "Martin."

"What up babe?" he asked in a half-tired voice. Shaniece noticed that Derek hadn't been very energetic for the last few weeks and thought it was because of work, but she was starting to sense that something else was going on.

"Never mind." She wasn't feeling his demeanor and turned to leave the room. Derek sat up and gently grabbed Shaniece's wrist to stop her as she walked back past him.

"No, go ahead. I want to hear what you have to say." He let go of her wrist, turned the TV down, and put both feet on the ground. Shaniece hesitated but then started smiling. She climbed over the top of the armrest and got in his lap. The long t-shirt that she was wearing draped over the sides of his legs. He looked her in the eyes and noticed how she was even more beautiful with no makeup on. He put his hand up to push a piece of hair out of her face then held her thighs. "What's up, babe?"

She paused then blurted, "We're pregnant!" Derek nearly knocked her off the couch as he tried to get up. He went to reach for his bottled water on the table to clear his throat before he responded.

"What?! We're having a baby…are you for sure?" he asked with hesitation.

"Yes, I'm a thousand percent sure! I went to the doctor yesterday for my regular check-up and told them I had been feeling under the weather lately. They ended up doing a pregnancy test, and it came back positive. The doctor did an ultrasound, and we found out that I'm eight weeks!" she said excitedly as she handed him the ultrasound image that she had hidden from his view on the side table when she came in.

"That darn honeymoon. That's when it happened…" Derek sat back on the couch, with one hand behind his head and the other now on the armrest.

"Yes, that's what I told the doctor. Are you excited?" She expected for him to jump up and do a happy dance, back flips, or something, but none of that happened.

"Of course, I'm happy," he said, rubbing her belly. Shaniece leaned forward and gave him a kiss, then laid her head on his shoulder.

"I was going to tell you tomorrow at Sunday dinner while Justin was here, but I just couldn't wait, plus it's better you knew before everyone else." Derek kissed Shaniece's forehead, but his mind was elsewhere. He really was excited, but the thought of having two kids scared him. He wanted to be a good dad and a decent person. He didn't want to be a deadbeat. It just didn't run in his blood.

✳ ✳ ✳ ✳ ✳ ✳

The next day, Derek and Shaniece attended church. After the assault the couple's attendance was sporadic due to the legal proceedings but also because Shaniece was not comfortable being around people yet. However, when they returned from their honeymoon, they started going back and had been more active attendees, attending every service they could on Sunday and Bible study during the week when Shaniece wasn't too tired.

On the way there, Shaniece was in the passenger seat and rubbed her stomach for a moment, then turned to Derek. "You think I should tell the ladies at church?" Shaniece asked.

"About what?" he responded, confused.

"Uh, the pregnancy."

"Oh, oh, oh. Yeah, why not?.......Well maybe not because we haven't even told our family yet." Shaniece thought about it and remembered reading in a magazine that a pregnancy announcement shouldn't be made until the second trimester because the chance of miscarriage is lower.

"Yeah, you're right, I'll hold off. I think I might just tell Justin, Mom, and our in-laws for now."

Derek reached over and touched Shaniece's belly, and she placed her hand over his. He didn't move his hand until they pulled into the church parking lot ten minutes later. Derek parked as close as he could to the building, got out, and shut the door. He was about to walk around to open Shaniece's door, but he paused for a moment and closed his eyes, as he could hear the harmony of the choir and melodies of the organ and piano. He thought to himself, *God, I need your help...please. Show me what to do.* He thought God heard him, as he immediately felt like some weight had been lifted off his shoulders. He took it all in and exhaled. Derek then walked around the front of the vehicle and helped Shaniece out of the car. They walked into the sanctuary hand-in-hand, greeted by a song of worship being belted out from the other members of the church.

* * * * * *

"Service was so awesome. God is really going to bless us even more before the year is out," Shaniece stated with enthusiasm as she pulled out a mirror from her purse and checked her lipstick and hair. Derek grunted briefly to acknowledge her statement while he drove them to meet up with another couple from church for lunch at a nearby restaurant.

Shaniece really wanted to know why Derek was clearly distant and had been less talkative for the last few weeks. Since they had this time alone, she sighed and spoke up. "Babe, can I ask you a question?" she asked as she grabbed Derek's right hand while they were sitting in the restaurant parking lot.

"Sure, babe. You can ask me anything," he told her, looking out his window for the other couple's vehicle.

"Okay…are you happy with me?" He turned his head quickly and looked at her with a confused look on his face.

"Why would you ask me a wild question like that?" Shaniece looked at him with a serious face.

"I need you to answer the question, Derek." Derek didn't think he had to, but he needed to appease Shaniece.

"I'm extremely happy. Never been happier in my life," he assured her. Shaniece smiled briefly because she knew he was telling the truth. It was something about the calm way he responded.

"Okay, last question. What's bothering you? And please don't tell me nothing because I know you and something is definitely on your mind." Derek started gazing out the window again as he looked at families walk from the parking lot into the restaurant. He had the opportunity to tell Shaniece about Danita at this point, but he held back – the timing just wasn't right. He lied to her instead.

"Babe, this high-profile client I have is just taking a toll on business. Nothing major, I just have a lot on my mind when it comes to making sure everything is on point."

"Well, I know we work in different fields but maybe I can help out in some way," she offered.

"Babe, it's nothing I can't handle. Thanks, but if I need you, I will let you know." Shaniece respected his wishes and left it alone. She looked at him and rubbed her stomach.

"We're hungry." Derek happened to spot the couple they were waiting on, and they hopped out the truck to walk into the restaurant.

DOWNHILL

"Man, this is too much to take in," Marcus remarked as he listened to Derek's problem from beginning to end. They were at Barry's, a popular cigar lounge and bar in downtown Jersey. Derek asked if he could meet him there to talk. Marcus knew about the fling with Danita, but the added story from that point was wild.

"I know, man. If I didn't talk to someone, I would literally go insane." Derek admitted. He was at a half bottle of whiskey after just one hour and drank glass after glass, back-to-back. Marcus had already made up in his mind after the second glass that he would be driving him home. He tried to stop him after the third one, but after Derek continually refused, he just let him go for it. Marcus thought, *If I was in his position, I would be doing the same thing.* Derek sat at the bar questioning his morals and what type of person he was. He tried to go back to his childhood to see where he may have gone wrong.

"I'm such a horrible person. How could I be so insensitive? This is payback for all the women I didn't commit to in the past. I know God is punishing me. I know it," he ranted. He mumbled over and over, "Bad things sometimes happen to good people. Bad things happen to good people." He was trying to convince himself that it was the devil attacking him and not his own wrongdoing because he was a good person. Marcus listened to Derek, but this time he really didn't know what to say.

"Look, man, hang in there. Just find out if the baby is yours or not and then move from there. You will make it through this." Derek listened and nodded his head in agreement as he gulped down his last sip of whiskey.

"Alright Derek, you ready?" Marcus asked as he stood up to put his jacket on. Derek started talking, but his words weren't making any sense. Marcus shook his head and told him, "Man, you're officially done for."

Marcus took the empty glass from Derek's hand. The next thing he knew, Derek had hit his head on the bar ledge, and he was out cold.

Marcus grabbed Derek and tried to get him up from the bar stool that he stumbled on. He was five inches shorter than his friend and trying to pick him up was more difficult than he expected. He tried forcing him to drink a few bottles of water before leaving, but he wouldn't open his mouth. Instead, he patted his face with ice, and Derek finally came to.

"C'mon, man. We gotta go," Marcus uttered as he tried to keep Derek from hitting his head again. Derek had his arm around Marcus' neck as they stumbled out the bar. Derek's phone had been ringing nonstop for the past ten minutes as Marcus tried to get him from the bar to the car. Marcus pulled Derek's phone out of his pocket once he got him settled in and saw, "Wifey," appear on his phone screen.

"Aww, man, it's Shaniece. Do I answer it? What do I say?" he asked himself. By the time he decided to answer, Shaniece had already hung up. He checked to make sure he had Derek's keys in his pocket before he pulled off. Once he got Derek into the passenger seat and strapped on his seatbelt, he called Shaniece back from Derek's phone.

"Honey, where are you?" Shaniece asked frantically on the other line. It was eleven thirty at night. The last she heard from Derek was at eight o'clock when he said that he was stepping out shortly and would be home before ten. Even if he didn't give her a time, he was always home by that time unless he was working on a business project.

"Hey, Shaniece this is Marcus." Her heart dropped. *Why is he answering Derek's phone?...What happened?........please, I can't take any bad news* were the thoughts that ran through her head all within five seconds.

"Marcus…where's Derek?" She didn't know if she wanted to know the answer to her own question.

"He's fine. He's right here in the passenger seat of my car. He had one too many drinks at the bar, and I wasn't going to let him drive." Shaniece was confused. She had all types of questions she wanted to ask because getting drunk to the point he couldn't drive was unlike Derek.

"Okay…are you on your way here now?"

"Yes, I left his truck at Barry's. He can go back and get it in the morning." Shaniece rode past Barry's a few times on Thursday nights and noticed the long lines outside. It was ladies' night on Thursdays, which explained the many men who waited in line in the cold to get in. She didn't trip too much and was glad that it was Marcus answering his phone and not some groupie.

"Thank you so much, Marcus. You really are a good friend." Shaniece hung up and waited patiently for them to arrive.

* * * * * *

Marcus pulled up to the Reeler household, and although it was not his first time his mouth always dropped every time he came over. The gold and white plated front door, tall windows with long drapes, beautiful flower garden, and Shaniece's new black-on-black Benz beside Derek's navy-blue sports car in the driveway were all what he noticed first when he pulled up. They lived in the elite area of Jersey alongside doctors and lawyers. Marcus still lived in a condo and thought maybe if he got married and pursued his real dreams and goals, he could live like this too. He had a decent paying job where he could afford to take nice vacations or wine and dine at the finest restaurants, but he certainly didn't have as much money as Derek and Shaniece. He admired Shaniece because she was a boss before Derek even came along, and she had her stuff together. When Derek first told him about Shaniece, he pushed him to go for it because not too many women like her would come around in a lifetime.

"Alright, man, we're here," Marcus said to Derek as he tried pulling him out the car. Shaniece saw the headlights beaming through the drapes and walked outside to where Marcus and Derek were.

She shook Derek's shoulder, trying to get him alert. "Babe, wake up." When he mumbled, she looked at Marcus. "How did you even get him in here?" Marcus hunched his shoulders.

"Trust me; it was a challenge. We're going to both have to get him in or we'll be here all night," he told her. Shaniece attempted to pull his arms from the car, but Marcus remembered that she was pregnant and recanted his statement. "Actually…no, I'll pull him out. Just help me walk him into the house." He managed to get Derek out the car without him hitting the ground. Once he got him on his feet, Shaniece walked on the other side and placed his right arm around her neck. They walked him up the three steps to the front door but struggled to get him through the foyer into the living room. When they finally got him there, they managed to prop him up onto the couch.

"You okay from here?" Marcus asked. Shaniece was standing with her hands on her hips, looking at Derek and shaking her head.

"Yeah, he'll be fine here for the night. I'll just bring down a blanket. Thanks for bringing him home." He nodded and headed to the door to leave. Shaniece followed him and was going to stay at the door to watch him go, but she stopped him before he slammed the door to his dark-colored Camry.

"Hey, Marcus! Wait." He paused as she came over to the car.

"Marcus, are you sure everything's okay with your boy? This is so unlike him." Marcus was caught off guard with the question but knew he had to have Derek's back.

"As far as I know everything is good except for some work issues, but nothing major that I know of." Shaniece exhaled sharply.

"Okay, thanks. Have a good night." Marcus closed his door and turned the car on, waiting until Shaniece entered the house before he pulled out of the driveway.

Shaniece closed and locked the front door, then leaned with her back against the door. She could hear Derek snoring already, so she made her way upstairs to go get a blanket. She didn't know if Marcus was lying or not. Still, she knew it was more than work challenges that Derek was facing; it was something more personal affecting her man. She thought maybe they were in trouble financially, and he didn't want to come out and tell her. The idea of him cheating entered her mind too, but she didn't want to let her mind go there so she tried alleviating the thought. She didn't know what it could be, but she was going to find out.

HURTING INSIDE

"Hey, bestie. What's up?" Shaniece was relieved that her best friend picked up the phone.

"Hey! what—is—uppp? I'm surprised to hear from you!" Karina expressed.

"Don't kill me, girl. I know it's been a while since we spoke. With the honeymoon, work, and Justin, I just haven't had the time to do much of anything." Karina understood because she was always busy and barely had time herself.

"So, what's the deal? Talk to me." She sensed Shaniece was calling her with more of a problem than good news. Karina had known her long enough to dictate how their conversations would go. Before Shaniece could get a word out, she started crying hard. "Shaniece, Shaniece! What's wrong? What is going on?!" Every time Shaniece tried to talk more tears flowed, and she bawled even more. Karina let her get it all out and didn't interrupt until she heard her let up some. "Shaniece, baby. I need to know what's wrong with you. I can count on one hand how many times I heard you cry, and for you to let it all out like this, it has to be serious."

Karina admired Shaniece for being so strong. From the time they were young, she had experienced so many setbacks, heartbreaks, and challenges. In all of those situations, Shaniece pretty much chucked up her deuces and kept it moving. She knew something wasn't right with her best friend this time.

"I'm pregnant," Shaniece announced.

"Wait. You're what? Yayyyy! I'm going to be a godmomma again. I'm so excited. This is the best news I heard all week!" Karina chanted. "So, tell me, what are we having? How many months? Wait......why are you not happy about being pregnant?" Karina was excited but didn't understand why Shaniece was so upset about it.

"I'm nine weeks. I'm happy about it, but you were more ecstatic than Derek was. When I told him, I was expecting for him to be overjoyed, ecstatic, or even excited. I don't know...maybe it's just me, but I was expecting a better reaction from him." Karina was now confused as to why Derek wouldn't be excited. She decided to ask less questions and just hear her out. "Derek got so drunk last night that Marcus had to drive him home. He's never been that drunk at least since I've known him. The last few weeks, he's been unengaged. When I asked him what was going on, he said he was having issues at work but nothing he couldn't resolve on his own. I even offered to help, but he said he got it. Things are changing between us and I'm pregnant and on top of it my emotions are all over the place." Karina really didn't want to elaborate too much because she didn't know much about their relationship. She hadn't spoken to Shaniece in some time; so many details could have been left out. As far as she knew, everything had been good for the happy couple.

"Look, girl, I know your emotions are all over the place, but if he said he got it then trust that he got it. Don't beat yourself up because it's not good for the baby." Shaniece thought to herself that she probably was overreacting, but that was until last night when Derek came in after midnight drunk.

"He's hiding something. I know it. I can feel it. I'm not sure if he's cheating or not. He's always at home unless he's at work but something isn't right."

"You don't have no hardcore evidence that he's cheating so don't let your mind start wandering and concoct a story in your head that may not even be true."

"You might be right. But Karina…I'm not only having the issue with Derek, I'm scared. I mean, I'm happy I'm pregnant and all, but I'm afraid of having a little girl. The day of the rape plays in my head every day, and I just can't imagine my daughter having to experience something so tragic. That man broke me…I know if I have a girl, I'm going to be extremely overprotective, and I don't want to be. I've been strong for so long because naturally I'm a strong person. I don't know if I can keep on. I'm drowning inside."

Karina wanted to forget about that day. She was beginning a press tour when Derek called her from the hospital. Her heart dropped, and she halted everything to be by her best friend's side. Karina couldn't fathom being a rape victim, especially after hearing the details of what happened once Shaniece came to. She had wanted to kill Julian herself. Regardless, Karina's heart went out to Shaniece. She felt so bad for her friend because she was completely out of it. She was in a state of shock and shutdown to the outside world for weeks. Karina didn't understand why Shaniece didn't confide in her about Julian, but she got it because she didn't tell all her own dirty secrets either.

"Listen, I know you're hurt, and I can't tell you to get over it. What happened to you was tragic, and no human should have to experience what you did, but if you have a girl, you can't punish her and shelter her because not every man is like that creep." Karina continued to talk words of encouragement, and by the end of the conversation their plan was for Shaniece to go back to therapy.

"Thanks, bestie, for your support. I always know I can count on you to make me feel better," Shaniece told Karina before they hung up.

I NEED TO KNOW

As the weeks passed, Derek developed more guilt deep down inside. He received a second picture in the mail from Danita of the now three-month-old baby boy. He looked at the picture and still saw no resemblance. The baby's features had changed much from the last picture, but he just couldn't be for sure if the boy was his. He locked it in his top drawer of his desk along with the other. Derek called Melanie and asked her to fill his schedule for the entire day, leaving no openings except for lunch. When he stayed busy, he tended to forget about all his problems. He worked for hours nonstop, and before he knew it, Melanie was walking into his office to check on him.

"Hey, you okay?" she asked with her belongings packed and her handbag hanging from her shoulder.

"Yes, I have a few more things to finish up, and I'll be out of here myself," he told her.

"Alright, good night." Melanie waved goodbye as she turned to leave.

"Goodnight, Melanie, and thanks for your hard work." After Melanie walked out of his office, his mind started to wander. He opened his top drawer and pulled out the baby pictures. He stared back and forth at both trying to make sense of it. After a few minutes he picked up the phone and went to dial Danita's number. He remembered that he threw her phone out the window but thought maybe she had gotten another one with the money he gave her and kept the same number. The phone rang a few times before going to voicemail. Derek hung up and didn't bother leaving a message. He placed the pictures back into the drawer and locked it. He finally wrapped up his work and was about to head out. As he was walking towards the door, his office phone rang. He walked back to his desk and looked at the number, asking himself if he should pick up the phone.

"Hello?" he answered.

"Hey, this is Danita. Did you call me?" she asked. He didn't know what to expect from the conversation. He remained calm and decided to drop the attitude.

"Yeah, I did," he told her.

"Well, aren't you violating the gag order? You shouldn't be contacting me," she reminded him in a sarcastic tone.

"I wouldn't if you stop sending baby pictures to my office." Danita was hoping he was willing to acknowledge her son at some point.

"I thought maybe you would want to see your son at least through pictures if you won't see him in person." Derek held his head down and looked down at the floor. Hearing the words "your son" was not registering with him.

"Look, before I even acknowledge him, I need a DNA test."

"I'm down for it. Let me know when and where, and I'll be there."

"I'll get all the details together in the next few days and give you a call back on this number. Whatever you do, do not call me."

"Alright, I'll be waiting for your call."

Derek hung up the phone and shut the door to his office. *I can't believe I've gotten myself into this,* he thought on his way out.

BABY TIME

"I'm beyond excited we're having a boy!" Shaniece exclaimed as she and Derek rode back from her doctor's appointment.

"Yes, he's definitely a junior. "You hear that, little man? You're going to be a junior." Derek had a wide smile as he placed one hand on Shaniece's stomach. Shaniece stared and smiled at the 3D ultrasound from every angle.

"I think he looks like me." Derek laughed while Shaniece giggled.

"You're seeing things!" she responded.

"Well, if he's a junior, he's definitely taking after his dad!" They both went back and forth about who baby boy looked like the most. "In all seriousness, you have to take the bed rest request seriously. You have to slow down, babe." Shaniece's doctor put her on bed rest when she started spotting, which he expected to stop after the first trimester. It hadn't, so he prescribed for her to stay on bed rest through her second trimester or longer if needed. She was scared at first, but her doctor reassured her that she would be okay if she kept off her feet.

"I will, I will…" Shaniece started smiling even more as she continued looking at the ultrasound.

* * * * * *

It had been a week since Derek spoke with Danita about their paternity appointment. He made a vow that if the boy was his, he would tell Shaniece right away. If the baby was not his, then he was going to keep his mouth shut. Derek arrived at the lab the next day, and his heart nearly dropped as he watched Danita walk through the office doors with the freckled-faced baby boy sleeping in her arms. She was dressed in dark jeans, brown knee-high boots, and a fitted brown leather jacket. She had let her hair grow out some, and it was pulled back in a short ponytail. Danita had a Mickey Mouse diaper bag on her shoulder as well, and Derek glanced at it a little more closely. The name "Tyler" was embroidered across the side in white letters. *Tyler...I figured she would have picked something with that started with a "D,"* he thought.

Something about Danita seemed off to Derek; she didn't look the same as when she worked for him, besides the weight gain. He shook off trying to figure out what was different about her and focused on the appointment at hand. Derek just wanted to get the test over and done with so he could know once and for all. He wasn't attracted to Danita in the slightest, so he was cool with being around her again. It was the baby he was the most nervous about.

"Hey, Danita. Thanks for being on time," Derek stated in a professional tone as he stood up and gave up his seat for her and the baby. She greeted Derek briefly and sat down with Tyler still asleep in her arms, focusing her attention back to her son. Derek wasn't much for small talk either, so he kept his head in his phone checking out his social media pages.

"Reeler......Reeler," the middle-aged lady from the front desk yelled out. Derek put his phone away and walked up to her.

"That would be me," he revealed with a slight smile.

"Hello, sir. I'm going to need you to come back through the blue doors to the left of me."

Before going in, he asked, "What about the baby and the mother? Do they come back with me too?" The woman looked at him with the same warm smile she greeted him with.

"This is a brief ten-minute information session before we start the testing. We will do this part individually so they will be called shortly after you."

After thirty minutes of questions, swabbing, and baby Tyler crying, they were finally done. Not once did Derek pick Tyler up or try to form any type of bond with him. He almost felt like a bad person, like he didn't have a conscience. He just couldn't get attached to a possibility. On top of that, Derek was even more nervous leaving than when he walked in. He knew it was no turning back now.

Derek walked Danita to her car just to be a gentleman, but they didn't speak much. As they got closer to the car, he discovered that she must've used part of the money to get a newer car; she went from driving a beat-up Toyota Corolla to driving a 2010 or 2011 Honda Civic. He thought to himself, *This is an upgrade for her.* When they got to her car, he watched as Danita strapped Tyler down into his car seat.

"Look, we'll wait on the test results in the mail and go from there," Derek stated. She nodded in agreement.

"I know, I know. You will call me and not to call you," she stated sarcastically before speeding off.

* * * * * *

Two weeks passed, and the test results finally arrived at his office. He sat at his desk staring at the envelope before opening it. He knew that his whole life could change for the best or the worst, depending on the results. If Tyler wasn't his, he could move on with his life. He started to think about his wife and his unborn son and really started worrying. "What if I'm a horrible dad and my son has to pay for my mistakes?" he asked himself. That and dozens of other questions went through his head. Finally, he took two deep breaths and built up enough courage to open the envelope.

HE LOVES ME, HE LOVES ME NOT

Shaniece was propped up on the bed in her silk pajama short set reading a Joel Osteen book while eating dry Cheerios and apple slices with caramel.

"Babe, this book is so good. You need to read it after me," Shaniece suggested with her head buried into the book. Derek was tired and ready to go to bed. He hated when Shaniece wanted to stay up all night reading. He wanted to go to sleep with fewer distractions, since his thoughts were always racing nowadays, but it obviously wasn't happening. When she got no response, Shaniece flipped the book over on her lap. "So, babe what did you want to talk to me about?"

Lying in the bed with his head turned upward at the ceiling, Derek uttered, "Huh?" He had no idea what she was talking about.

"Uh, remember yesterday when I called you at work, and I asked what was wrong. You told me you would tell me later. It's been a day now, so what's wrong?" she asked. Derek couldn't stand the fact that Shaniece wouldn't let things go. He had totally forgotten that conversation. He had so much on his mind that he didn't remember much of anything about that day.

"Oh, that was yesterday. Who knows what it could be," he responded. Shaniece didn't press the issue and decided to let it go for the time being.

"Alright then, Derek," she replied with a slight attitude as she picked up the book and continued to read. Derek put the covers over his head and went to sleep thinking, *Thank God, she let that go.*

Shaniece was really starting to take in the message in the book. *"Being unwilling to forgive is like drinking poison and expecting the other person to die,"* she mumbled under her breath. Her therapist had suggested that she go back to reading motivational books to keep her spirits up. She was all for the idea because before things really took off with her career, husband, and financial success, she had spent most of her time reading and contributed some of her success to what she learned from reading books. Once she found out she was having a boy and things started getting somewhat back to normal with Derek, her anxiety started to calm down. She continued to see her therapist to keep herself leveled. Derek knew she was back in therapy, but Shaniece hadn't quite shared with him as to why. She just mentioned that she needed emotional support with the pregnancy.

Shaniece finished her book shortly after 2 a.m. She wasn't ready for bed just yet and needed something else to snack on. Derek was knocked out next to her, and she knew he hated when she would stay up all night but thought, *I'm pregnant so he's just going to have to deal with it.* Shaniece slid out of bed and waddled down into the kitchen.

"What can I snack on?" she asked herself as she held opened the refrigerator door. Her eyes popped like a kid in a candy store.

"Straaaawberries," she squealed quietly, smiling ear to ear as she popped them into her mouth. She grabbed the Reddi Whip out of the side of the refrigerator then shook it up, threw her head back, and pushed the nozzle down. She laughed to herself because she had always wanted to do that but never got to when she was a kid. When she finished snacking, she walked back upstairs into the bedroom.

"Ugh, he drives me crazy," she stated with frustration as she picked up Derek's suit off the end of his office chair. She noticed his briefcase sitting on his desk, and it was unlocked. The last few weeks, especially since his drunk episode, she couldn't help but think about if his business was in trouble. She was bringing in twenty-five to thirty-thousand monthly and was well able to maintain the household bills with just her income alone. However, she was nervous but never mentioned it to Derek because he told her that everything was fine. She stared at the briefcase for a good forty-five seconds. *I wonder what he's hiding?* she asked herself. *Open it......no, don't open it* played back and forth in her mind. She walked away from it and went to the bed. She propped herself up to get comfortable and turned on the television. She flicked through the channels, and nothing was on, so she decided to listen to the Music Channel. She laid in bed listening to nineties R&B throwbacks as all types of thoughts raced through her mind. She turned over to look at Derek, and he was out completely cold. She couldn't resist the temptation.

"Let me just see what's going on," she stated as she carefully got out of the bed with her eyes locked on Derek. She needed to know what they were up against. She walked over to the computer desk and took a deep breath before she made the decision to be nosy. "Okay, what's the problem..." she whispered to herself. She started rambling through paperwork. She viewed a few office bills. Some were paid, and some were past due. *No biggie,* she thought. She kept digging and pulling papers out, placing them on the floor. She finally came across an envelope and blurted out, "Paternity test!" Derek started to move around. She covered her mouth hoping he wouldn't wake. A minute passed, and she saw that he was still sleep. She opened the envelope to view what was inside. She read it from top to bottom, and each second her chest tightened. "This can't be. This can't be. This can't be," she uttered over again. She couldn't believe what she was reading. "Baby…My husband…No, this can't be."

The last thing she thought would happen at this moment was the Joel Osteen chapters that she just read a few hours ago would be flooding her mind full force. *"Being unwilling to forgive is like drinking poison and expecting the other person to die,"* was the quote that came to her mind several times again. She wanted to forget everything and go over to the bed, place a pillow over his head and smother him. Her next thought was to go down in the kitchen, get a knife, and stab him, but she felt numb. She was mad at herself because she wanted to spazz out, but something down inside wouldn't allow her to. She quickly placed the paternity results back into the envelope and put everything back to how it was. She decided to take a different approach: she wanted to see how long Derek would go without telling her he had a baby by another woman.

Shaniece was surprised by how calm she was, despite the thoughts she had just moments before. She was starting to think her behavior was abnormal. She thought to herself, *Is this how people typically act before they're about to commit a murder?* Shaniece climbed up on the bed and turned to look at Derek. She stared at him for a good five minutes thinking about their future, their past, if he really loved her, and if he really wanted another baby. A ton of thoughts hit her all at once as she tried to get her mind adjusted to another baby being involved in their lives. The thought of it made her want to puke. She ran to the bathroom and put her head over the toilet seat, and the only things that came up were small strawberry particles. She felt her anxiety increasing to the point where her heart felt like it was skipping beats. She immediately thought about how the stress would impact her son and knew she had to pull herself together quickly. She managed to pull herself up from the toilet and go over to the sink.

"Get it together, get it together," she whispered to herself while slumped over the bathroom sink patting cool water onto her face. She stared into the mirror looking back at her own reflection. "Does he love me?" she asked. She then shook her head while walking out the bathroom. "I will not do this to myself. I will not."

* * * * * *

The next morning Derek woke up refreshed ready to hit the gym. He grabbed his suit from the closet, grabbed his briefcase, kissed his wife, and was out the door by 6:20 a.m. While driving, the results of the paternity were on his mind but not more than his wife and her feelings. He loved Shaniece and couldn't imagine not having her in his life. He knew he couldn't keep this from her forever and had to share the heartbreaking news. He just didn't know how and when due to her high-risk pregnancy. He turned up his music and started singing Anthony Hamilton to the top of his lungs, "As you criiied in my arms. You wooookee up my heart. And I saw again what I found in yoooouuu. 'Cause her heearrrrttt, her hearrrttttt won't let me lose herrrrr. No matter how I try. I just can't say goodbye and lose herrrr." Derek turned into the gym parking lot and put "Her Heart" on repeat while his own heart was nearly broken thinking about what he was about to put his wife through. After listening to the song nearly three times in his car, he switched it up and put gangsta rap on his phone before hitting the treadmill. He was lost in another world, and he would've continued if he didn't have to get ready for work. He hit the shower after his forty-five-minute workout, suited up, and was out the gym door by 8 a.m. He looked down at his Armani Exchange watch and noticed he had some time to spare. *Let me call my wife,* he thought to himself. As soon as he got in the car, he dialed Shaniece's number and heard her pick up.

"Hey, sleepyhead," he joked.

"Hey, what's up?" she asked in a groggy voice. Immediately when she heard his voice, the episode from a few hours ago played back in her mind.

"I just wanted to check on you and Junior. You were out cold this morning. What time you end up going to bed?" he asked. Shaniece looked at her alarm clock to see the time.

"Ugghh, maybe two or three," she lied.

"Wow, did you finish the book?"

"Yes, it was good too."

"I bet. I need to read it next," he stated.

"Yes, it's a must," she agreed in more ways than one.

"Alright, babe, I just wanted to check in before I head into this office. Enjoy your day and remember bed rest. No exercising, you hear me?" Shaniece rolled her eyes.

"I know, I know. I will follow the doctor's orders." They both exchanged "I love you's" before hanging up. Derek sat in the parking lot in his car listening to music for a good five minutes before walking into the office. Every song he heard reminded him of his wife, and his heart broke even more.

* * * * * *

When the phone call ended, Shaniece hung up feeling so emotional after talking to Derek. She loved him so much and just couldn't imagine their marriage being jeopardized because of some side chick. She sat on the bed with her hair all over her head. She was not only emotional about what she just found but also about being on bed rest and not being able to go to the office. She still worked from home, but she still couldn't get used to being away from the office longer than a few days. She rubbed her stomach as she sat on the bed with the morning sunlight shining through the curtains onto her bronzed skin. The nice days out made it even harder to adjust because she wanted to hit the track and at least go baby shopping.

"C'mon, little man. What we going to eat?" she asked her unborn baby as she made her way down into the kitchen.

* * * * * *

"Hey, Danita. What's going on?" Derek decided to call her and check in on his son. He knew his loyalty was to his wife, but this was his own flesh and blood. There was no way he could ignore that no matter how he felt inside.

"Hey, Derek, I'm getting Tyler dressed and then I'm on my way to work," Danita responded. She was surprised to hear from him. When she received the results, she waited for his call and was willing to go at his pace. She didn't want anything but for him to be a father to their son. "So, how do you feel about everything?" Danita asked out of curiosity. Derek sat in his black leather chair and swirled to look at the city view from his office before answering.

"I mean it is what it is. I can't change the fact that he's my son. I will take care of him and be there for him the best that I can." Danita was cool with that. It was close to what she wanted to hear. She gave up the fact of wanting him and just wanted him to be involved with their son.

"So, does your wife know?" she asked. Derek didn't want to get too personal with her, so he ended the conversation.

"Look, I have a meeting I have to get to. I'll call you back later," he stated as he quickly hung up. Derek was feeling even guiltier than before. He knew he had to stay in contact with her, but it wasn't what he really wanted. He knew things would change quickly on both ends for the sake of his son. It wasn't part of his life plan, and he didn't want to deal with her for the rest of his life. He continued his day working on projects, returning calls, attending meetings, and replying to emails. He had Melanie fill his schedule to the point he didn't have time to even eat lunch. When 4 p.m. came around, he was starving and decided to call it a day.

"Alright Melanie, I'm outta here," he told her as he walked past her desk with his hand in the air waving goodbye.

"Okay, Mr. Reeler. I'm headed behind you shortly. See you in the morning."

Derek walked to his car, and when he got in, he sat with his head laid back on the head rest for a few minutes before pulling off. He wanted to go home but didn't want to face Shaniece. It was hard for him to look at her, and he knew if he went straight to bed two days in a row, she would start overreacting. He decided to tell her he was going to stop and get something to eat but would make it home in another hour. The thought of calling Marcus crossed his mind. He decided against it, knowing that if he headed out to the bar, he would have another crazy drunk episode. He also knew Shaniece wasn't having it, and he didn't want to upset her in any way possible due to her high-risk pregnancy. With a long exhale, he gave her a call.

"Hello, beautiful. What you doing?" Shaniece immediately had an attitude when she heard his voice.

"Ummm, what you been doing today? You didn't have time to pick up the phone to call me?" she yelled.

"Sorry, babe…I've been so caught up with work and meetings, I didn't have a chance to do much of anything. Not even lunch. That's why I'm leaving work early because I'm starving." Shaniece's mind started to wander, and she automatically thought he was lying.

"So, you mean to tell me not once did you think, *Let me call my pregnant wife who is on bed rest?*......Not once did you think that to yourself?" she asked, expecting an immediate response.

"Look, babe, it wasn't that I didn't think about you or Junior. I just didn't have the time. It was hectic today." Derek tried to calm her down, but she was on him like white on rice. He just listened to her rant.

"You're right. I'm wrong. I should've called. It won't happen again," Derek assured her. His words didn't make Shaniece feel any better.

"Yeah, whatever," she stated as she abruptly ended the call.

Derek knew there would be drama when he walked into the house, especially if he stayed out longer than an hour. He stopped by the restaurant close to their house, picked up a Supreme-style Pizza, and headed straight home. At this point, Derek just wanted to keep as much peace between them as possible.

BONDING TIME

"Hey, man, you alright?" Marcus asked. Derek and Marcus were on their way to spend time with Mr. Reeler. It had been a while since Derek last spent time with his dad. He decided to bring Marcus along with him because Marcus was having some trouble in paradise with his own lady, so a guy's day out was needed. Natalie was starting to hang out more with her friends and was giving him a dose of his own medicine. He cheated early into their relationship and pretty much ran over her. She had been his girlfriend, not even his fiancée, for nearly fourteen years, and he realized that he may be losing her for good.

"Yeah, man, I'm alright, but I haven't told you the latest though," Derek prepared him. Marcus wasn't sure if he wanted to hear the latest; what he knew already was enough. He braced himself and made a guess about what had happened.

"You got the DNA test done." Derek nodded his head briefly.

"Yeah, I did."

Marcus, with his eyes squinted, asked, "So, I'm assuming that's your kid." Marcus sort of knew the answer but was hoping deep down that Derek would deny it. Derek confirmed his assumption by nodding his head once again. Marcus put his hand over his face. "So, what you going to do man?" he asked out of concern as he slid his hands down off his face lifting his head back up to hear Derek out.

"I'm not even sure what to do. Since we found out, I have been taking care of him." For the last few weeks, he had been there for Tyler financially by taking care of his entire spring wardrobe, paying for doctor co-payments, and paying his childcare expenses but hadn't spent much time with him. It was extremely difficult with having his own family to tend to, and his wife being on bed rest required a lot of his time. He was surprised about how patient Danita had been with him, but he did what he could for now. Marcus was more curious about what he was going to do as it related to Shaniece.

"I know you haven't told Shaniece about it because you're in one piece," Marcus joked. Derek chuckled.

"Yeah, I'm still trying to figure that out. I think it would be best to tell her after she gives birth because she's high risk, and I don't want any complications." Marcus nodded his head in agreement.

"Yeah, that's your best bet, but you definitely have to break the news and tell her." Derek dreaded thinking about that day. He dreaded having to see her with a broken heart. She just got herself back on track since the rape and didn't want to see her broken once again. He was over the conversation and wanted to move on to bonding for the rest of the day. "You'll be alright, man," Marcus assured him as he patted him on his back.

"I don't have no choice but to be alright. What they say?....What don't strike you make you stronger," Derek stated.

"Um, you mean.... What don't kill you make you stronger," Marcus corrected him.

"Yeah, that," Derek agreed as they both laughed.

* * * * * *

They pulled up to the lake, and Derek always felt a sense of peace when he went there. Derek and his father had fished at the same lake since he was a kid. When he was eight, he caught his first fish and felt like the man. Ever since that day, he looked forward to going fishing with his father. His brother, Jeffrey, was more like their mother. Derek and his father would return home from the lake, sweaty and reeking of fish, to see his mother and brother in the living room with their faces planted in a book. That was their idea of having a good time. Derek figured that was why his brother was such a smart and successful architect. As they got closer to his father's car, Derek saw Mr. Reeler waving to them. When they parked, the two got out of the vehicle and made their way over to him. Both Marcus and Derek agreed that they would not mention the Danita situation and would instead focus on other topics such as work and sports during their bonding time.

"Hey, gentlemen, nice for you to join the old man today," Mr. Reeler yelled out. He was already prepped with the fishing rods and worms for bait.

"Hey, Dad." Derek hugged Mr. Reeler tight and let go when his dad patted his back a few times.

"Hey there, Mr. Reeler," Marcus responded, giving him a handshake.

"Glad to have y'all here. But Derek, I'm so happy we're finally having a grandbaby. How many months we have left until we meet Junior?" Mr. Reeler asked. Derek smiled.

"Three more months, and he'll be here, Dad." Derek wished he could tell his father about baby Tyler and that Junior would not be his firstborn. The thought of having to break the news to his family hurt just as much as having to tell Shaniece.

"My first grandbaby. Mom already knitted five blankets for him so far. He's all she talks about."

Derek listened to his father go on and on about how he couldn't wait to meet his grandson, but he was excited himself. He couldn't wait until he laid eyes on his son. He thought about how he would react in the delivery room. He hadn't had the opportunity to see Tyler being born. After a conversation with Danita, he learned that when she started reaching out to him, she was scheduled to have her labor induced and wanted him to be a part of the experience. Even if he had answered her calls, he wouldn't have believed her anyway and still would've missed out. For a moment, he had zoned out thinking about Junior, but he snapped out of it and listened in on Marcus being in the hot seat of interrogation with his father.

"So, Mr. Marcus, when you going to pop the question? I mean, what you waiting for?" Mr. Reeler asked. Marcus wanted to continue to focus on actually catching a fish and skip over his personal issues. He hated when he got asked the same question time and time again from different people.

"Well, Mr. Reeler. I'm not sure. It's complicated," Marcus gave him a brief answer. Mr. Reeler laughed out loud as he threw back the baby fish he caught into the lake.

"It's always going to be complicated. You have to determine if it's worth it or not. If so, marry the girl. If not, let her go and allow someone else to marry her." Marcus had never had anyone tell it to him like that. The thought of Natalie leaving and marrying someone else had never played through his mind.

"Mr. Reeler, I hear you, but if she's not complaining then I must be good, right?" Marcus asked hoping he would agree, and they could move pass the entire marriage ordeal. Mr. Reeler turned and looked at him then shook his head.

"You don't get it. She may not say anything to you but she's definitely complaining to someone and you want to know what they're telling her?...They're telling her to leave your ass and look for better." Marcus scratched his head and thought, *She does hang out with her friends a lot more.* Mr. Reeler continued to drop knowledge on Marcus. Derek laughed a little while listening because he saw that his father was starting to get through to his friend.

"Sir, thank you for keeping it real with me. I have to really do some rethinking."

"Well, that's not all." He went down memory lane and talked about how he met Derek's mother. "I was an engineer, and Angie worked for the clerk's office in the county building. One day, I had to pick up some building permits for my boss, and it was like love at first sight. I asked her out, and she surprisingly said yes. We were inseparable ever since. I knew that day she would be my future wife. Fast forward to two years later, I put a ring on it, and we got married at the courthouse. If I didn't make the right choice with anything else in my life, I know I did when I married her. She helped me be the man I am today." Derek nodded and smiled as his dad told his story. Mr. Reeler didn't want to just share and talk about the good times; he wanted them to know about the tough times too. Derek wanted to hear what his dad had to say because he didn't know too much about the hard times. He wanted to learn something too.

"About ten years into our marriage, that's when things started getting really hard. My union went on strike, and I wasn't bringing in any income. Bills were piling up and Angie couldn't handle them all on her salary. We fought all the time, and I even started drinking because

I was upset that I couldn't provide. We got through it though. We didn't quit and give up. We worked it out. That's what you need to learn when the tough times come. Don't give up."

Derek heard stories from his dad plenty of times. He looked up to his parents and wanted his love to last like that. No matter what, through better or worse, through thick and thin, they continue to love each other. Derek knew it was a different time, and Shaniece was a new-aged woman who handled things on her own for many years before they met so, he figured it would be easy for her to walk away at any time. Still, he took away that no matter what happened, he would never give up or quit on his marriage.

* * * * * *

After two hours of much needed bonding, they packed up their fishing rods and headed to the dirt field where their cars were parked.

"Alright, gentlemen, we're going to have to do this again real soon," Mr. Reeler stated as he headed over to Derek's truck. Marcus was sitting in the truck texting his girlfriend while Mr. Reeler and Derek talked briefly outside.

"Yeah, Dad, maybe in two weeks we can meet up again?" Derek suggested. Derek attempted to give his dad a hug before leaving, but Mr. Reeler stopped him.

"What's going on with you, son?" Derek looked at him with a look of guilt.

"What do you mean?"

"Well, for starters when I call, you're always busy and never have time to talk to your old man. It took nearly two weeks to get in touch with you about today," Mr. Reeler went on to say. Derek was partially relieved because he thought his troubles were starting to appear all over his face.

"Ahh, Dad. It's just work stuff. Just very busy with my high-profile clients, that's all." Derek's father knew there was more to the story. He had raised him for thirty-eight years and knew when something wasn't right. His mood swings were a dead giveaway. Whenever Derek stayed away, it was always because a heavy burden was harboring him. Some years back, he had done the same thing. Mr. Reeler kept telling his wife that something was wrong, and Derek finally broke down and told them what was going on. After a few months of struggling financially, he finally revealed to his family that he had lost his corporate job. They had to loan him close to seven-thousand dollars to dig himself out of a hole. His father wanted to prepare himself again in case he needed money. He figured that may not be it this time around because Shaniece ran a successful business, and Derek had taken on some reputable companies as clients.

"Alright, son. You know if you need me, I'm here to talk." Derek nodded his head.

"I know, Dad, but everything is fine," he reassured him. Mr. Reeler still didn't believe him but decided to give up trying to get answers from his son. He knew he would revisit the conversation soon or eventually Derek would come to him, so he parted ways. "Alright dad. Love you." Derek hugged and patted his dad on the back before jumping into his truck and pulling off.

PROMISES

"Hey Derek, can we talk?" Derek was caught off guard when Danita called into his office.

"Danita, what are you doing calling me at work?" he asked, very annoyed.

"I'm sorry, but I really need to talk with you. I knew Melanie was out to lunch. That's why I called now."

"Okay, okay, what's up? Is everything alright with Tyler?"

"Yes, yes, he's fine. I just really need to talk to you about something." Derek didn't want to be rude, but if it didn't concern his son, he could care less. He didn't want to be that way, but that's how he felt.

"Okay, what's going on?"

"I need to talk to you in person, not over the phone." Derek wasn't with all the games.

"Look, I don't have time to meet you. Just spill it."

"I have to speak with you in person. Would you please meet me somewhere? Give me twenty minutes tops, that's it." Derek was curious what could be so important that she needed to meet up. The last time he met with her, she told him he had a son. He couldn't see what else she would want from him.

"Alright, I have twenty minutes to spare after work. I can come over briefly and we can talk."

"Alright, thank you. I'll be home."

Derek hung up confused wondering what it could possibly be. He noticed how she had been more than patient and respectful, but he couldn't help but wonder if she had another trick up her sleeve. It was just too easy for him with her, and he didn't trust her. He handled his usual business throughout the day and headed out his regular time. Melanie left an hour early for a doctor's appointment, so he made sure everything was taken care of before he left the office. He had a long stressful day and didn't feel like meeting up with Danita. He decided to call Shaniece before leaving out.

"Hey, babe, you alright? You need anything before I come home?" Derek asked, secretly hoping she didn't give him a long grocery list of items. Shaniece was miserable. She just wanted to have this baby and be back to her normal self. She had been on bed rest for four months and was going insane.

"Yes, can you stop at Scoopers and get me a strawberry sundae?" she asked. Derek laughed because that was her normal. It was either a strawberry sundae or a shrimp roll from the Chinese restaurant down the street from the house. There was no in-between. It was like night and day with her cravings.

"Alright, babe, I'll be home shortly. I'm just tying up some loose ends here at the office." He hung up, locked up, and made his way over to Danita's.

* * * * * *

Danita didn't live in the most elite neighborhood like Derek but didn't live in the hood either. He thought to himself that it was the best she could do. As long as he didn't see thugs, drunks, or prostitutes hanging around her building, he was good. Danita met Derek at the entrance of her apartment. Whenever he came over, he never stepped foot past the living room. He noticed how small but tidy her space was, so he felt comfortable with his son staying there.

Danita noticed that Derek walked in suited up like a GQ model in his navy-blue suit with a fresh haircut, well-trimmed beard, and an aroma of a cologne Danita had never smelled before. Before she got too entranced, she quickly turned her attention to Tyler sitting in his bouncer and sucking on his pacifier with a onesie on. Danita kissed his chubby freckled cheeks, then took him out of the bouncer and handed him to Derek.

"Hey, little man, it's Daddy," Derek stated as he held Tyler up to the ceiling. Whenever he saw him, his heart melted. He didn't know who Tyler looked like because he didn't have his features, and he barely looked like Danita. Both he and Danita were brown-skinned, and Tyler was fair-skinned with big and bright brown eyes and sandy brown curly locks. He figured he must look like someone in her family, even though he didn't know too much about them. He had never had the chance to connect with her on a personal level.

He wouldn't admit it to Danita, but it felt good to see his son's face and hold him in his arms. His love for his son grew deeper whenever he laid eyes on him. The situation wasn't ideal, but at this point he knew he wouldn't trade him for the world. He just wished he could spend more time with him but knew it wasn't possible now. Tyler giggled and laughed out loud while Derek kissed and hugged on him. Derek eventually sat down on the couch while holding Tyler in his arms. He looked over at Danita sitting beside him and felt uneasy because it looked like she'd been crying. He didn't want to be too straightforward, so he decided to wait until she started talking. After no conversation on her end for a few minutes, he spoke.

"He's getting so big." Tyler was wriggling around and trying to sit up on his lap.

"I know he is," Danita agreed as she smiled with tears streaming down her face at the same time. She wiped her tears and slowly looked into Derek's eyes. Derek was starting to feel uncomfortable because he knew this was about to be a serious talk. He was nervous, and his heart started pounding while his hands started to sweat. He had a feeling she was about to deliver some upsetting news.

"Danita, take your time. Get it out," he told her. Danita now had her head held down halfway into her lap. Derek shifted in his seat as he wiped baby Tyler's slobber off his slacks. He focused his attention back to Danita and waited for her to speak. She took a deep breath.

"Derek...I...I have cancer." Tears were streaming down her face even more, and they started hitting the couch. Derek couldn't respond. He couldn't believe what he just heard. He cleared his throat and shifted in his seat.

"I'm sorry, Danita...I don't even know what to say...what kind?" he asked eventually. She tried getting her tears under control.

"Stage four breast cancer," she told him with a look of shame on her face. Derek stood up and placed Tyler back into his bouncer. He felt bad for Danita and thought it was only right to console her at a time like this. He grabbed her closer to him and hugged her tightly. "Derek, they're saying I have a month, maybe two, left." Derek looked at her with no words. Instead, a river of tears dripped from his eyes one by one. He didn't know what to do, what to say. All he could do was hold Danita in his arms as she cried nonstop. After five minutes of no words and letting Danita cry it all out, she broke the silence.

"Promise me. Promise me. My son won't go to foster care when..."

Derek intentionally cut her off, "Yes, of course. He's my son. I would never let him go to foster care," he promised. "How long did you know?"

"I knew a couple months now. When I found out, it had already progressed. I tried chemo, but it didn't work for me." Derek listened as she talked while staring off at Tyler sitting in his bouncer, still sucking on his pacifier without a care in the world. Everything started to make sense. He now understood why Danita had been more than cooperative and patient with him. It also explained her recent changes in appearance that he had noticed in the last few months. Derek looked at his watch and saw the time. He thought to himself, *Shaniece is going to kill me. I should've been home an hour ago.* He didn't want to appear as a total jerk, so he continued to talk with Danita while holding her in his arms a little while longer. She had an entire plan together regarding Tyler and wanted Derek to be onboard. Danita finally asked the million-dollar question.

"How do you think your wife would feel about taking on a baby?" Derek hadn't even thought that far. He was still processing the fact that she had cancer.

"Well, she won't have a choice really," he told her. That was what Danita wanted to hear. Even though it had been a couple months, she felt that Tyler would be best off with his father. She didn't have family that she could depend on to help her either way. Derek was pretty much it, and she was okay with that. She hadn't spoken to her mother in over four years due to some unresolved childhood issues she never forgave her for. Her father died in a car accident on his way to work when she was fifteen. When she lost her father, life changed for her. Her mother depended on him financially so when he passed, they received some benefits but not much. After the money ran out, they were evicted from their home and had to move in with her grandmother. Her mother fell into depression, and Danita had to fend for herself. She was the only child growing up, so she didn't have any sisters or brothers to share her time with. Instead, she started manipulating and using men for money by using her best asset, her body. She slept with married men because they were the easiest to con. She could get money out of them after threatening to expose them to their family. She became devious and didn't care about who she hurt in the process. Despite her selfish ways, she did go to school and continued her education. That was the one thing that kept her grounded for a while without having any support.

At this point, she was used to being alone until Derek started coming around to see Tyler.

After an hour and a half of talking and discussing Danita's game plan Derek heard enough for the night and was ready to go home. Tyler had fallen asleep in his bouncer. Derek picked him up and laid him down in his crib, kissed him on his forehead, and headed to the door.

"Alright, Danita. Whatever I can do…." Derek had to think about his wording and corrected himself. "Danita, I want you to hang in there. I will do what I can for you. I'm going to continue to pray. You know prayer works, right?" Danita cracked a smile and completely agreed with him.

She wanted to tell him that was all she had been doing the last few months. She definitely knew prayer worked because she prayed that he would be a part of her son's life even though she had planned the pregnancy, and if revealed, he had every right to walk away from her forever. She prayed every night after she found out she had cancer that, despite her selfish ways, her baby would be taken care of by someone who truly loved him if she didn't make it. She knew she didn't have long, so she spent her time praying to God about her son's future and eventually came to terms with death.

BABY SHOWER TIME

"Baby bag – check, change of clothes – check, baby clothes – check."

Derek and Shaniece were prepping for their future hospital visit. She was eight months pregnant now, and they were ready to meet their little one in the next few weeks. Shaniece thought about Derek, his side chick, and baby every day. She needed him more than ever now, so she decided to keep what she knew to herself until the timing was right for her. She woke up with an attitude some days and didn't want anything to do with him, and some days she was happy to see him. Her emotions went back and forth, up and down. Derek thought it was due to the pregnancy, so he dealt with her mood swings.

"A few more weeks and we'll meet our baby boy," Derek expressed excitedly. Shaniece sat up on the couch waiting for Justin to bring her food.

"Justin, where's my pizza? What's taking so long?" she asked in a cranky voice, completely ignoring Derek.

"Mom, hold up. Here I come." Justin waited on his mom hand and foot whenever Derek couldn't. He usually was out with his friends on a Friday night, but the last few weeks, he decided to stay home and help out more. When his mom and Derek made the announcement, he didn't know how to react. He was shocked. He didn't think his mom wanted another baby because he didn't hear her talk about it. Plus, she was so into her career, he didn't think she would have the time. Shaniece had no plans on getting pregnant so soon. She knew Derek wanted at least one child, but she wanted to enjoy married life without any little ones for at least two years before trying.

"Here, Mom, here's your pizza," Justin stated as he stood in front of her. The two started having a conversation after Shaniece finished the pizza. Derek sat up on the couch and listened to Justin and Shaniece talk about school, sports, and his new girlfriend. Derek usually engaged in their conversations when either Justin or Shaniece asked for his input. This time around, they didn't bother so he didn't have much to say. He felt like somewhat of an outcast but didn't want to complicate things, so he let it go.

In the last few weeks, he felt Shaniece's energy towards him starting to shift. Justin was around more waiting on her hand and foot and even though he didn't want to feel this way, a part of him was jealous. He felt like Shaniece was relying more on Justin than him through her pregnancy and deep down it bothered him. He didn't mention it to her, though; he felt he didn't have that right.

* * * * * *

The next day, Shaniece got ready for her baby shower. Derek looked at Shaniece once she was fully dressed. She was wearing a long ankle-length grey and canary maxi dress. Her long, chestnut brown locks flowed down to the middle of her back. She wore a tad bit of makeup and had freshly manicured nails with grey polish. Lately, Derek had been used to seeing Shaniece in house robes, slippers, and her hair pulled back in a bun, so he appreciated her efforts.

"You look amazing, babe," he stated as he admired her look. Shaniece looked at Derek with a fake smile and thanked him for the compliment. She didn't feel like being bothered or being around people today. She had been in the house so much; she had gotten used to being by herself. She especially didn't feel like being around Derek; she woke up with the burden of him having another child on her mind and knew she had been living a lie. Regardless, she decided to try and put her feelings aside.

Derek helped her down the steps into the living room. Her mother, mother-in-law, and sister-in-law had come by earlier that morning to decorate. Shaniece didn't see the setup until now and was rather impressed. The house was covered with baby blue balloons, and the tables were twisted with blue and canary yellow strings. She sat in the decorated rocking chair in the living room and waited for her guests to arrive.

Within ten minutes, family and friends started to show up. Karina, her in-laws, mother, a few employees, some college friends, aunts, and cousins were all in attendance. Her father-in-law and Jeffrey were also there to keep Derek company.

"Shaniece, you look pretty amazing to be pregnant," Karina stated as she sat on the couch diagonal from her. "I mean your hair, body, and skin are just flawless." Karina hadn't seen Shaniece since the rape and was rather surprised how beautiful she looked. It was a drastic change from how she looked when she was pregnant with Justin. Shaniece hit the gym every other day for years before she was pregnant so the weight she picked up didn't look bad on her. Her skin had a glow, and her hair had grown like crazy.

"Thanks, bestie. But girl, every day it's a struggle," Shaniece told her as she rocked back and forth trying to get comfortable in the chair.

Shaniece was excited to see her assistant, Karen, and a few of her employees in attendance.

"So, do you guys miss me?" she asked as she batted her eyes and smiled. Karen looked at her with her head tilted.

"Now you know this baby not stopping nothing. You be on it. We can't even tell you're not there." Shaniece laughed at Karen's comment and shook her head because she knew that she had been over the top since being on bed rest. She was a hard worker, and she didn't want to see what had taken so long to build crumble just because she was going to have a baby. She had been in business for nearly five years, and this was the first time she had been out this long.

Morgan rounded everyone up to head into the family room. "Okay, it's time to play the infamous baby shower game," she stated as she handed Karina a roll of toilet paper. After several minutes of fun, laughs, and small talk, Morgan announced, "Mom Reeler, you're the winner!"

Her mother-in-law had the closest guess of how big Shaniece's stomach was. Mrs. Reeler was excited that she won and started dancing in front of everyone. She walked over to Shaniece and placed her hand on top of her stomach.

"You hear that, grandson? Grandma won!" Shaniece shook her head and laughed at her competitive spirit. Mrs. Reeler kept her hand on Shaniece's stomach and softly patted for Junior to kick. "Does he still kick after lunch?" she asked.

"Yes, he's always moving around in there. Keep your hand there another minute, and he'll kick." Mrs. Reeler held her hand on Shaniece's stomach for close to two minutes and still didn't feel anything.

"Grandma going to have to have a talk with him already," she joked as she headed back to her seat.

* * * * * *

Three hours passed, and everyone continued to play games, eat, watch Shaniece open gifts, and take pictures. After close to five hours, her guests started leaving one by one. Her mother, mother-in-law,

Morgan, and Karina stayed after to help clean up while the men went outside to smoke cigars.

"So Shaniece, who's going to be in the room with you?" Karina asked. She knew she may not be one of the people present even though she was the godmom but was curious. Shaniece was tired and wanted to call it a day. She was overwhelmed and didn't feel like answering any more baby questions. She didn't want to appear rude, so she went on like usual with an indirect but good enough answer.

"Girl, Derek and I haven't even discussed it yet," she responded. Her mother-in-law was in the next room and overheard the conversation. She walked in with her hands on her hips.

"Oh, for sure I'll be in there seeing my first grand born. I wouldn't miss it for the world." Shaniece didn't expect Mrs. Reeler to come popping into the room or conversation the way she did. Shaniece smiled.

"Yes, Mom, it's your first grandbaby so it's only right you be there," Shaniece agreed. Her mom then came into the room to join the conversation.

"What's going on in here? We might as well talk about this right here, right now." Shaniece rolled her eyes in the back of her head because her mom was over the top at times. She realized that's where she may have gotten it from, but her mom tended to get bent out of shape over the littlest things.

"Mom, it's already established. It'll be Derek, Mom Reeler, and yourself in the room." Shaniece was done talking about it. She felt herself getting agitated, and her body was starting to wear down, but she was glad that she had gotten that conversation out the way. Both her mother and mother-in-law came by to visit once or twice a week ever since she had been on bed rest. Still, that conversation was never brought up, maybe assuming both parents thought that it was a no-brainer. She spoke with Derek about it early into the pregnancy, but they didn't make a final decision as to whether they wanted others in the room with them. She decided she would tell Derek what happened later so he could be aware of her decision.

119

"I'm sleepy. I'm going to go upstairs and rest for a bit," she told everyone as she tried getting up from her seat. They all waited on her hand and foot and catered to her every need. She tried going to sleep, but all she could hear was her mother and mother-in-law talk about how they couldn't wait to meet Junior and all the plans they had for him. They talked about taking him to the zoo to pushing him on the swings at the park. One thing Shaniece knew for sure was that her son wouldn't want for anything and had a lot of people in his life who loved him.

BROKEN HEARTED

"Derek, Derek! Wake up," Shaniece voiced over and over. He finally came to.

"What's wrong? You in labor?" he asked as he frantically sat up on the bed. Shaniece was paranoid now.

"I haven't felt Junior move in hours. That's unlike him. He's always moving."

"When was the last time you felt him kick?" he asked. Shaniece thought back.

"Uuuh, at the baby shower yesterday," she told him.

"Do you think something is wrong?"

"I don't know. I just know that he usually kicks me around the same time every morning after I drink my tea. I drank it an hour ago, and he's still not moving." Derek placed his hand over Shaniece's stomach and started shaking her belly.

"Little man, do something, come on kick for Daddy." Derek waited a few minutes, and he felt nothing. He knew something wasn't right at that point because that was his usual morning routine with Junior. They both got dressed right away and headed to the emergency room. On their way, Shaniece kept her hand over her stomach hoping that she would feel baby Junior move so they could turn around and go back home but still nothing. She didn't want to panic and add any stress, so she inhaled and exhaled, taking deep breaths until they pulled up to the hospital doors. Derek left her in the car and ran in to get help. Two nurses came out with a wheelchair and wheeled Shaniece in. They checked in at the information desk where they were asked numerous questions.

"Mrs. Reeler. Why do you feel something is wrong?" Shaniece gave the nurse the worst look.

"Uh because I can't feel my baby moving. I haven't felt him move since yesterday," she told them. The nurse saw that Shaniece was starting to freak out and didn't want to make matters worse, so she started directing the minimal questions towards Derek.

"How many months is your wife?" she could hear the nurse asking. Before Derek could respond, Shaniece yelled out.

"I'm thirty-two weeks. Can we please see a doctor now?" The nurse placed a hospital band around both of their wrists. Three minutes later, they were directed by another nurse through double doors to the Maternity Emergency wing. They waited in the lobby for an available room. Once in, the nurse and Derek helped prop Shaniece up onto the hospital bed.

"Alright, Mrs. Reeler, we're going to do an ultrasound on you," the on-duty nurse stated. The nurse placed the cold gel onto her stomach and rolled the transducer probe around to find a heartbeat. Shaniece kept her eyes on the nurse's face because that would be the determining factor if something was wrong or not. She saw the nurse's hazel eyes get big.

"What is it?" she asked slowly. Derek followed up.

"What's wrong?" The nurse continued scrolling around on Shaniece stomach without saying a word. She then told them to hold on while she walked out the room. She walked back into the room a few minutes later with a doctor. The doctor introduced himself as Dr. Dunn and picked up from where the nurse left off, continuing to scroll around on Shaniece's stomach. After a long two minutes, he looked at the couple and broke the sad news.

"Mr. and Mrs. Reeler, I'm afraid your baby does not have a heartbeat." The doctor saw the instant pain in their eyes and knew Shaniece was going to lose it. Shaniece couldn't believe what she heard.

"Keep looking," she asked. The doctor showed her the ultrasound on the screen.

"There's no heartbeat to find…" he assured her. Derek was in disbelief. He sat down in the chair and was completely speechless. He wanted to punch a wall, but he walked to the door and left out instead. Shaniece was in the room with the doctor and nurse as they gave their condolences. She was in denial, and their words still were not registering with her. She finally cried out. Derek hurried back in when he heard her cries become louder with every step he took. He walked in and looked at Shaniece slumped over on the hospital bed with her face covered with her hands. He put his head over hers and cried with her. Shaniece felt his tears running down the side of her face. The nurse gave them a few minutes to themselves to grieve.

The doctor and nurse returned to the room, giving their condolences again. When Derek looked at the nurse, it looked as if she'd been crying too. He wondered if she felt the pain they felt.

"Mrs. Reeler, just want to inform you that we contacted your doctor, and he'll be here in an hour or so." Shaniece heard Dr. Dunn speaking, but her mind was in another place. Derek tried to stay strong for his wife, so he took over with the doctor and nurse.

"So, how did this happen?" Derek asked. He wanted answers. He knew his wife was high-risk, but she followed bed rest orders, and everything was normal at their last doctor's appointment.

"Well, Mr. Reeler, according to the ultrasound, the umbilical cord disrupted the baby's blood supply to his brain causing him to lose oxygen, and that's why the heart stopped. It's what we call umbilical cord compression." Derek shook his head as the doctor went on to explain what took place.

"She went to her weekly check-up last week; why didn't the doctor catch this?" Dr. Dunn looked at Derek and placed his hand on his shoulder.

"Some things doctors can't catch. At the time of your wife's appointment, there may not have been a problem. The baby could have shifted and moved since the last appointment, putting her in a more severe state. There are a number of reasons this could've happened," the doctor went on to explain. Derek wiped the tears from the cracks of his eyes.

"So, what happens next?" he asked out of deep concern for his wife. The doctor looked over at Shaniece.

"Well...your wife is going to have to be induced," the doctor advised him. Derek looked at Shaniece and knew she was out of it. It was the same look from when she was raped; he thought that he might not get his wife back this time around. Derek told her what needed to be done. She hunched her shoulders.

"It doesn't matter. Do whatever you want to do," she told both Derek and the doctor nonchalantly.

"Mrs. Reeler, we called your doctor and he's on the way but for the time being we would have to induce you and get you dilated. We'll check you first to see if you're dilated any already." Shaniece nodded her head in agreement with tears in her eyes. She wasn't in touch with the moment and followed the flow of whatever her mind and body directed. Derek had called their parents when he was out in the hallway, so they were already on their way.

* * * * * *

A few hours later, Shaniece was in the labor room propped up on the bed breathing in and out. Her doctor, Dr. Myers, had arrived and was prepped for the delivery. He gave her an epidural to relieve some of the pain. She heard his voice and wanted answers, but she couldn't speak. Her mother and mother-in-law were both in the delivery room for support. She could feel their presence on each side of her. One was rubbing her head, and the other was rubbing her shoulder. More hours passed, and Shaniece was finally dilated enough to deliver. She could hear the nurse and doctors talking louder than usual in the background. "Alright, here we go," the doctor blurted out as he strapped on his blue medical gloves. After twenty minutes of pushing, baby Junior was delivered. Immediately after, she heard the doctor give his final words: "1:48 a.m., time of death." At that point, Shaniece, Derek, her mother, and mother-in-law felt the pain all too well. Shaniece looked up and saw her lifeless son in the nurse's arms. She felt like she was in a nightmare and couldn't wake up to reality.

"Do you want to see him?" the nurse asked as she somewhat cleaned and swaddled him in a hospital blanket. Shaniece didn't know what to do. Her mother nodded her head for her and answered the nurse. She could see the fear and sadness in her daughter's eyes.

"Yes, we would like to say our final goodbyes." The nurse laid baby Junior on Shaniece's chest. She noticed his features right away. His slanted eyes and silky jet-black hair resembled both her and her father. She touched his toes and fingers and every part of his body, hoping some sort of life would come from him, but nothing. With tears strolling down, she held him tight to her heart with her eyes closed. She had looked forward to this moment but never imagined that it would be like this. She didn't want to let his lifeless body go. Derek stood by her side and placed his hand on top of baby Junior's back. He tried to stay strong up to this point, but he couldn't any longer. He was sobbing nonstop. Shaniece then passed baby Junior to Derek. Everyone in the room looked as he held baby Junior, rocking him back and forth in his arms. The nurses and doctors couldn't ignore the moment and put their heads down, attempting not to shed tears. Mr. Reeler and Karina were out in the lobby, and the nurse let them in to say their goodbyes as well. A chaplain came in to bless baby Junior and pray for comfort in the family's heart. They were offered to have pictures taken but Shaniece opted out because she felt she would never overcome the grief. She wanted the memory in her heart to remember him by instead.

Once the doctor took the lifeless body away, Shaniece immediately looked at Derek with anger in her eyes. She was furious and blamed him for their son's death. With the rest of the strength she had left she yelled out, "You did this. You did this. It's your fault." The doctors, nurse, and family all looked at her in shock. They knew she was in pain but couldn't understand why she would blame Derek. Her mother, Ms. Brown, tried calming her down.

"Shaniece, baby, please not here." Shaniece wouldn't listen.

"Mom, you don't understand. Derek has a son already. Baby Junior wasn't his first child. He cheated, Mom. He cheated." The entire delivery room was quiet, and everyone looked like the air was knocked out of them. Derek stood there in the most shock. His first thought was, *How did she know?* Derek was embarrassed not only because her accusations were true but because she put him on the spot in front of their family. Everyone in the room including the doctors and nurse looked to see Derek's response. He couldn't face the judgement, so he walked out the room and raced to the stairwell. His father chased behind him.

"Derek, get back here. Get back here now."

Shaniece told everyone left behind what she knew and how long she knew. Derek's mother was shocked that her son was hiding a child from them all this time. She couldn't take the pressure and started having chest pains. She could barely stand. Karina was standing beside her and grabbed her before she hit the floor.

"Doctor, doctor," Karina yelled while trying to hold Mrs. Reeler up. The doctors rushed over, and the nurse ran out to grab a wheelchair. When they returned, Mrs. Reeler was out cold. The doctor rushed her out the room, but the mayhem in the room was at an all-time high. Shaniece panicked when she saw her mother-in-law being whisked away, perhaps unconscious. She started crying, yelling, and fighting anyone who tried to console her. She couldn't take another heartbreak.

Derek ran down the steps to the last floor of the stairwell. As he was running, he heard his father from three flights up yelling his name. "Derek, stop, son. Stop!" Derek couldn't face his father because he knew he lied to him. He knew eventually he needed to tell someone other than Marcus what was going on in his life. It needed to be someone like his father who could help him think rationally and offer support, but he was drowning. Derek finally stopped and waited for his father to catch up. Mr. Reeler was out of breath by the time he made it to the final floor. Derek was sitting on the last step with his head held down. His father sat down beside him attempting to catch his breath. After thirty seconds of silence, Derek spoke.

"Dad, I'm ashamed and feel like the worst man in the world. I never meant for any of this to happen." His father shook his head because Derek had just confirmed that Shaniece's accusations were true.

"Well, son, we all fall short. The problem is you dug yourself in a bigger hole by not saying anything. I mean we're talking about another baby for God's sake." Derek knew his dad was disappointed and had to accept the responsibility that by keeping his secret, he had caused more damage.

"Dad, the situation is so complicated. I didn't even know I had another son until a few months ago. Only reason, and I mean the only reason, I didn't tell Shaniece was because she was high risk, and I didn't want to cause any more stress."

"But look what happened. She knew all along and that woman lost your son, my grandson. Can you imagine how she feels?" Derek knew he had damaged his wife, and the thought of having to face her again was something he was not looking forward to. Derek pulled his phone out to check the time. His phone was on silent, and he noticed multiple texts and voicemail from an unknown number. While listening, he jumped up and helped his dad up from the last step. His dad was nervous after looking at Derek's face.

"Quick! We gotta go up, something's wrong with Mom." They both ran out the door and hopped onto the elevator. They made it into the lobby and saw Karina standing there in tears.

"Karina, where's my mom?" Derek asked as he walked up. Mr. Reeler ran over to the front desk to get more insight into what happened to his wife. Karina was in tears and shaking as she told them what happened after they left the room. After finally getting the story out, she went back downstairs to be with Shaniece. Derek and his father sat in the waiting room for nearly three hours before the doctor finally came out. He walked up to Mr. Reeler and confirmed he was the husband. Mr. Reeler's heart dropped because he didn't know the status of his wife.

"Mr. Reeler, your wife had a mild stroke. She went in and out of consciousness a few times. She seems to be okay for now, but we will have to monitor her for a few days. Good thing she was here when it happened." Mr. Reeler was relieved that he didn't hear the words, "We're sorry, but your wife is gone" because he couldn't take any more bad news for one day.

"Well, can I see her?" he asked as he tried pushing past the doctor. The doctor nodded his head.

"Yes, you may but she's resting for now. She's going to need a lot of sleep." Derek was happy to hear his mom was okay. He wanted to go back downstairs with his wife but didn't want to cause anymore drama, hurt, and pain than he already did. He knew she needed him but also knew at the same time that she hated him right now, so he decided to wait it out.

* * * * * *

A few hours passed, and Derek decided to face his fears. She wasn't the only one who was suffering. He walked past the front desk headed to her room. He noticed security was on the floor this go-round. He walked into the room, and Shaniece was lying in the bed sleep. Her mother was resting on the couch beside her. It was dark in the room so they couldn't make out that it was Derek who walked in. He walked over to his wife and rubbed her head. Her mother jumped when she saw him.

"Derek, what are you doing?" she asked in an angry tone. Derek looked at her and replied with a whisper hoping not to wake his wife.

"Coming to see my wife…look, I don't want to cause any trouble. I just want to see my wife." Ms. Brown pushed her blanket back from over her lap and walked over to him.

"Well, she doesn't want to see you. Don't you think you have done enough damage? Just leave," she told him. Derek didn't want any more drama, so he kissed his wife on her forehead and walked out. Shaniece heard what was going on and cried silently into her pillow thinking about all that she had been through.

* * * * * *

Derek went back to be with his mother and father. He walked up to his father and doctor in the lobby as they were speaking. He heard the doctor ask his father if his mother was worried about anything or had any stress at home that would cause her to have a stroke. His father went on to explain the incident that took place in the delivery room a few hours ago. Derek was embarrassed when the doctor looked over at him. He was starting to think he was the talk of the hospital staff. His main concerns at this point were his mother and his wife.

"Mr. Reeler, I'm afraid there must be something else worrying your wife. A single event like what happened today wouldn't have caused your wife to have a stroke. It's most likely a buildup of stress that may have taken place over months or years is why your wife had a stroke." The doctor didn't want to pry but warned Mr. Reeler to figure out what it was so it wouldn't lead to an even more severe stroke later down the line. There hadn't been much trouble at home, besides quarrels about small things like him forgetting to take out the trash, but other than that he couldn't think of what could be bothering his wife to the point of a stroke. The doctor left out, and Mr. Reeler remained heavy in thought, worried about his wife and her condition.

* * * * * *

It was early in the morning, and Derek nor his father didn't get much rest. Derek had been at the hospital since 10 a.m. Sunday, and it was now 7 a.m. Monday morning. He had been up for close to twenty-four hours, and his body was starting to give out on him. He fell asleep in a small uncomfortable chair as he waited for his mother to wake. After a few hours of rest, he woke up and saw his mom still resting in the bed and his father sitting in a chair slumped over on the end of her bed. Derek checked his phone for the time and saw that he had multiple missed calls from Danita. He walked out into the hallway and called her back. "Danita, hey, what's going on?" he asked in a concerned voice. Danita didn't sound like her usual; he noticed it from the time she answered the phone. She went on to tell him that she was being admitted to hospice and needed him to come pick up Tyler. Derek put his hand over his eyes trying to hold back tears once again. "Okay, I'm leaving the hospital now," he told her.

"Why are you at the hospital?" she asked, concerned. Derek didn't want to be rude but didn't feel like talking about it.

"My mom was sick, but she's fine now. Look, I'm on my way," he told her before hanging up. Derek tipped toed back into the room and saw his parents still asleep. He walked back out and rushed over to Danita's.

* * * * * *

Derek pulled up to Danita's apartment and banged on the door. Danita let him in, and right away he noticed her apartment was practically empty. He didn't question why because he pretty much knew the answer.

"Hey, I have all of his belongings here," she told him. Derek looked down at a play pen, stroller, baby bags, and a few other items next to the door. Derek's mind was wandering all over the place, and he had so many questions.

"Who said you need to go to hospice now?" he asked hoping she would give him a concrete answer.

"Well, I went to my doctor and the cancer spread and I don't have that much time. I can't care for Tyler in the condition that I'm in. I could go any day now and who would know?" Since Danita had broken the news some weeks ago, he had been over and calling her nonstop because he knew she was caring for Tyler alone and feared himself the same thing, so he understood.

"Okay, well let me take you there at least," he offered. She shook her head and told him a friend was going to take her in a few hours. Derek wanted to do more for her. He asked if there was anything he could do, and she told him she had everything under control. Derek respected the fact that she was so brave and prepared to leave this earth. What he didn't understand is how she could stay so strong. The biggest obstacle life could throw at someone was looking her directly in the face, but she hadn't lost her mind. Her courage actually gave him strength in all he had been dealing with and was part of the reason why he's been able to keep going. Derek packed all of Tyler's belongings into the back of his truck. He watched Danita give her goodbyes, and it broke his heart because so many hours ago he had to do the same thing with baby Junior. He hugged her tightly and said goodbye. "We'll be there every day to visit you until the time comes," Derek told her before pulling off. Danita shook her head in agreement and waved goodbye until his truck was out of sight. Derek drove halfway to his house before realizing he couldn't take Tyler there. Shaniece would kill him without discussing it with her first. He knew he couldn't have that conversation now. He looked back at Tyler sleeping in his car seat so peacefully. He didn't want to go to a hotel, so he called Marcus. He pulled his car over and dialed his number.

"Hey, man, what's good? Where you been? I've been calling you. I did it man, I did it," Marcus shouted on the other line. Derek had no idea what he was talking about and was curious to know.

"You did what, man?" he asked.

"I proposed to Natalie! I finally did it after fourteen years." That was the last thing Derek expected to hear from Marcus.

"Congratulations, man. I'm proud of you! You finally stepped up to the plate," Derek told him. He wanted to tell him about Shaniece losing the baby but didn't want to ruin his moment. He knew he had the right to know as the godfather and would tell him once he got things settled with Tyler and finding a place to stay.

"So, what's the deal? Why the heck are you calling me in the middle of the day? I never hear from you until after five—slow day at work or something?" Marcus asked.

"I'm hitting you back from the missed call yesterday, but after hearing the good news I suspect this is why you called. At that point, he changed his mind about getting his help because he didn't want to intrude. Congrats again, man!" Derek stated before hanging up. He banged on his steering wheel with his phone still in his hand. "Who can I call? Who can I call?" he asked himself while scrolling through his contacts. He finally realized who would be the biggest help to him.

"Hey, Melanie, how's things going in the office?" he asked for small talk.

"Well sir, things are quiet today. I have everything under control," she assured him. He asked if she could take a late lunch and meet him across town at a coffee shop. Melanie knew that something must been going on. She replied, "Yes, of course sir," with no questions asked.

"Good I'll see you at 1 p.m.," he stated before hanging up. An hour later, Derek met up with Melanie at a small shop distant from the office. He came clean about everything from the time of the meet-up that they had planned with Danita months back until now. Melanie was in shock just like everyone else about Tyler. Her heart went out to both Shaniece and Danita. She was loyal to Derek and was naturally a problem solver; that's why Derek compensated her so well. Melanie brainstormed and thought of a last-minute solution. She told him that she and her husband had a home they were planning to sell and put on the market soon. She offered Derek the chance to live there with Tyler until he figured things out and gave him the key to the house along with the address. When she looked at Tyler, she immediately thought about her son and wanted to help in any way she could. She couldn't imagine her son being in that position and felt bad for both him and Derek.

* * * * * *

A week had passed, and Derek was still staying at Melanie's home. He took Tyler to see his mother every day until she passed. During the last few weeks of speaking with Danita, he was able to get all the information he needed. She gave him his medical and social security card, insurance papers, court documents, childcare contacts, and picture album for baby Tyler to remember her by. Derek also begged Danita for her mother's contact information for weeks because he wanted his son to know someone from her side of the family. Danita refused to give it to him up until her last few breaths. She gave him her mother's name and state where she lived. He decided that that was enough information to start his search.

Things really got real for him after losing baby Junior and Danita's passing. He knew he had to be strong, especially for Tyler. He called Shaniece every day since her mother kicked him out the hospital room, but she wouldn't pick up. He sent numerous texts begging for her to call him back but got no reply. His mother was doing better after she was released from the hospital. He knew she was disappointed in him, but he promised that he would come over and explain everything, including how he now had custody of baby Tyler.

FINAL FAREWELL

Shaniece was released from the hospital a few days after giving birth. Her heart was broken, and she didn't know what to do with her life at this point. She had to stay strong just a bit longer to plan her baby son's funeral. She decided to keep it private and invite close family and a few friends. Shaniece's mother helped her pick out a tombstone and come up with a funeral service program. Even though it was hard to speak to or hear about him, Shaniece knew it wouldn't be fair to not include Derek. She picked up her phone and finally returned his hundreds of calls. She dialed his number, listening to each ring and secretly hoping that he wouldn't pick up.

Derek was sitting on the couch and slowly looked up at his phone on the coffee table after it started buzzing. When Derek saw Shaniece's number pop up, he didn't know what to do or say. He grabbed the phone and stared at it for a moment, then straightened up and answered as calmly as he could.

"Hello?" Derek said in a surprised voice. He had been calling nonstop and wanted to talk to Shaniece but had no idea of what to say now that the time had come. At first, Shaniece sat on the other line in silence without saying anything. She heard his voice repeat "Hello? Shaniece?" over and over, and eventually all the hatred came back to her. She couldn't talk to him so she hung up the phone. Derek looked at the phone, devastated at the words "Call Ended." He called her again, back-to-back, but Shaniece wouldn't answer. She wasn't prepared to deal with him yet.

* * * * * *

The next day, Derek decided to go to the house after work. He had done enough calling – it was time for a face-to-face conversation. He used his key and walked right in. Shaniece was lounging on the couch in the living room while her mom was in the kitchen cutting up fruit and vegetables. They were both shocked to see him walk through the door. Shaniece got up and met him at the doorway so he wouldn't come any further into the house.

"What are you doing here?!" she screamed. Derek looked at her in her soft pink sweats and wrinkled t-shirt with her hair standing all over her head. Seeing her this way made his heart drop even more because he knew then that she was really struggling. He wanted to do nothing but grab her and hold her close to him.

"I can't do this. I can't take it. I'm hurting. I need to talk to you, see you," Derek blurted out. Shaniece shook her head in anger, covering her ears and trying not to listen to what he had to say.

"I want you out. Get out now!" Shaniece yelled as she turned away and pointed to the front door. Derek begged her to give him a chance to speak. Shaniece's mother walked out the kitchen with a knife in her hand.

"What did my daughter say? She wants you out!" she barked as she walked toward his direction. He saw her knuckles were starting to turn lighter from gripping the handle so hard. Derek knew he couldn't compete with a knife, so he turned away and grabbed the doorknob but then paused before he opened the door. He turned around and looked at both women.

"Before I leave, I just want to let you know I will be at the funeral. Both me and Marcus. He was my son and his godson too." Shaniece figured his parents had told him about the service but didn't say a word.

133

She crossed her arms while eying the door, giving him the cue to leave. He got the point and didn't bother pushing things any further. Shaniece slammed and locked the door behind him then went back to the couch for another attempt to get some rest. Her mother stood in the room briefly but retreated back to the kitchen to finish cutting up the rest of the fruit and vegetables.

"He had some nerve showing up here like that," she said to Shaniece. Shaniece didn't respond. She was curled up on the couch, tears still streaming down her face.

* * * * * *

On the day of the funeral, family and friends gathered inside the funeral home chapel. Shaniece opted to have a closed casket service; she couldn't bear to see her deceased baby again. She sat in the front row between her mother and Karina, who held Shaniece as she alternated between sobbing quietly and wailing out loud. Derek had arrived with his parents, brother and sister-in-law and sat toward the back with Marcus and Natalie. Melanie stepped in and helped him out with Tyler while he attended the funeral. Derek was unsure of where Shaniece was mentally and knew it wasn't the time nor place to find out, so he kept his distance. Derek's family and friends gave their condolences and were grieving just as hard as Shaniece was. They lost a part of them as well. Baby Junior's death had taken a toll on everyone connected to them both.

After the funeral, Shaniece held a small intimate dinner back at her home, and, for her in-laws' sake, she allowed Derek to come. During dinner, Derek tried whisking Justin off to talk with him alone, but his stepson gave him the cold shoulder. He wanted so badly to come back home and make things right, but he knew it wasn't happening any time soon, especially with him having Tyler now. He sat quietly eating his meal, when he heard Shaniece speaking to his mother.

"Mom, I'm so glad you're okay. I was so worried about you," Shaniece said. She didn't want to talk about what happened but wanted her to know that she was still thinking about her since their communication had been limited over the last few days.

"Thank you, sweetie. I almost scared myself. I'm just glad that you're starting to feel better," Mrs. Reeler went on to say. Shaniece smiled briefly, but deep down, she was far from feeling better, not even close. Derek wanted to talk to Shaniece too, but he decided against it, instead he slipped out to go wait in the car until his parents were ready to leave. His heart just couldn't take the sight of seeing Shaniece in so much pain. He could see right through her, and it killed him that he wasn't able to be there for her like he wanted. Mrs. Reeler and Shaniece continued talking, while Mr. Reeler looked on as he finished his plate. He shook his head as he happened to see his son go out the door. He wondered if and how he could help fix the whole situation; he hated seeing his son like this.

* * * * * *

After a few hours, everyone left except for Shaniece's mother, Ms. Brown. Shaniece was sitting in her recliner, tired but relieved that the day was over with. She just wanted to be in the house and left unbothered.

"Mom, Justin and I will be fine for tonight," she told her mother, who was standing by and fixing one of the cushions on the loveseat.

"No, no, no. I'm going to stay tonight in case you need anything." Shaniece sighed. She appreciated her being there but was starting to feel smothered. She wanted some time alone without someone waiting on her and asking if she was okay every ten minutes.

"We're alright, Mom. There's really no need—"

"Look, Shaniece, I'm not going anywhere, and that's final." Shaniece knew not to argue back. She just crossed her arms and closed her eyes as she rocked back and forth in the recliner, staring at the wall. *I'm so done with everyone and everything,* she thought.

* * * * * *

Shaniece tossed and turned all night long. She couldn't sleep thinking about all that she'd been through. She eventually sat up and started crying silently. "Why me, why me? I really don't understand why I keep trying in life and everything, I mean everything, just doesn't seem to turn out right. God, why are you punishing me? Are you even listening?" she lashed out in an angry, tear-strained voice. She cried into her hands for a while attempting to be as quiet as she could. The last thing she needed was for her mom to hear her from the other room and come bursting in with her cape on like Captain Save-a-Daughter. After ten minutes, she dried her face with the comforter and laid back down, trying to close her eyes and go back to sleep.

As much as she hated Derek, she couldn't ignore the fact that she still loved him. She was mad at herself because it was typically easy for her to walk away from a relationship if something went wrong, but this time around, it was much harder for her to do. She thought heavily about giving up on their marriage and starting her life over again. She thought back about the rape as well as her prior relationships and connected the dots. Every time a tragedy happened in her life, it always seemed to involve a man. She was starting to think that she was better off by herself. It would be less painful that way. She didn't want to be that woman who, after a terrible experience, painted all men the same, but she understood why some women did.

She clutched her pillow tightly as more thoughts about herself and her decisions came rushing into her mind. She knew she cheated as well and messed up with Julian but thought she at least was woman enough to admit to her mistake. She didn't know all the details about Derek and his side chick. She didn't even attempt to find out who the mysterious woman was due to being high risk at the time and now grieving her son's loss. She did want to hear him out but was still too fragile at this point and knew she wouldn't be able to handle the full truth. She was just unsure of when the right time would come around for them to talk.

* * * * * *

"Shaniece, can we please talk? It's been three weeks, and I really need to talk to you" were the words Derek uttered on Shaniece's voicemail. She listened to his messages one after another, and every time she thought about it, she realized she wasn't ready. She continued to work from home and kept herself busy around the house to keep from thinking about her life. Justin stayed home from school for a few days after the funeral just to keep her company. She didn't want him to, but he insisted.

"Mom, are you okay being by yourself today?" Justin asked as he handed her water jug from out of the fridge. He was about to leave the house to go to school.

"Yes, son, your mom is a strong woman, so don't you worry, okay?" she told him. Justin always looked at his mom with pride because, as long as he could remember, she had always been strong. He had seen her look adversity in the face and overcome it so many times, and he respected her for it. He experienced some things during his high school years but could move past them because of his mom's example. Still, that didn't keep him from being worried about her. This was the first time she had dealt with something like this, and he saw how much of a toll everything had taken on her. He was afraid that her strength was no longer enough now.

"Alright, I'm heading out for school. I'm going to the skate park after to practice so I'll call when I'm headed home," he told her as he kissed her cheek before walking out the door. Shaniece felt partially guilty because she was so mad at Derek that she shared what she knew with Justin. She figured he was old enough to know what was going on. From that point on, Justin didn't want anything to do with Derek. They both agreed that he wouldn't be able to move back in. Justin was now a junior and would be attending an out-of-state college soon. He didn't want his mom to be alone, but at the same time, he didn't want her to live the rest of her life with cheating Derek either.

After Justin left, Shaniece stood in the family room and looked around. She didn't know what she was looking at or looking for. She suddenly fell to her knees in the middle of the floor and started praying.

"God…please take this pain, anger, and hatred away from me. I'm bitter and mad as hell. I can't handle this pain on my own…I need you now more than anything." She remained on her knees for a few minutes, bawling her eyes out. She yelled and screamed to get all her feelings and hurt out. The next thing she knew, she awoke in the middle of the family room floor hours later with the imprint of the carpet on the side of her face. She sat there for a few minutes massaging her cheek with her hand, attempting to get the wrinkles out.

"Alright…I'm ready to talk to him," she told herself as she grabbed her cell phone off the middle shelf of the bookcase. She closed her eyes as the phone rang.

"Hello?" Derek answered on the second ring.

"Hi, Derek…I guess I'm ready to talk now," Shaniece started off.

Derek was happy she called but didn't want to sound too excited. He cleared his throat before speaking.

"Thank you for calling me. Is it okay if I come over after work? Is that fine?"

"Yes." Shaniece abruptly replied.

"Okay…I miss you so much," he whispered into the phone. Shaniece didn't want to hear that from him. She just wanted to know how the baby came about and more of what she didn't know.

"I'll see you later," she said, hanging up the phone quickly.

* * * * * *

Immediately after work, Derek dropped Tyler off to Melanie while he went to go meet Shaniece. He drove as quickly as he could, pulling into the driveway and practically forgetting to put the truck in park. He used his key and entered the house. "Shaniece?" he called out.

"I'm up here," she answered. He walked upstairs to the bedroom and tapped softly on the bedroom door.

"Come in," Shaniece stated as she waved her hand for him to walk in. Shaniece was propped up on the bed with sweats and her company T-shirt on. Her long curls were pushed behind her ears, and her face was makeup-free. Derek cracked a small smile at her as he took off his suit jacket and loosened his tie and collar before sitting on the edge of the lounge across from the bed. Shaniece muted the television as she waited for him to get adjusted.

"So…tell me everything and I mean everything." She got right into it. Derek went on to reveal everything from beginning to end, not leaving out any details. When Shaniece heard that the side chick was Danita, she was dumbfounded. She didn't put two and two together that the last name on the paternity results were the same as Danita's. At that time, her mind was frazzled and all she could think about was her pregnancy and not causing any harm or stress to her baby boy. She immediately went back to the day when she came to the office and Danita had disrespected her. She didn't think Danita was his type and now realized he didn't have a type, which instantly became a turn off to her. Derek told her it was only about the sex, but she figured if he gave in more than once, there had to be more to it. When he got to the part about Danita passing, she couldn't believe what she was hearing. She didn't know if she was still living in the same nightmare. Derek also told her that he was now caring for baby Tyler and actively looking for a place. She wanted to hear the truth but she wasn't prepared for this. Shaniece then shared how she found out and how she was waiting for him to break the news to her. Derek hung his head, feeling even more disappointed in himself that he didn't just tell her sooner. After they were done putting everything out in the open, they both sat in silence staring off into space. The sound of light rain against the windowpane was the only thing either of them could hear in the room. Shaniece finally spoke and broke the silence.

"I want to see the baby." Derek looked at her, confused.

"You do?"

"Yes, I want to see him," she told him again.

They talked more and eventually agreed that she would come over to the house the next day to meet Tyler for the first time. When they finished talking, Derek got up and gathered his things. He wanted to show Shaniece some type of affection, but he could tell that they were not back to that point yet. He nodded his head on his way out attempting to shut the bedroom door behind him before Shaniece directed for him to leave it open. Shaniece unmuted the TV and turned up the volume to drown out the soft sobs that had started up once again.

* * * * * *

Two weeks passed, and Shaniece never made it to see baby Tyler. En route that day she turned back around because she realized she wasn't ready to see a baby that her husband had fathered with another woman when she just lost her own. She was bitter and mad at the fact that she didn't have his first child. She thought she would be able to handle it, but she couldn't. Derek understood that she would need more time and took things at her pace. He knew it was a complicated situation that would take some time getting adjusted to.

Shaniece and Derek had spoken twice since the night he came over. The communication was mostly one sided: Derek was the one doing the calling to check on her wellbeing. He mentioned to her that he had found a condo and that he would be coming to get his belongings in a few days. Shaniece was heartbroken because she didn't want to live in a big house alone, especially with Justin leaving soon. The thought of her meeting another man never crossed her mind. However, the thought of selling her home, moving into a condo by herself, getting a cat, and being alone for the rest of her life did.

When it finally came time for Derek to move into his condo, he came over almost every day for a week to get different items. Whenever he stopped by, he wanted Shaniece more and more. They had small talk when he was there but never deep conversations like they did in the past. Whenever he left, Shaniece would sit in the middle of the doorway with her arms folded looking at him pull off. He almost wished that she would beg for him to stay, but he knew that wouldn't happen. At his last trip to the house to get his belongings, he decided to give it one last try with Shaniece.

"I'm sorry…I'm sorry about everything. If you could only forgive me like I forgave you…" he pleaded. Shaniece thought about what he said several times before he even stated it. She thought about how she cheated too, and if he was able to forgive her, why couldn't she forgive him? She felt like she lost so much more than he did. If he would've come clean and told her then maybe, just maybe, she would be a little more forgiving and willing to work things out with him. She thought the whole time she was feeling guilty about Julian when what she thought all along was true. Derek had been cheating. Shaniece looked at him with big raindrop-sized tears falling from the corner of her eyes. She didn't bother wiping them away.

"Derek, please go. I can't do it. I'm bitter. I'm mad that I lost my son. I've been through enough, and I can't take any more pain. Anyone who causes me unfathomable pain must be eliminated from my life…so you'll be hearing from my lawyer in the next few weeks because I want a divorce." Derek wasn't expecting to hear that. He looked at her angrily.

"A divorce?! A divorce?! Are you serious?" He was under the impression that they were taking a break until everything died down. He noticed she wasn't wearing her wedding ring, but he never would've guessed that she wanted a divorce.

"Yes, I thought about it long and hard, and I have to move on and change the course of my life."

"What? What does that mean?"

"I'm making some serious changes to stop this cycle of pain and hurt that I encounter every few years. Getting a divorce has to be one of those changes." Derek was hurt and didn't want to hear anything else she had to say. He grabbed the rest of his belongings, hopped in his truck, and sped off. Shaniece turned quickly and rushed into the house, slamming the door behind her and locking it. She laid her back against the door but burst into more tears as she slid to the floor, covering her face with her hands.

* * * * * *

"Whyyyyyyyy?! Why?! Why? Why?" Derek yelled out as he banged the steering wheel driving back to his condo. He knew he made a mistake with Danita and should have been able to resist the temptation. He was furious with himself that he didn't dismiss her. "How could I be so stupid?" he asked himself. "I mean I had a small stupid fling. I never would've imagined it would lead to this." Derek was questioning himself and God about the entire ordeal. After he calmed down for a moment, he began to think about other men he knew had been unfaithful. His buddy Omar from college cheated on his girl with a stripper and contracted HIV. One of his father's friends cheated on his wife with her sister, and she murdered him. He continued thinking of various times where men he knew of cheated and life dealt them their cards. He just wished he would've thought about all of these situations before he made the same mistake. He then tried to make sense out of his problem and wondered if it was fate. He thought about losing Junior and thought maybe baby Tyler was part of the plan all along. He considered how Tyler needed him but also how he needed Tyler. If he didn't have anything else, he at least had his son. Even if he couldn't get the chance to do right by Shaniece, Derek was determined to at least do right by Tyler -- no matter what.

SECRETS

Shaniece headed out the door to her in-laws' house. Mrs. Reeler called her the night before to come over for lunch while her husband was out fishing. She turned into their driveway and parked. When she saw her mother-in-law at the door, she exhaled before she exited the vehicle. Mrs. Reeler waved as Shaniece looked toward the house after shutting her car door. Shaniece always joked with Derek about growing up in a neighborhood like the Brady Bunch – just without all the brothers and sisters. Mr. and Mrs. Reeler lived in a modest, close-knit community. The neighbors were friendly, and the homes were kept up nicely. Shaniece wondered if the neighborhood would be fined if their landscaping wasn't kept up to par because she never saw one home or yard out of place.

Shaniece knew Mrs. Reeler likely wanted to talk to her about her decision to divorce Derek. Her mind was made up, and no one could change it. She wanted to start her life over. It had been eight weeks since she lost her son, and, instead of crumbling under pressure, Shaniece decided to get her life back on track and keep going. Her sales team did a remarkable job while she was out and picked up some new clients, so she was returning to the office in a few days. She'd been in talks with her realtor about putting her house on the market. She returned to therapy and had attended two sessions thus far. She even visited different churches to get the Word, hoping she would find a new church home she could join.

* * * * * *

"Hey, Mom." Shaniece greeted her mother-in-law as she walked up to the newly renovated front porch. Mrs. Reeler was all smiles as she opened the screened door to let Shaniece in.

"Hey, my beautiful daughter." Shaniece knew that her decision to divorce Derek would impact her relationship with her soon-to-be ex-mother-in-law and that broke her heart. She tried not to think about it too much.

"I'm loving the porch. The renovation came together rather nice," Shaniece stated as she took a double look when the two broke from their embrace.

"Thank you. I'm enjoying it so far." Mrs. Reeler motioned for Shaniece to join her in the kitchen where lunch was prepared. She looked at the warm rolls, grilled chicken and salad on the table then made her plate.

"I'm so happy you joined me today for lunch." Mrs. Reeler went on to say.

"Well, you used to come to me when I was on bed rest; now, I finally get to come visit you," Shaniece responded as she struggled putting dressing on her salad. "So, are you alright? Did you have any complications?" Shaniece followed up out of concern.

"No, I must say that I was one of the lucky ones. It could've been much worse. Good thing I was in the hospital at the time."

"Well, what did your doctor say? What caused it?" Shaniece had been wondering if it was something other than all the drama in the room that day.

"They say stress, but who knows? It could be a number of things," Mrs. Reeler told her. While eating, they continued to chat about the new renovations and how Shaniece was excited to be returning back to work. After they were done, they walked out to the porch to enjoy the sunshine. It was May, and the weather was perfect. It was hard to be depressed when the sun was shining every day.

"I'm loving those shades," Shanice expressed as Mrs. Reeler placed her Louis Vuitton sunglasses on her face.

"Oh, Morgan bought me these glasses for Christmas. I finally get a chance to wear them." They sat out on the porch enjoying the view of the neighborhood. One of the neighbors slowed down as she was walking her dog, and Mrs. Reeler called out to her.

"Hey, Delores! How are you today?"

"I'm doing well, just out walking Shiloh. I'm glad to see you're doing better, Angie! Also, who is this beautiful woman next to you?"

"Yes, I'm doing well. And, this is my daughter-in-law, Shaniece! I don't believe you met her." Mrs. Delores acknowledged Shaniece and waved.

"Nice to meet you, dear!"

"Same here, Mrs. Delores," Shaniece responded. Before Mrs. Delores could speak again, Shiloh started barking and pulling forward.

"I guess Shiloh says we're done here. I'll see you later!" She waved goodbye and kept going.

Mrs. Reeler loved her daughters-in-law. She was glad that her sons had found women who lived up to her standards. Both Shaniece and

Morgan were beautiful, smart, educated, and successful in addition to having morals and respect. Whenever she had a chance to brag about them, she took full advantage. She just hated that she didn't get to talk to Delores longer; she had so many wonderful things to tell her about Shaniece. At least doing that would have made it easier for the conversation she was about to have. After a few minutes, Mrs. Reeler decided to get to the point of the visit. She poured two glasses of lemonade and handed Shaniece one.

"Oh, well thank you," Shaniece stated as she lifted the glass and sipped on the bitter drink. *This could stand to have a little more sugar,* she thought. Mrs. Reeler looked at her with a half-smile.

"So, Shaniece, tell me…what are your plans?"

"Well, what exactly do you mean?" Shaniece asked as she went from sips to gulps. She knew they would end up talking about her relationship with Derek, but she didn't want to give up too much information, so she wanted her to be more specific.

"Well, what I meant is…what do you plan to do now that you know about Derek and the baby?" Shaniece took a deep breath because she was still fragile. She was strong, but when someone talked about the situation, she became weak all over again. It was like kryptonite to her.

"Well, I'm pretty sure Derek told you how I decided to handle it. I'm filing for divorce." Mrs. Reeler held her chest after the word "divorce" came out. She cleared her throat.

"Yes…he did tell me you were filing for divorce…and I can understand why. The entire situation is a mess. He did tell me that he told you everything…correct?" Shaniece sank down into her chair and began to share some of the details of what Derek shared with her the night he came over. She decided to tread lightly because she didn't want to disrespect her mother-in-law in any way.

"After losing Junior, I gave up on our marriage. I just can't do it anymore," Shaniece admitted.

"Well, sweetheart, we were all hurt to the core when we lost Junior. It was painful for us all." Shaniece wanted Mrs. Reeler to get to the point; she was becoming agitated with her mother-in-law.

"No one knows how I felt. What's tragic is losing my baby and finding out my husband fathered another child and didn't tell me. Now that's a low blow." Mrs. Reeler shook her head back and forth as she stared off into the sunlight listening to Shaniece share her feelings. She gently placed her glass down on the table.

"Well, I do know how you feel," Mrs. Reeler went on to say. Shaniece looked at her with a side eye.

"How so?" Her mother-in-law sat there for a few seconds, contemplating if she wanted to have this talk with her daughter-in-law. She took a deep breath and looked at Shaniece.

"I'm about to share a secret with you and only you. The only reason I'm sharing it with you is because I felt your pain and can still feel it. What I'm about to tell you will not leave here, do you understand?" Mrs. Reeler looked into Shaniece's eyes. Shaniece was scared and nervous to hear what she was about to say.

"Yes ma'am." Mrs. Reeler took another sip of lemonade and began speaking.

"Okay…a few years back, maybe three years ago, our house phone rang, and I answered it. A young lady on the other line asked to speak with my husband. She identified him by his first and last name. I asked her name, and she stated 'Cassandra.' I asked what she wanted with my husband and then she hung up. Well, I redialed the number and wrote it down, and every day for nearly a month, I called sometimes twice a day until I got an answer. Finally, the woman with the same voice picked up. I asked who she was and why she hung up, and she told me she was Joe's daughter. She then went on to tell me that her mother passed, and on her death bed, she revealed to her who her real father was. The pain I felt that day was indescribable. The young lady at the time told me she was twenty-nine. Joe and I had been married for forty-two years so that means he cheated on me. The bad part is he didn't and still don't know about her." Shaniece was shocked but confused about Mrs. Reeler's last statement.

"What do you mean still don't know?" she asked. Mrs. Reeler stared down at the concrete outside the porch, embarrassed to finish the story.

"Well…I promised the young lady that I would keep her contact information and when Joe came home I would have him call her, and we would work out a meeting. Well, I didn't do that. I changed our number the next day so she couldn't get in contact and hid the information. I never told Joe about the call, and still until this day, he doesn't know he has a possible daughter. I've been stressing about what I've done for years, and when I heard you yell out that Derek fathered another child in the hospital that day, I immediately thought about his father, and that's what caused my stroke. Shaniece…I know what my son did was wrong, but we all make mistakes, and everyone deserves forgiveness including me."

Shaniece was speechless. She now saw Mrs. Reeler in a totally different light. She wanted to blurt out how she was dead wrong and that was the worst thing she could do to someone she loved, but she was pretty sure she knew it by now. After minutes of silence, Shaniece finally spoke.

"You're right, but what you did was wrong."

"I know I was wrong and I'm going to make it right, but you've made mistakes yourself. Derek forgave you, didn't he?" Shaniece looked over at her because she knew what she was implying. *Derek must have told her about the affair,* she thought.

"Yes, I have but I paid for it in the worst way!" Shaniece stated angrily.

"I know that, dear. On the night of…what happened to you…Derek called me and told me what happened. He wanted to know if I could help bury the story and keep it under the radar to protect your reputation and business. I called in a few favors to the media and the courthouse. Who do you think was behind the guy getting the maximum sentence? What I'm getting at is my son loves you and the only reason he didn't tell you about the baby is because you were high-risk. All I'm asking is please reconsider the divorce because my son needs you. That baby needs you." Mrs. Reeler kept going nonstop about how Shaniece shouldn't be like her, how she should forgive and let bygones be bygones, and how she should help raise baby Tyler instead of walking away. Shaniece couldn't take it anymore.

"Stop, please stop!" she yelled out. She looked around because she was rather loud and didn't want to bring any drama to the neighborhood. Shaniece grabbed her purse and walked to her car without saying another word. Mrs. Reeler got up quickly and rushed over to the stairs of the porch.

"Please think about what I said. That's all I ask," she mentioned again before Shaniece hopped in her car, slammed the door, and sped off.

* * * * * *

A week came and went, and Mrs. Reeler was starting to think that she should have taken her secret to her grave. Still, she had kept it to herself for three years, and it was killing her inside. Shaniece was the first person she told, which made her feel a little less guilty about confessing what she did. She called Shaniece a few hours after she left her house that day, but her daughter-in-law didn't answer. The last thing she wanted was for Shaniece to be mad at her. Her intentions were pure when she invited her over for lunch. She just wanted Shaniece to understand how her son really loved her and did what he could to protect her. On top of that, Mrs. Reeler felt that Derek wasn't fighting hard enough for his marriage, so she had to step in. She couldn't help herself because that's what she had done all her life. If something went wrong, she was the one who made it right. When she worked at the county building before retiring, she always had a solution to any problems that arose in the office. When her husband lost his job, she pulled some strings to get him a better-paying job. When Jeffrey received bad grades and was failing in school, she set him up with a tutor, and he started making the honor roll every year afterward. When

Derek was out of work and he was on the verge of losing his home and car, she gave him money to get out of the jam. She didn't mean any harm, but she just wanted the best for her family. She knew Shaniece was best for her son and wasn't going to let up until she got her way.

She tried calling her daughter-in-law one more time a few days later. The phone rang three times, but when she heard a live voice on the other line, Mrs. Reeler sat straight up in her chair. "Hi, Mooommm," Shaniece answered with a strain of annoyance in her voice. Mrs. Reeler could picture Shaniece's eyes in the back of her head when she greeted her, but she was happy that she still acknowledged her as "Mom."

"Hello, daughter. How are you?" Mrs. Reeler uttered. Before giving Shaniece the chance to respond, she went directly into her reason for calling. "Shaniece, I want to apologize first. I never meant to hurt you. I know our conversation the other day had to be a bit uncomfortable and maybe too much for you. You've been through enough and putting more of a burden on you was wrong. Will you please forgive me?"

Shaniece was glad that she started off with an apology. It made her a little more receptive to listen to what else Mrs. Reeler had to say. She had enough troubles to deal with, and now this was one more thing she had to think about. She actually thought about it every day since she left the house and felt bad for her father-in-law. She understood why her mother-in-law told her about the secret child but wished she would've used a different strategy.

"Well, thank you for the apology. I appreciate the fact that you had enough trust in me that you could share a burden so big, but it's been really bothering me. I mean, what you did was dead wrong and not fair to Dad. You need to tell him…"

Mrs. Reeler listened to Shaniece and was expecting the response she gave. "You're right and that's why I'm calling you…because I decided I'm going to tell him. I'm driving myself crazy trying to protect my sons." Shaniece didn't quite understand.

"What do you mean? Protect them from what?"

"Well, I'm protecting them from the image they will have of their father once they find this out. You know they look up to their father, and for them to find out he cheated on me and had another child outside of them, they will hate him. I know it."

"With all due respect...don't you think that you would be the one they hate for being deceitful?" Shaniece wanted to retract the words that came out of her mouth and wished she used a different word other than "hate" because it sounded so harsh. Still, she wasn't the type of woman to hold back about things she said.

"It is possible that they'll hate the both of us..." Mrs. Reeler told her.

The gears in Shaniece's head started going as she thought about how she would respond. She had some time to think about how she wanted to handle the situation with Derek and Mrs. Reeler, and she felt this was the perfect time to use what she knew as leverage for dealing with them. So, she offered her mother-in-law a proposition.

"Look, if you're serious about telling your family about your secret, then I promise that I will come around and try to work things out with Derek. I want to change my life so bad and start over, but I can't help but to think, 'What if?' The thought of Derek starting over with another woman after all that we've been through literally breaks my heart." Shaniece could hear Mrs. Reeler smiling through the phone.

"Really?.... You got yourself a deal." She was excited to hear that Shaniece was willing to give her marriage another try.

"Okay, we got a deal. So, when do you want to do this? You know, sit down with your husband and sons," Shaniece asked. Mrs. Reeler was so focused on Shaniece changing her mind about the divorce that she suddenly came to terms with what she agreed to.

"Well, let's see. Not next week because it's Joe's birthday...the following week is Derek's. Jeffrey and Morgan will be away on vacation the week after that...so maybe when they come back." *Her timing is almost a month out...plenty enough time for her to change her mind,* Shaniece thought.

"I'm willing to risk it all and walk away from this marriage forever. I'm prepared to start over. The sooner you have the talk, the sooner I will reach out to Derek. I'm going to continue moving forward with the divorce until you share your secret with the family." Mrs. Reeler didn't like where the conversation was headed because she thought she had agreed more to a deal. This was starting to sound more like blackmail. It was either her secret or her son's marriage, and she would have to give up something to make someone else happy.

"Shaniece, I just can't break this news to Joe on his birthday." Shaniece didn't want to hear it.

"Well, I'm sure you're aware that I told Derek I had an affair on our wedding night, so if that's not bad timing I don't know what is. In most situations, the timing will never be right." Shaniece instantly had a flashback to that night and wanted to cry. She had never forgotten the sad look in Derek's eyes.

"I guess you're right. The entire family will be here on Joe's birthday...so that's when I'll tell my secret."

"Sounds like a plan...I'll talk to you later." Mrs. Reeler hung up without saying a word and stared at the phone in her hands.

She was hoping that she wouldn't have to agree to next week but did want to get it over and done with. Her husband needed to hear that he possibly had a daughter out there. *It could be a birthday gift to him in disguise*, she thought. *That's the only way I'll feel better about doing this.*

"HAPPY" BIRTHDAY!

"How old are you now, how old are you now, how old are you nooooowwww? How old are you now?" the Reelers sang to Mr. Reeler while standing around the dining room table.

"I'm sixty-three and blessed beyond measure," he yelled out. Everyone laughed and clapped while Mr. Reeler yelled out, "I'm sixty-three!" again. Afterwards, Mrs. Reeler cut large slices of cake for her sons and husband and small pieces for herself and Morgan. Shaniece wasn't in attendance for her father-in-law's celebration because she still wasn't ready to face Derek yet. She wanted to hear how everything went and then reach out later. Jeffrey and Morgan knew bits and pieces of why Derek and Shaniece weren't together anymore, so they didn't question why she wasn't there. They knew Shaniece miscarried but was left in the dark about baby Tyler. Derek decided he would reveal his secret when he was ready and arranged to leave his son with the sitter for the evening.

Everyone sat at the table eating ice cream and cake while taking a trip down memory lane. Every year whenever they got together for a birthday, the old days always came into conversation. Derek got everything started by picking on Jeffrey. "So, Jeffrey, remember when you wore braces, and you ate that apple and your braces got stuck on it and Mom had to rush you to the hospital?" Derek laughed out loud while thinking back to that day. Jeffrey chuckled but had a comeback.

"Yeah, I remember that, but remember in high school you went to the bathroom, and the seniors turned the lights off on you, and you had to run into the hallway with your pants around your knees because you couldn't find the toilet paper to wipe your butt?" Everyone at the table laughed. Their parents had heard that story so many times before, but every time they thought about it, they couldn't do anything but laugh.

"Okay, boys, stop it. Let's quit while we're ahead." Mrs. Reeler laughed but didn't want them to spend hours going back and forth embarrassing each other. There were so many stories to share, and they would be there all night. Besides that, she thought if they kept going, she would never get a chance to say what she had to say.

A half-hour later, everyone was done with dessert and filled up on wine. Morgan helped Mrs. Reeler clean up, and she noticed that her mother-in-law was drinking more than normal.

"Mom, you alright? I never seen you drink a full glass of wine before, let alone two glasses." Mrs. Reeler smiled without saying a word and walked out into the living room where her sons and husband were seated. Morgan followed behind her, confused but intrigued, and watched as she turned off the television and stood in front of it with her half-filled glass in hand for comfort. The men sighed with their hands up asking what she was doing.

"Okay, gentlemen…now that we've had dessert, I want to speak with everyone as a whole." Mr. Reeler looked at his wife's face and immediately became concerned because she looked like she was on the brink of crying. He immediately thought she was about to share a bad medical report and knew he wasn't prepared for it.

"Honey, are you alright?" he asked with hesitation.

"Yeah, Mom…is everything okay?" both Derek and Jeffrey asked at the same time. They both turned and looked at each other because they sounded like Bobbsey twins. Morgan was wondering what was going on and sat on the couch beside her husband. She grabbed his hand for support because she thought the worst was going to be revealed too. Mrs. Reeler took one last sip of her wine before placing it on the end table.

"Before anyone's blood pressure goes up, I'm fine…I just want to talk with you about something that's been weighing heavy on my heart." Mr. Reeler was confused at this point. *If it's not a bad medical report, then what could it be?* he thought to himself. Mrs. Reeler went on to speak, and after a few minutes of beating around the bush, her secret was out. She shared the entire story the same way she shared it with Shaniece. Before she could tell everyone that she kept the contact information, Mr. Reeler jumped up and ran outside, leaving everyone else in the living room still in shock. She tried consoling and explaining herself to her sons about how she tried protecting them, but they didn't want to hear it.

"Mom, I don't get it. Why would you tell us like this? You should've told Dad first. He didn't have to find out like this," Derek expressed. Jeffrey was dazed, and Morgan was sitting next to him quietly continuing to hold his hand until Jeffrey pulled away and stood up, turning away from his mother.

"You don't understand…this secret has been haunting me for years. I couldn't take it another day. It's so hard to get everyone together, so I figured I would use this opportunity to put it out in the open." She kept looking at everyone around the room, hoping someone would be on her side, but to no avail. She covered her face with her hands and began crying, retreating from the living room to her bedroom upstairs.

Derek shook his head with frustration as he watched his mom leave the room. He jumped up from the couch without saying another word and went to look for his dad. Derek knew the pain his father felt and wanted to be there for him the same way he was there for him at the hospital. Derek walked within a two-block radius both ways, and there was no sight of his father. His car was still in the driveway so he knew he couldn't have been too far. He thought of calling him but realized his own cellphone was in the house. He didn't want to go back in just yet, so he went to the end of the sidewalk, staring both ways hoping his father would walk up. After a few minutes, he decided to go back into the house. When he walked in, he saw Jeffrey and Morgan gathering their belongings.

"Hey, did you try calling Dad?" Derek asked as he looked at Jeffrey checking his phone.

"Yes, I called his cell over and over and he's not answering. We're going out now to look for him." Derek didn't understand why Morgan had to follow along but kept his thoughts to himself.

"Alright, I'm going to drive with you," he told him as he grabbed his cell and keys from off the table. Mrs. Reeler was now sobbing audibly in her room, drowning in all the hurt and pain she had caused. Everyone left the house without saying a word to let her know they were leaving and jumped into Jeffrey's vehicle.

They drove for more than ten minutes, and there was still no sight of their father. Suddenly, an idea popped into Derek's head.

"Jeffrey, pull into the park," Derek yelled out.

"Huh? The park for what?" Jeffrey asked confused.

"Remember Dad used to come to the park and sit in the field whenever he needed to get away?" Jeffrey immediately thought back to a time when their parents were arguing about finances, and when their dad walked out and was gone for hours. When he returned, Mrs. Reeler demanded to know where he had gone, and he told her that he was at the field in the park down the street. After that day, they always knew where to find him when things went wrong.

They hadn't been to the park in over twenty years. When they pulled into the parking lot, it was dark out, and the lights were dim.

"Morgan, wait here," Jeffrey told her. Morgan looked around at the darkness and refused.

"No, I'm coming with you. I'm not sitting here by myself." Jeffrey looked around at his surroundings and reconsidered what he had told her. Derek led the way and walked past the swing sets and slide into an open field. He walked back toward the lake and noticed his father sitting on a large rock.

"Hey, Dad," Derek stated as he got closer and sat on the gigantic rock beside his father. Jeffrey and Morgan remained standing close by.

"Hey, Dad," they both repeated after Derek. It was an awkward moment because they didn't know how to approach him or what mind frame he was in. Mr. Reeler sighed heavily before he responded.

"I figured you guys would be running away from me…not towards me…" His deepest hurt at that moment was thinking his sons hated him because of what he had done.

"Nah, Dad…we're not mad at you," Derek assured him while looking at Jeffrey for confirmation.

"Dad, that was the past. Everyone makes mistakes. This doesn't change how great of a dad you are," Jeffrey followed up. Mr. Reeler opened his mouth to speak but hesitated. After a few minutes, he cleared his throat and spoke.

"Let me ask, how do you feel about me pursuing and finding out if the girl is blood or not?" There was another moment of silence before any of them spoke. Morgan nudged Jeffrey's arm to speak.

"Um…Dad, it's up to you. We're here to support you no matter what." Mr. Reeler turned to look at Derek.

"Dad, you already know I support you." Mr. Reeler knew exactly what Derek meant and responded with a slight smile. Derek felt since secrets were coming out, he might as well tell his brother about Tyler.

"I got a confession as well," Derek blurted out. Jeffrey looked at Derek like he was crazy.

"Man, what are you talking about?" Jeffrey asked. Derek could see Morgan's eyes ready to pop out her head.

"Mom and Dad already know, but Shaniece and I are getting a divorce, and I have a ten-month-old son named Tyler. There…I said it. I put it out in the open. No more family secrets." Derek looked his brother in the eye waiting for him to respond. He was already on the defense and ready to shut him down.

"Wait, wait, wait…come again?" Jeffrey stated. Jeffrey and Morgan assumed the two had grown apart after the death of Junior. They weren't aware of the divorce or about baby Tyler, so it was a shocker to them. Mr. and Mrs. Reeler felt like it was Derek's place to share his secret not theirs, so they kept it to themselves.

"You heard everything I just said, and yes, it's all true." Jeffrey and Morgan squeezed each other's hands tight.

"So, who's the other woman you had an affair with?" Morgan questioned with slight anger in her voice. Derek went on to explain in more detail about the situation. He told them about Danita passing away from cancer and him now having custody of his son. They held on to Derek's every word as they listened to his story. Morgan then looked at Jeffrey and whispered in his ear.

"Should we tell them?" Jeffrey picked his head up and returned her question with an "I don't care" look. Morgan took a deep breath.

"Well, now that we're getting secrets out…we have one too." Mr. Reeler and Derek both looked at each other with their eyes squinted and stood up with their arms folded to hear what Morgan was about to confess.

"We're moving to Thailand in two weeks."

"What the hell you mean in two weeks? And why so far?" Mr. Reeler yelled. Jeffrey interjected.

"Dad, calm down…now we knew we would get this type of reaction…that's why we waited to say anything. I landed a really big project to work on the country's poor infrastructure. It has multiple projects which will take years to complete. Morgan and I visited last year, and after doing some research we decided to make it a permanent move." Derek stared closely at Jeffrey as he talked.

"So how often will you be back home?" Derek asked.

"Well, to be honest, probably not until another year or so. The first year will be the busiest for me."

"Morgan, what about your school? You're just going to give that up?" Derek asked.

"I gave up my stake, and it's now under new leadership. I landed a teaching job there at one of the private schools." Derek shook his head; they had the right to do what they wanted to do, but he never thought they would have made a move like this.

"Wait until Mom hears about this. She's going to be livid," Derek told them as they all headed back to the car.

* * * * * *

They made it to the house and before entering they all agreed that they wouldn't make Mrs. Reeler feel any worse than she already did. They knew she was wrong but decided to move past it for now and focus on reuniting their family. They all walked in to find Mrs. Reeler asleep on the couch. Derek, Jeffrey, and Morgan all decided to let their dad take it from there. Everyone hugged one another and left to head home.

Mr. Reeler walked into the living room, grabbed the empty wine glass off the table, and took it into the kitchen to be washed. He returned to the living room and sat in the chair adjacent to his wife, staring at her while she slept. He cried because he loved his wife, but he also cried tears of anger because he was so upset at what she had done. His gaze shifted focus when he saw something move slightly on the floor from the fan above the table.

"What's this?" he whispered to himself as he bent down to find a folded paper next to the couch his wife was sleeping on. He opened it up and saw a name and number. He looked at it confused but suddenly realized that his wife kept the information he needed to connect with his daughter. He took the paper and placed it in his pocket then returned to his seat and sat there for a few more minutes. He grabbed a plush throw blanket off the arm of the couch and placed it on his wife before heading upstairs. When he made it to their bedroom, he knelt to the floor beside the bed and clasped his hands together. He hadn't prayed in so long and almost felt guilty. For the most part, everything went well in his life, so he never had to ask God for much. The Reelers didn't go to church; they spent most of their Sunday mornings watching television preachers and had praise and worship in their own home. Still, they loved the Lord.

"God, I know you hear me...I know I haven't come to you in prayer in a while. Please God help me. My mistake from years ago has come back to haunt me and I don't know what to do. My wife hid this secret from me for three years God, three years. How do I forgive her?" Immediately, all the answers to his questions he asked for in prayer came right back to him. He heard in his spirit to forgive his wife the same way he would want her to forgive him for his affair, which is the reason why the secret even existed in the first place. He also received that he needed to contact the young lady right away because if he waited any longer, she may be broken for good. Mr. Reeler sat in the same position for close to twenty minutes with tears falling. He knew what he had to do. He walked downstairs to his wife, picked her up, and took her upstairs. He changed her clothes carefully as not to wake her up and placed her in the bed. Mrs. Reeler woke up as he was laying her down.

"Honey, I'm so sorry. Please forgive me," she asked as he headed to the other side of the bed to lie down.

"You're already forgiven my dear. Go back to sleep and we'll talk in the morning."

I CHANGED MY MIND

Morgan called Shaniece the day after Mr. Reeler's birthday fiasco. Shaniece and Morgan didn't speak much outside of family dinners or events. Shaniece liked Morgan as a person, but neither one of them took the initiative to call or link up beyond spending time with their husbands. Morgan happened to call this time because she wanted to know more about the divorce and now baby. Shaniece wasn't prepared to talk about it but knew it would eventually come up in conversation. After the two discussed that situation, Morgan shared the details of the party. *Mom did it...she told,* Shaniece thought.

"Girl, I can't believe what you're telling me! So, Mr. Reeler has a daughter out there, huh?" Shaniece played like she had no idea and was hearing the story for the very first time.

"I know...crazy, right? I couldn't believe it when I heard it myself," Morgan replied. The two shared more thoughts on the whole situation until Morgan changed the topic. "Well, I have some more news for you. Kinda the reason I'm calling you," she confessed. Shaniece was surprised there was more to the call other than what happened at the Reeler house. She hoped it didn't have anything to do with Derek. "Jeffrey and I are moving." Shaniece thought, *Okay, what's the big deal?* until Morgan blurted out, "To Thailand." Shaniece didn't understand why they decided to move to another country.

"What? Wait, Thailand? Why there?" Shaniece asked simply confused. Morgan went on to explain the reasons why they decided to move to another country. It made sense to Shaniece, and to her, it seemed like it was the best bet for them financially once Morgan shared that Jeffrey's salary would increase three times as much. "So, when will it be official?" Shaniece asked. Morgan had forgotten to share that piece of information up front to get the shock out in the beginning. "See that's the thing...we're leaving in two weeks."

"Two weeks...like the week after next?" Morgan laughed.

"Yes, the week after next. Jeffrey's first project is starting next month, and we have to leave now to get things in order." Shaniece knew

Jeffrey was a well-respected architect in the surrounding states but didn't know he could do that caliber of work outside the country. Derek and Shaniece barely got chances to see them and now that they would be moving, they probably would see them once a year if that.

"I'm really going to miss you guys. Family dinners at the in-laws won't be the same."

"Wait, I thought you and Derek were getting a divorce? You changed your mind that quick?"

"Morgan…I'm not sure what I'm going to do to be honest. I go back and forth about it, but after hearing the story about Mom and Dad Reeler, I'm considering maybe giving it another shot. If Mrs. Reeler can accept an illegitimate child, then maybe I can too." Morgan thought both stories were completely out of touch for her. She couldn't imagine being in either of their shoes.

"Listen, girl. It's up to you. If you still love Derek, then give it another shot. I've known Derek for ten years now, and I never saw him so in love with any woman. He brought women around but the way he is when he's with you is like he came alive. He loves you, girl, and you can't walk away from a love like that even if you wanted to. He made a mistake, and I'm sure the last few months he felt the pain of it all." Shaniece respected Morgan's input, and it made her decision to give her marriage another round that much easier. They said their goodbyes and promised to stay in contact at least once a month to check in on each other.

Days after Mrs. Reeler's secret was out, Shaniece decided to reach out to Derek. She had given much thought to how she wanted to approach him. She knew he was up at the gym by 6 a.m., at work by 8:30 a.m., home by 6:15 p.m., and asleep by 11 p.m. She knew he had his hands full with Tyler, so she had to consider that as well in order to figure out what would be the best time to talk. It had been three months since all hell broke loose. Eventually, she just took the chance and called. The phone rang several times before going to voicemail. She hung up and threw the phone down on the bed.

"Why didn't he answer for me?" she asked herself. She was mad because she thought he would be standing by the phone waiting for her call and pick up on the first ring. She quickly picked up her Joel Osteen book from the nightstand and sunk down into her covers to feed herself inspiration. After reading half of a page, she glanced over and saw her phone light up with Derek's number displayed. After a deep breath, she answered.

"Hello?"

"Hey, I saw that you called. I'm sorry; my phone was in the kitchen," Derek stated in a perky voice. When Shaniece heard Derek's voice, she wanted to melt and immediately felt better. She was happy that he still was excited to hear her voice.

"How're things going?" she asked. She had a whole plan as to how she was going to address him, but now she couldn't think of any of it.

"I'm hanging in there. Things are definitely a lot different for me, but I'm learning to manage," he told her. She heard Tyler talking baby talk in the background, and she immediately thought about Junior. Shaniece closed her eyes, and tears started to stream. She tried to hold back any indication that she was crying in hopes that Derek wouldn't notice through the phone.

"Well, same here. You crossed my mind today, and I wanted to reach out." she admitted. Derek was surprised to hear that from her.

"Wow…I didn't think you thought of me anymore." Shaniece still attempted to hold back more tears.

"Well, as of late, you've been on my mind quite a lot actually. I can't believe I'm admitting to this right now, but I miss you." Derek was completely caught off guard. The last they talked, she wanted a divorce and that was it. He received his first piece of paperwork from her attorney the other day, and at that point, his mind was prepared for divorce. He didn't want to accept it, but he took her serious.

"Shaniece…you're in the process of filing for a divorce. How can you miss me when you want to divorce me?" he asked in a high-pitched tone.

"Well that's why I'm calling…because I don't want to go through with it. I don't want a divorce anymore. I had a chance to think about it long and hard, and it's not what I really want." Derek was confused, and his emotions were starting to take over.

"Shaniece, don't get me wrong. I love you. I want to be with you. I want to grow old with you, but I don't know if you're having a weak moment and then later down the line you hate me again and want to continue with the divorce. My heart can't take it and I would rather for us to be done now instead of the back and forth." Shaniece thought it was rather cocky for him to react this bluntly since he was the one who had put the final bullet into their marriage. She was the one who was fighting to resuscitate it. She took a deep breath before she responded because she didn't want to come off as defensive.

"Derek, that's a chance you have to be willing to take. I'm telling you today and right now that I'm serious and want to work things out with us. I love you…and when we took our vows we promised for better or for worse…and I'm not a quitter. Are you?" Derek chuckled and was happy deep down inside that his wife had come back around. He immediately thought about what his dad told him sometime back about not quitting on marriage.

"Hell no, I'm not a quitter. I'm a fighter, baby…I'm a fighter." They both laughed out loud. They continued talking briefly about Tyler and Derek's new place. By the end of the conversation, Shaniece agreed to come over in a few days, which happened to be on Derek's thirty-ninth birthday to meet Tyler – for sure this time.

* * * * * *

Shaniece went all out to prepare to see Derek on his birthday, as it also had been a while since she decided to take time out to pamper herself. She made appointments to get her hair, nails, and feet done, and she hit the mall to buy a nice new dress. She wanted Derek to see her in something he had never seen before, but she wanted more for him to see what he was missing. When she returned home, she got dressed and did her makeup, vibing out to some old school R&B. Before leaving the house, she did some final tugs and pulls on her dress as she checked herself out in the full-length foyer mirror. She paused to get a good look at herself, pushing a piece of hair in her face behind her ear and smiling briefly at her reflection, and then made her way out the door. She put Derek's address into her GPS, which led her to a gated community that required a passcode to get in. When she pulled up, she entered the code on the keypad, and the gates opened revealing a flowing fountain surrounded by gorgeous flowers. "Very nice," she whispered while driving around the lighted fountain into the parking lot in front of his condo. She didn't expect anything less from Derek. She looked in the rearview mirror and checked her makeup before she got out of the car. It was a nice summer night, and she took it all in as she strolled up the steps to his door. She tapped the door twice with her knuckles. Derek knew it was her and opened the door right away. She stuck out a bottle of wine and handed it to him, yelling out, "Happy Birthday!" When Derek laid eyes on her, he was blown away as always by her beauty. *She looks incredibly gorgeous, probably the most beautiful I've ever seen her,* Derek gushed in his mind. He didn't want to drool too much because he didn't want to do anything that would ruin the night. He knew Shaniece saw his reaction and could sense the flattery.

"Thank you, thank you," he stated as he grabbed the bottle from her hand and let her in. She walked in and looked around at his décor. The living room was decorated with vases, various sized candles, and abstract paintings in shades of brown and hints of navy blue. The chocolate leather L-shaped couch as well as the espresso-colored coffee and end tables added a nice touch to the room too. *I love this setup,* she thought to herself while nodding her head giving her unsolicited approval on his style. She followed Derek into the kitchen, where he was checking on the steaks, roasted red potatoes, and asparagus for their meal. Shaniece sniffed the air to smell the mixed aromas.

"I taught you well," she joked. Derek nodded his head in agreement and laughed.

"Yeah, I guess you did." He dimmed the lights in the kitchen and led the way back to the living room. He gestured toward a spot where she could sit. He couldn't resist.

"You look gorgeous," he told her as he sat extremely close to her on the couch. Shaniece felt like it was a first date and scooted over a little to give herself some breathing room.

"Well, thank you." She had decided to wear a knee-length floral dress that fit her body like a glove with some wedge heels. Her hair was parted in the middle, straightened and flowing down to the middle of her back. She had on minimal makeup because she knew he loved to see her natural beauty.

"So…where's the baby?" She was ready to get it over and done with. She figured this would be the hardest part.

"He's asleep. I tried keeping him up, but he couldn't hang." Shaniece nodded her head indicating she understood. Derek turned off the television from where he had been watching sports and turned on Shaniece's favorite, some old school R&B music. He went into the kitchen to grab two wine glasses and sat them on the front room table. Derek poured Chardonnay into both glasses and handed one to Shaniece. He put his glass in the air signaling a toast, and Shaniece followed.

"This is to the future," he stated. Shaniece laughed.

"This is to the future." Derek downed his entire glass in one gulp. Shaniece could tell he was nervous because she could see it in his face. He was also going back and forth from the living room to the kitchen every five minutes. She decided to help calm his nerves. When he sat down beside her after coming from the kitchen again, she looked over at him, grabbed his face, and kissed his lips. She had her glass in one hand and held the side of his face with the other, brushing her thumb back and forth against his cheek. Derek wasn't expecting any of that but was glad that she did all of it. She removed her hand from his face and placed her glass on the table. She pulled him toward her and kissed him again. Once he felt her soft lips for the second time, he couldn't keep his hands off her. He grabbed her thighs gently then moved his hands to the hem of her dress. He tried pushing it up her legs to lift her dress off, but Shaniece pushed his hands away.

"Not now," she told him in a hushed voice. They continued kissing until Derek stopped so he could check on the food.

"Dinner's done!" he announced. He escorted Shaniece to the dining room table and pulled out a seat for her to sit in. He pushed her in and went back to the kitchen, where he fixed their plates. When he came back, he sat both plates on the table after lighting the candle in the middle then retrieved their glasses from the living room. He felt like the luckiest man in the world as he sat across the table from Shaniece. They blessed their food and began to eat.

"Babe, this is so good." Derek looked at her and smiled.

"I'm glad you like it." They sat at the table for close to two hours talking about everything from losing baby Junior to his parents' situation to Derek adjusting to life with Tyler. She was surprised that she could face reality without shedding a tear. She knew she was growing and that God was working on her. Her feelings for Derek were also slowly coming back to their original strength. The more time they eventually spend together, the more she felt like she would fall for him all over again.

After dinner, dessert, and an empty bottle of wine, Shaniece was ready for Derek, but Derek wanted her even more. Derek walked Shaniece into his bedroom and left back out to check on Tyler. Shaniece sat on the bed and took in the scenery of his Jacuzzi, fireplace, and flat screen in the bathroom and bedroom. His king bed was covered in chocolate brown satin sheets with a brown and gold comforter with matching pillows. Derek walked in, laid Shaniece back, and climbed on top of her.

"I thought you would've taken this off for me," he joked. She had removed her wedges but still had her dress on. Shaniece rolled her eyes and smirked at him.

"I want you to do it for me." She scooted from under him and stood up. Sitting on the edge of the bed, Derek unzipped the side of her dress, and it fell to the floor. She climbed out of her panties in front of him and he unsnapped her strapless bra after she turned around. They switched places as Derek stood up next while Shaniece laid naked on her back in the bed with her hands behind her head, looking at him get undressed. Derek took off his jeans, button-up shirt, and underclothes in less than thirty seconds, but he took his time getting to Shaniece. He climbed on the bed slowly and slid his coffee brown muscular body in between Shaniece's firm thighs. She wrapped her arms around his neck as she invited him in. He kissed her softly and gradually slid himself between her walls. Shaniece let out a loud moan, and Derek covered her mouth. She figured it was because he didn't want her to wake up Tyler. Derek went slowly in and out of her. He missed her wet vagina and loved that he had another chance to take a splash in it. Shaniece moaned repeatedly but quietly, wrapping her legs around his lower back.

"I love you so much," she confessed emotionally, with tears flowing. She couldn't imagine having any other man inside her but him.

"I love you too, babe…I miss you so much," Derek told her. They stared into each other's eyes and exchanged words of affection back and forth. Ten minutes later, Derek finally exploded like a firecracker and released all that he had built up from the last few months. He usually warned Shaniece so she would release at the same time, but he couldn't this time around. He laid on her chest still moving his mid-section slowly in circular motion. Shaniece hadn't reached her peak yet and hoped he knew.

"I'm sorry, babe. I couldn't hold it," Derek apologized. Shaniece was happy that he still knew her body and knew that he would make it up to her. Derek slid out of her slowly and fell to the side of her body. He grabbed her hand, and they both laid there quietly. After five minutes, Derek got up to get a wash rag from out of the bathroom and used it to wipe in between her thighs. Once he had her cleaned up, he went down using his tongue in every way possible. He grabbed

Shaniece's nipples and played with them to get an arousal out of her. Shaniece loved when he did that. Suddenly, Derek popped his head up, and Shaniece looked down at him.

"What you doing?" she asked annoyed. Derek hopped off the bed, grabbed a pair of basketball shorts from his drawer, and ran into the bathroom, flipping the light on without saying a word. She laid there with her arms blocking her eyes from the bright bathroom light. She heard water running, and when it stopped, he walked out the room after turning the light back off. Once he opened the bedroom door and rushed out, she heard Tyler crying at the top of his lungs and figured he had been in the bathroom to wipe his face. She sat up and grabbed a pillow to hold in front of her body. She could hear Derek in the kitchen moving around and guessed that he was warming up a bottle. A few moments later, she saw him walking back into Tyler's room. *Maybe we can get back to business after Tyler's taken care of,* she wondered.

* * * * * *

Derek had been gone for more than ten minutes now, so Shaniece decided to help out. She got up, walked into the bathroom, grabbed a wash rag from his small linen closet, and wiped herself down. She found one of Derek's T-shirts, put it on, and walked into the baby's room. She saw him on the phone talking.

"I gave him a bottle and he's still crying, Mrs. Nixon," she heard him say. Derek hired Mrs. Nixon, Melanie's mother, over a month ago to be Tyler's nanny. She was a retired daycare provider with plenty of experience, so Melanie suggested Derek use her assistance on weekends or whenever he had to work late. Melanie would still step in and help occasionally but had her own family to tend to; helping Derek out as much as she did was starting to interfere with home.

Shaniece walked up to Derek and put her arms out for him to hand her Tyler, which he did without hesitation. She laid him on her chest as she walked around the room bouncing him and rubbing his back in circular motion. Derek, still on the phone, looked shocked as Tyler quieted down more and more by the minute. His look of shock turned into happiness because she reacted and jumped in to help him. After three long minutes, he stopped crying completely. Derek told Mrs. Nixon that everything was under control before hanging up. Shaniece looked over her shoulder at Tyler and saw that he was still awake but calm. She didn't know what to do at that point. She continued the same routine for another three minutes before giving him back to Derek. Derek continued rubbing and patting his back until he let out a loud burp.

"That's what was wrong with you. Your tummy was hurting," Derek stated as he rubbed his back again. Shaniece stood there admiring how Derek was with him. She had no doubt that he would be a great father. Tyler finally went back to sleep, and Derek laid him down in his crib. Shaniece stared at his precious face and saw a reflection of herself. She almost thought that he could pass as her son. It looked like he favored her more than his actual parents; he didn't look like Danita in any way, and he didn't look completely like Derek either. After confirming that Tyler was fully settled, Derek grabbed Shaniece by the hand and tipped out the room.

"You thirsty?" he asked. Shaniece followed behind him into the kitchen, and Derek grabbed them both a bottled water out of the side of the fridge. They both stood still in the middle of the kitchen floor, chugging.

"He's beautiful," Shaniece stated while screwing the cap back on her bottle.

"Yeah, he is." Derek wanted to keep the conversation short because he didn't want Shaniece's emotions about losing baby Junior to overwhelm the moment. "C'mon let's go back into the room," Derek stated as he grabbed her by her hand. She followed hesitantly and laid back on the bed. Derek tried to pick up from where he left off, but before he could get back to it, Shaniece pulled his head back up.

"I'm not feeling it no more. How about we just lay in each other arms for the night?" Derek didn't know what came over Shaniece because when it came to sex, she never wanted to be left out.

"You sure? I have more from where that came from, you know," Derek joked. Shaniece laughed.

"No, I'm serious. I just want to lay here with you," she told him as she laid on his chest and intertwined her hands with his. Derek kissed her on the forehead.

"This is the best birthday ever!" he exclaimed quietly. They slept the night away until 6 a.m. when they were both awakened by their little human alarm clock.

BLENDED FAMILIES

Mr. and Mrs. Reeler were slowly starting to work things out together. It was quiet in the house for a few days after his birthday, but eventually the couple had a long talk about their situation. Mr. Reeler expressed to his wife how he was disappointed in her. To make it up to him, he demanded that she accept his daughter as their own. He knew he needed to get a blood test, but as of now, he considered the mysterious young lady to be his daughter. The timeline was consistent with when he had his only affair and knew it could be a possibility, he may be the father. He made his wife promise that she would follow through on all his demands. He knew she was more than capable of doing so after seeing how she was with Shaniece and Morgan.

Because of what his wife did, he thought about the fact that his daughter would not want to come around because of how she had been treated. Still, he figured he would try his best and reach out. For a week, he tried picking the phone up to call but hung up before he dialed the number because he didn't know what to say. He finally struck up the courage because it was bothering him more day by day. He needed to know if she was his daughter and if she still wanted to get to know him. He called the number and let it ring. On the second ring, a female voice answered.

"Hello, may I speak with," he looked down at the folded paper to glance at the name again. "Can I speak with Cassandra?" he asked, hoping that it was her that answered.

"This is she. Who's calling?" she asked. His eyes immediately started watering up.

"This is Joe, your father." He heard silence on the other line, which he expected.

"I don't have a father named Joe. You have the wrong number," she told him with an attitude. He was confused and looked at the number on the phone, then looked at the number on the paper and knew he dialed the right number.

"I get it...I would see why you wouldn't claim me. You have to believe me, but I just found out about you less than a week ago." He heard the woman's throat clear on the other end.

"How's that when I reached out to you over three or four years ago? You made it very clear that you wanted nothing to do with me so I'm good now. I'm over it."

"Please don't hang up. Let me explain," he begged. He then went on to tell her how he found out. He apologized on behalf of his wife and said that she was scared too and didn't know what to do. She listened to what he had to say, and from what he stated, it made sense.

"That wife of yours is something else. I would never do that to anyone," she told him. He couldn't disagree with her because it was the truth.

"Well, I hope you can forgive both of us...I really want to be in your life if you'll let me. I would love to meet you and your family and talk some more," he requested. He wanted to see her face-to-face and meet her kids – if she had any.

"Give me a few days to work out a date, and I'll call you back on this number...is it okay with your wife?" she asked sarcastically.

"Yes, this is my cell. I have it on me all the time. If I don't answer, leave a voicemail."

"Okay...thanks...I guess I'll be seeing you soon."

"Yes...see you soon."

✳ ✳ ✳ ✳ ✳ ✳

Mr. Reeler and Cassandra met up a few days after their phone call. They decided to meet over coffee at a local diner to learn more about each other, but it would just be Cassandra this time. Cassandra didn't want to bring her kids until she had an idea of what type of man he was. Mr. Reeler arrived first and was seated. He looked at his watch, hoping time would speed up. He was nervous and excited at the same time.

"Hello," Cassandra greeted him as she walked up to the table, following the waiter. Mr. Reeler took off his glasses and took a good look at her. She was noticeably taller than him, and he was surprised because he was average height for a male. Her hair was cut into an ear-length sleek bob. He noticed she had a lot of make-up so from what he could see he considered her to be fair skinned.

"Well, hello…I don't know, should I call you daughter?" he asked with a huge grin on his face. Cassandra smiled.

"Well, let's just go with 'Cassandra' for now," she told him. They hugged each other tight before they sat down. They began to get acquainted five minutes in, and Cassandra decided to get straight to the point.

"So, tell me why would my mom mention your name on her deathbed?" Cassandra asked.

Mr. Reeler sat there dumbfounded because it had been so long ago, and he didn't remember too much about her mother. She was pretty and looked like a model – close to how Cassandra looked but with a browner tone. On top of that, she was a party girl. He found that out because he was having a tough time financially in his marriage and started drinking and partying to void out his issues. Whenever he went out, she was always around. The next thing he knew, they were in the back of his Chevy making out. He felt horrible about it and was almost on the verge of telling his wife until his buddies talked him out of it. He went out again across town, hoping she wouldn't be around, but she ended up at the same place he was. He tried avoiding her for the night, but she wouldn't let up. He remembered once again making out with her in the backseat of his Chevy and things really got hot and heavy afterward. He left her alone after that and stopped going out to party. Still, he never would have thought a child would have come out of their rendezvous.

"Well, Gloria and I met at a party and got acquainted there. We ran into each other a couple of times after that, but we were never very close..." Cassandra wasn't one hundred percent satisfied with his answer, but she caught the gist of what he was trying to say.

"I see."

"Yeah...but I have a question...who did you think was your father all this time? You know, before your mother said anything about me."

"Well, I had always thought that my stepfather Torrance was my real father. He was very abusive towards my mother. I was confused and couldn't imagine how someone like that could be my dad. One day, my mom had enough and started fighting back and wasn't scared of him no more. I don't know why she was in the first place because she was way taller than him. Anyway, when I was around fifteen years old, he never came home from work. The next thing we knew days turned into weeks which turned into months which became years. My mom didn't even bother looking for him. When he left, life was good. My mother and I were close, and she took good care of me." Mr. Reeler listened as Cassandra talked about her mother. He could see the pain in her eyes going back down memory lane. He felt bad himself because he wished he would've known from the beginning that he had a daughter. He missed out on so many years, and it hurt him deep down.

"Well, I'm glad that you two were close...that's a blessing." Cassandra smiled and nodded her head.

"Yes...yes, it is."

They sat for hours discussing just about everything they missed out on. Cassandra also shared more about her family. She had a seven-year-old daughter named Mikayla and two-year-old son named Myron. She ended up becoming a single parent through tragedy, as her children's father had been struck by a bullet while trying to calm a neighbor's domestic disturbance last year. Mr. Reeler's heart really went out to her when she heard the entire story. He then went on to talk about his own personal history and his family, mostly about Jeffrey and Derek. He wanted Cassandra to know that she had siblings and that they were open to meeting her one day, if she felt the same way.

After hours of catching up, Cassandra and Mr. Reeler both agreed that they would meet up soon – except this time, he would be able to meet her children.

MISSING YOU

Jeffrey and Morgan's going-away party was scheduled to start at two o'clock., but an hour before it was to begin, Mrs. Reeler was freaking out.

"Everything has to go right, but I feel like everything is going wrong!" she cried.

"Honey, calm down. Everything looks beautiful. You've done an excellent job," Mr. Reeler responded. He knew when his wife got into her frenzies, it would easily get to the point of no return. He had to calm her down before she started hyperventilating.

"Hun, the chicken is still not done, half of the balloons are popping, and people will start coming in less than an hour!"

"How about this: you go get dressed, and I'll take it from here." he told her. She looked at him and then looked around at all that she did accomplish. Mrs. Reeler took a deep breath.

"Alright…thanks, honey. That's a great idea – I'll just go get dressed," she stated while taking off her oven mitts before making her way upstairs.

* * * * * *

Morgan's parents, sister, brother-in-law, and baby niece were the first to arrive. A few of Jeffrey's college friends and co-workers came in next. Mr. Reeler welcomed them in and made everyone feel at home. Shortly after, Mrs. Reeler was downstairs, ready to start hosting. She hugged everyone in the room and went into the kitchen. She saw that everything was completed and in its proper place. "Good job, honey," she whispered in his ear as she pecked him on his cheek while they were prepping the dining room table.

Derek and Shaniece eventually walked in; Derek was carrying Tyler in his car seat. When she saw them, Mrs. Reeler's face lit up. She had spoken to Shaniece over the phone after she shared her secret and was elated to hear that things were getting better with their marriage. This was their first time together as a family with Tyler in public, and it made her heart melt seeing them walk through the door.

"Son, you need help with that car seat?" Mr. Reeler asked.

"No, Dad, I'm good. I'm used to the struggle by now." Everyone in the room laughed. Derek and Shaniece knew they were going to have to do some explaining at some point. Still, they didn't care what others thought about their relationship. They loved each other, and as long as that was priority, nothing else mattered. Mrs. Reeler glided over to the couple and hugged Shaniece for the longest time. Derek took Tyler out of his car seat, and soon as the last buckle was off, Mrs. Reeler whisked him away into the family room. Shaniece followed behind her with a smile on her face, and everyone was cooing about how cute Tyler was.

"He looks just like his mother," Morgan's mother, Mrs. Burroughs, stated out loud. Shaniece opened her mouth to correct her, but Mrs. Reeler cut her off.

"You know what? My husband and I say he favors Shaniece also." Shaniece's genuine smile turned to a fake one, and she didn't respond. Derek was in the dining room but soon made his way over to Morgan's family. He had met Morgan's family a few times, and they were a lot like he expected. He understood where Morgan got her hospitality, genuineness, and beautiful spirit from. He thought about how it must have been something that was passed down from generation to generation.

"He is so handsome," Morgan's mother stated again.

"Thank you so much," Derek acknowledged while holding his hand out to Tyler, who grabbed and held two of his daddy's fingers as he babbled. After playing with Tyler for a few minutes, Derek walked off into the living room to greet a few of Jeffrey's college buddies.

"Congrats, man, your brother told me the business is doing really well. That's good. Keep it going," one of the guys mentioned. Derek was happy his brother was proud of him. He put a lot of pressure on himself so to hear it from someone other than his wife made him happy.

"Thanks, man, it's been a struggle, but things are finally starting to look up." He glanced over his shoulder back at Shaniece, who now had Tyler and was talking and laughing with his mother and Mrs. Burroughs. He smiled to himself and turned back around to make more conversation with Jeffrey's friends.

* * * * * *

"They're here," Mrs. Reeler yelled out as she saw Morgan and Jeffrey pulling up in front of the house, and everyone simmered down. The bell rang once, and Mrs. Reeler flung it open. Jeffrey and Morgan walked in and looked surprised when they saw all their family and friends. They noticed a few of them standing up while holding a "We'll Miss You!" sign. Morgan started crying right away, and Jeffrey laughed out loud. They thought they were coming over for a small intimate dinner party but never imagined it would be of this caliber. When Morgan saw her family, she really lost it and broke down crying even harder. Her father had to grab her and walk her over to the couch to sit down.

"Now that they are here, everyone can eat," Mrs. Reeler announced. Everyone walked into the dining room to prepare their plates. After a few brief conversations with his buddies and family members, Jeffrey finally had a chance to chat with his brother.

"So, this is my nephew, huh?" he asked while grabbing Tyler out of Derek's arms.

"Yeah man, this is him," Derek confirmed. Jeffrey held Tyler while looking at him gum down on his fist. Jeffrey raised Tyler's slobbery hand up to Derek.

"I think he might be hungry," he told him. Derek laughed.

"Nah, man, he's teething. He gnaws on any and everything." Jeffrey laughed himself because he didn't know much about babies. He then looked over at Shaniece, shook his head, and smiled.

"What?" she asked when she turned and found him looking at her.

"Nothing. I'm just happy you guys worked it out, that's all."

"Yeah, I am too."

Morgan finally was able to get herself together and walked in to join Jeffrey while he was holding Tyler. She looked at him then looked at Shaniece.

"Wow…what a resemblance," she remarked.

"Yeah," Shaniece responded. She thought that she may have planted the idea that he favored her in her head because she lost Junior and because this was the first baby she saw thereafter. She realized she wasn't crazy for thinking he looked like her after hearing it from other people as well. Still, she was tired of the comparisons of her and Tyler by now. Hearing about it in such a short time span was starting to get on her nerves. She didn't say anything else but watched Jeffrey and Morgan playing with Tyler, kissing him all over.

"You guys look good with a baby you know," Derek mentioned. Jeffrey and Morgan laughed it off and gave him an "I don't think so" look. They had a plan for their life, and right now a baby wasn't a part of it. Mr. Reeler walked in on Tyler getting loved on.

"Hey, guys, what's going on in here?" he asked while eating the last of his fried chicken leg.

"Nothing, we're just discussing how Tyler looks like Shaniece," Morgan blurted out.

"Yeah--everyone's saying that" Mr. Reeler agreed. Shaniece sighed quietly then decided to change the subject.

"So, are you guys all ready to leave?" Shaniece directed to Jeffrey and Morgan hoping that they'd get the point. They went on for the next ten minutes talking about how much more they needed to do before they left in the coming days. Discussing all they needed to do out loud made them realize they were more behind than they thought, so they wanted to dismiss the conversation before getting overwhelmed again.

"Alright, let's go join the rest of the party," Jeffrey suggested. Everyone got back together in one room and spent the next few hours eating, drinking, and talking about memories of Jeffrey and Morgan.

FORGIVE OR NOT TO FORGIVE

"Hey, Cassandra. It's me, Joe. I wanted to see if you wanted to meet up at the park and then head out for ice cream with the kids," Mr. Reeler suggested. It had been a week since their first meet up, and he wanted to make up for lost time. Since she had come into his life, he didn't want to go weeks without seeing or talking to her.

"You know what? That sounds like a good idea. We didn't have anything planned today. The weather is nice, so why not?" she agreed.

"Good! Let's meet at Fox Park on Lattimore Street."

"Alright, sounds good. What about two o'clock?" she asked.

"That's perfect. I'll see you then," he confirmed. He hung up the phone and put it in his pocket then walked outside to wash his truck and get ready for his playdate with his grandkids. About ten minutes later, Mrs. Reeler came out and sat on the porch.

"Oh, I didn't get a chance to tell you, but I'm meeting Cassandra again today and this time she's bringing the kids," he went on to say when he noticed her sitting in one of the rocking chairs. Mrs. Reeler smiled, but he knew that she wasn't too happy about the idea.

"What is it?" He looked up at her briefly while he rinsed the driver's door.

"Oh, it's nothing. I'm happy that you're bonding with your daughter," she told him. Mr. Reeler knew she didn't really mean it but didn't bother going down that road. He was happy about it, and that was all that mattered to him at this point.

"Thank you…me too." He turned his attention back to the truck, put down the water hose, and started soaping up the hood. Mrs. Reeler was quiet for a moment then spoke up.

"Joe…maybe you should get a paternity test just to see if she's really your daughter. I mean you really don't know." He wasn't offended by her comment because he had already thought about it himself. He knew that was part of the process but wanted to enjoy spending time with her for now.

"Yeah, I know, honey. The time will come soon. Just be patient with me." Mrs. Reeler respected his decision. If he knew what needed to be done, she was okay with it. Mr. Reeler spent the next hour and a half cleaning his vehicle before heading to the park.

* * * * * *

He arrived at Fox Park, and it was packed with little ones running around the sliding board and swings. He checked the time, and it was two o'clock on the dot. He looked over and saw a dark grey Dodge Charger pull up. He realized it was Cassandra, and two children were sitting in the back. A big smile came across his face as he stepped out of his truck and closed the door. He walked over to the car as Cassandra was getting out.

"Hey, lady," he stated as he greeted and hugged her.

"Hey, Joe," she replied as she hugged him back. She walked around to take Myron out of his car seat, and Mikayla climbed out behind him. Mr. Reeler looked down at them, and small tears fell into the crack of his eyes. With Myron on her hip and Mikayla standing by her side, she gave an introduction.

"This is Mikayla, and this is Myron." Mr. Reeler stuck his hand out to greet Mikayla first. She looked at her mother to get her permission, and Cassandra nodded her head.

"Hello, my name is Joe. You are beautiful, I tell you." His heart melted when he saw her long pigtails and small eyeglasses. He then looked up at Myron and rubbed his head.

"Hey, little man. You are a handsome little fellow." Myron turned his curly top into his mom's chest and started whining. Cassandra apologized.

"He just woke up not so long ago so he's cranky." Mr. Reeler could fully understand because he felt like that at sixty-three whenever his naps were interrupted. They walked through the field headed toward another part of the park. Cassandra put Myron down, and both he and Mikayla dashed toward the sliding boards.

"Hold up, Mikayla, watch your brother," Cassandra yelled out across the field. She and Mr. Reeler sat down on a bench in close proximity and talked about her life as a single mother.

"I commend you because being a single mom is a big job," Mr. Reeler went on to say. Cassandra nodded her head because she couldn't agree more.

"Yes, it is…some days I don't know how I do it," she confessed, watching Mikayla help Myron make his way down the slide. While talking, Shaniece came to Mr. Reeler's mind, and he imagined that she knew how Cassandra felt.

"I have a daughter-in-law, and she was a single mother for years before she met my son, Derek. Maybe one day you could meet and talk with her. I'm sure you two would have something in common." Cassandra didn't dismiss the idea. She didn't have a lot of family and her friends were few, so meeting new people was something she looked forward to.

"Yeah, maybe." Mr. Reeler nodded, and the two of them sat quietly while watching the children run and play. Cassandra eventually got up and started playing with them too. Mr. Reeler smiled and teared up again when he saw the little family together. He sat and took in the scene, listening to Myron and Mikayla's laughter as Cassandra went back and forth pushing them on the swings.

* * * * * *

After the park, they drove to the ice cream parlor down the street. Everyone got ice cream cones with different flavors and sat outside at one of the sky-blue picnic tables. After a few minutes, they all laughed as Myron was eating his vanilla ice cream, which was all over his mouth. Without thinking, Mr. Reeler took a napkin and helped clean his face. Cassandra was surprised but not upset. When Myron finished, Mr. Reeler took everyone's trash and threw it away. The whole group left the table and headed back toward their vehicles. After Cassandra buckled Myron in and monitored Mikayla putting on her seatbelt, she leaned on the top of her car door facing Mr. Reeler.

"I really enjoyed today. It looks like the kids enjoyed it too," Cassandra stated. Mr. Reeler was glad that she was starting to feel happier. He could see the sadness in her eyes was starting to dissipate from when they first met. He was grateful he had something to do with it.

"You have no idea how much I enjoyed this day. I can't wait to do something like this again. That's if you don't mind us planning another outing," Mr. Reeler suggested. Cassandra agreed and gave him a big hug before getting in and pulling off. He watched her go then started waving when he realized two little hands were up waving at him through her rear window.

* * * * * *

Mr. Reeler arrived home shortly after five o'clock and found his wife sitting on the couch, knitting a baby quilt. When he saw it, he immediately thought about baby Junior. His wife had spent months knitting all types of blankets for him. Instead of giving them away, she kept them in a drawer. He walked over and pecked her on the lips.

"So, how was it?" she asked. He smiled ear to ear; he couldn't hide it even if he wanted to.

"It was great. I met the kids: Mikayla and Myron. They're really great kids." Mrs. Reeler smiled because she could see he really enjoyed himself.

"That's great, honey. I'm really glad that you're happy. If you're ready to eat, dinners on the stove for you." Mr. Reeler walked into the kitchen and warmed his plate up. He returned to the living room and turned on the television. He looked at the almost-finished quilt and thought, *My wife got skills.*

"Tyler is going to love it," he assumed as he watched his wife finish up the last lining of the quilt. Mrs. Reeler nodded her head and grinned.

"You know his first birthday is next month, so I figured I would knit him something nice." Mr. Reeler then started to think about how he met Tyler less than six months ago, and now he would be getting ready to turn one in another month. They continued to have small talk for a few minutes until Mrs. Reeler left to go upstairs to rest. Mr. Reeler remained downstairs watching television.

"Alright, hun, I'll be up in a few," he yelled as she walked up the steps. He fell asleep off and on while the television watched him. After a while, he woke up fully and checked the time. He thought he would take some time to call Derek and Shaniece.

"Hey, son. What's going on there?" he asked. Derek was happy to hear from his dad. Admittedly, he was a little concerned because it was nine o'clock at night, and he never really called that late.

"Hey, old man. What you still doing up?" Derek asked.

"Aw, man, I dozed off and on the past two hours so I'm up now." Derek laughed.

"You sound like me. Tyler finally fell asleep, and Shaniece and I are just sitting here."

Mr. Reeler heard Shaniece's name and remembered he wanted to talk to her.

"I'm not intruding, am I?" he asked.

"No, Dad, nothing not going down here tonight. We too tired." They both laughed.

"Remember I told you I met up with Cassandra last week?" Mr. Reeler asked.

"Yes, you said it was nice, and you were happy you went."

"Yeah, well we met again today but this time at the park with the kids." Derek held the phone closer to his ear.

"Oh, really. How was it dad?" Derek asked out of curiosity. Mr. Reeler went on to explain his day and gave Derek the latest updates on Cassandra and where they stood. He found it so easy to talk with Derek about his situation.

"Oh, speaking of Shaniece, I wanted to talk with her about meeting Cassandra. I feel that they could really connect. Shaniece was a single mom for a long time before you came along so maybe she could guide

Cassandra a little." Derek listened as his dad was looking out for the best interest of his daughter.

"I'm sure she wouldn't mind. She's dozed off now, but you mentioned she has a two-year-old son. Maybe she can bring them both to Tyler's birthday party next month?" Derek suggested.

"That'll be great. I'll call her and see if she would like to come, and I'll introduce her." Mr. Reeler loved the idea of inviting Cassandra and the kids to Tyler's birthday party. The only problem would be getting Cassandra to agree to be in the same room with his wife. He had close to a month to straighten that issue out.

"Alright, son. I'm going to let you get some rest. Your old man going to get in the bed himself."

"Alright, Dad. Have a good night." Mr. Reeler disconnected the call, turned off the television, and made his way up the stairs to lie down.

* * * * * *

Two weeks passed, and Mr. Reeler had worked out a plan to bring his wife and Cassandra together before the party. He spoke to his wife and advised her that he was inviting Cassandra and the kids over for dinner. He reminded her that she owed him and needed to be apologetic as well as sympathize with Cassandra and their situation. Mrs. Reeler agreed that she would welcome Cassandra and the children with open arms. She had reached a point where she regretted her decision to block her out for years and wanted to finally apologize in person.

Mr. Reeler was able to convince Cassandra to come by for a 4 p.m. dinner, but he practically had to beg her. She was hesitant because she knew how his wife felt about her. Still, she figured she would spend more time with Mr. Reeler, so she was willing to tolerate the visit. When she arrived, Mr. Reeler met her and the kids outside the house. They walked into the living room, and Mrs. Reeler was standing there waiting to greet them. When she laid eyes on Cassandra, she didn't blink. She was trying to see if there was any resemblance to her husband. She noticed how tall she was but couldn't say if she looked like her husband or not. On top of that, Mrs. Reeler never saw her mother, so it was hard for her to make the determination in who she looked like. She welcomed her in with open arms, and after the brief meet and greet, everyone stood in the middle of the front room with awkward silence not knowing what to say next. Mr. Reeler decided to break the ice.

"Alright, let's eat! I'm starving." They all walked through the living room and into the dining room to a beautifully prepared table. Cassandra and the kids sat on the left side of the table. Mr. Reeler sat across from them, and his wife sat at the head. They started to dig into the fried chicken, mac-n-cheese, candied yams, string beans, and rolls. Five minutes in, Mr. Reeler noticed how Cassandra was engaged with her kids, cutting up food and making sure they were taken care of. He waited until they were settled before starting any type of conversation. Mrs. Reeler beat him to the punch.

"So, Cassandra I hear you work in the medical field. How do you like it?" she asked. Cassandra wondered why she wanted to know but to be respectful, she went along with what she felt like was a charade.

"Thank you for asking. I like it. I'm a medical assistant now. Looking to go back and finish my nursing degree to become a registered nurse. I guess I'll get there one day." Mrs. Reeler smiled. She was happy that she had goals and wasn't looking for a handout.

"That's awesome. I'm sure you can do it. You seem like a bright young lady and if you're anything like Joe, you're determined for sure." Cassandra smiled and nodded in agreement. Mr. Reeler was glad that they could be in the room together and have a decent conversation – at least for the moment. When everyone finished, Cassandra and the kids went into the living room while Mrs. Reeler put away the dishes. Mr. Reeler put up the rest of the food and went into the living room.

"You alright, Cassandra?" Mr. Reeler asked as they sat on the couch.

"Yes, Dad, I'm good." She caught herself and looked at him like a deer in headlights. He smiled and grabbed her close to him.

"That's great, daughter," he replied with a genuine smile.

"Did either of the kids ask who I was yet?" he asked.

"Yes, the day after the park. Mikayla said 'Mom, is that our pop pop?' I just told her maybe. I didn't want to get her hopes up high like I did and then her spirit get crushed." Mr. Reeler respected how she handled the situation and understood what she meant. Mrs. Reeler walked in and joined in on the conversation.

"Who spirit get crushed?" she asked making the tail end of the conversation. Mr. Reeler looked over at her slightly annoyed.

"We're just talking about Mikayla asking who I was, that's all." Mrs. Reeler nodded her head but didn't push the conversation about it any further.

"Cassandra, your kids are so well-behaved," Mrs. Reeler acknowledged. Myron and Mikayla were sitting on the couch, quietly trying to make each other laugh by making funny faces at one another.

"Thank you. They have their moments, but for the most part they are great kids." Mrs. Reeler wanted to connect with her but didn't know what she could talk about to strike up a conversation. She didn't want to try too hard and come off as a detective asking so many questions about her life, so she treaded lightly.

"Cassandra…want to help me in the kitchen with dessert?" Mrs. Reeler asked. Cassandra looked down at her kids who were now watching a cartoon Mr. Reeler turned on for them on the television. She saw that they were content.

"Sure," she stated as she stood up to follow her into the kitchen. Mrs. Reeler walked over to the stove to pull out a warm apple pie. She placed it on the counter to cool off.

"Would you like anything else to drink?" Cassandra, sitting on the edge of the one of the stools, politely declined. Mrs. Reeler pulled out a bottle of red wine from the wine holder and poured herself a glass. She took a sip and proceeded to speak after gently placing the glass back down on the countertop. She decided now's the time to get out what she's been wanting to say for some time now.

"I'm sure you probably…hate me. What I did was awful, and I beat myself up about it every day." Cassandra put her head down because she didn't want Mrs. Reeler to see the anger in her eyes but took a deep breath and responded looking Mrs. Reeler directly in the eyes.

"When you changed your number that day, it wasn't you that I hated. It was Joe. I thought he was behind it and didn't want anything to do with me. I just lost my mom and was lonely and depressed. When you shut me out like that, I went into a deep depression and almost took my life. I found out the man I thought was my dad was not my real dad then my mom tells me some stranger I didn't even know was my dad. On top of all of that, I was having serious issues in my relationship with my kids' father and on the verge of losing my job. It was the worst time of my life. I guess what I'm saying is when you make a decision to intentionally hurt someone, sometimes it's a matter of life and death." Mrs. Reeler's heart sank as Cassandra spoke. If she felt bad before, she felt even worse now.

"You're absolutely right. At the time, I didn't even consider you or your feelings." Mrs. Reeler began to tear up as she held her hand over her mouth. Cassandra shook her head.

"Look, I don't want you to take pity on me...I just want you to know the damage you caused." Mrs. Reeler looked down at her half-empty glass with the worst look on her face. She walked around the counter to Cassandra and gave her a big hug.

"Please forgive me...I want to start over again from today." With tears in her eyes, Cassandra laid her head on Mrs. Reeler's shoulder and released built-up tears. The hurt and pain she felt over the years finally came to the surface.

"I forgive you. I forgive you," Cassandra repeated. Mrs. Reeler held Cassandra's head, and they cried and sorrowed together. Mr. Reeler happened to walk in and took in the moment. He laid his head onto Cassandra's upper back and grabbed her hand, and they all cried in unison.

1ST BIRTHDAY BASH

"Babe, everyone will be here soon. Is everything in order down there?" Derek yelled from the top of the stairs. Derek still lived in his condo but was back and forth between the house and his place until his lease was up. He spent the night to help Shaniece prepare for the party but ended up oversleeping and was rushing to get himself and Tyler ready. Shaniece was putting last-minute touches on everything.

"Yes, hun, everything is under control. You two just get dressed!" Shaniece yelled back.

Around two o'clock, their guests started to arrive, and Shaniece's mom was among the first to be there. Shaniece was happy that her mom had finally gotten over what Derek did to her. She had to explain that she couldn't help her feelings and had to follow her heart. Her mom wasn't thrilled about the idea but had to respect Shaniece's decision. Shaniece knew her mom would be the hardest to convince because when her dad messed up, her mom kicked him to the curve and put him out the house. She wasn't a three-strike-rule kind of woman. She didn't think her mom would show up to the party. It was her first time in Derek's presence since the day he came to the house when she was ready to slay him with a kitchen knife. Shaniece laughed to herself thinking about what happened because her mom was not playing with him that day. Not long after her mother arrived, Marcus, who was now Tyler's godfather, walked in with Natalie. Shaniece could see the glow on them. Things were looking up in paradise from what she could see, as she heard that they were now engaged. She didn't know Natalie too much but knew she wasn't going nowhere so they had plenty of time to get better acquainted.

"Hey, sis!" Shaniece knew that voice no matter where she was. She turned around to see that Karina had arrived with bags of designer gifts.

"Girl, what is up with all these designer bags?" Shaniece asked, shaking her head.

"Girl, you know godmom always have to show up and show out. I got both of my godsons something. Who knows the next time I'll see them?"

Shaniece and Derek had asked Karina if she would be the godmother of Tyler after they got back together. Karina was a little hesitant due to the circumstances but agreed to be his godmother regardless. Karina was ecstatic about Junior just like everyone else was, and when Shaniece lost him, she felt the same pain. It was like a child was taken from her too. She felt she had no choice but to give the same energy when it came to Tyler. After all, Shaniece was her best friend and sister, and she couldn't let her down.

"Well too bad you won't see Justin today because he's away on a college tour trip." Karina stopped in her tracks playfully holding her hand to her chest.

"Oh, Lord, I'm getting old. My baby is going to college." Shaniece couldn't believe it herself. She was proud of her son – especially since he grew up to be a fine young man. At the same time, Shaniece couldn't shake off knowing that Justin wasn't completely onboard with her getting back with Derek. When she first told him about the situation, he was upset with her about Derek returning, but he realized that she had a right to be happy. If his mom wanted to forgive Derek, she had that right to. His relationship with Derek wasn't like it was before, but he still grew to respect him again.

The great thing was that it actually didn't take much for Tyler to grow on Justin. When he saw him for the first time, Tyler lit up and stuck his hands out for Justin to pick him up. Justin would play with him making funny faces and doing character voices while Tyler would giggle hysterically. Shaniece and Derek would get a kick out of it because he only laughed like that when Justin was around.

The doorbell rang, and this time it was Shaniece's in-laws. Shaniece lit up when she saw the Reelers but then remembered that Jeffrey and Morgan couldn't be there. She was used to Morgan helping out at family functions, and it was odd not having her around.

"Hey, Mom; hey, Dad," Shaniece stated as she hugged both while walking in.

"You guys did an excellent job with this Mickey Mouse theme. It looks like Disney World in here." Mr. Reeler joked and complimented at the same time.

"Thanks, Dad. You know the same guy who planned our wedding helped me with the party, but I'm thinking maybe he went a little over the top." Her father-in-law looked at her, smirking.

"You think?" They all laughed as they looked around at all the decorations, food, and big Mickey Mouse cake sitting on its own table in the back of the kitchen. Mr. Reeler's phone rang, and he walked outside while answering it. A few moments later, he walked back in with Cassandra and the kids. Shaniece immediately walked over, stuck out her hand, and introduced herself.

"This is my daughter-in-law that I told you about, Cassandra," Mr. Reeler stated as he patted Shaniece on the back.

"Good to meet you. Your house is so pretty…" Cassandra noted. She was hoping her facial expression didn't give away the fact that she had never been in a house as beautiful as hers, but it was the truth.

"Thank you, Cassandra. Trust me it took us some time to get here. And are these your babies? They are so precious!" Shaniece remarked.

"Thank you so much," Cassandra replied, beaming with pride. Mr. Reeler grabbed both Mikayla and Myron by the hand and walked them into the family room, which had been turned into a play area filled with Disney toys, balloons, and a bouncer. Shaniece and Derek had also hired some actors and actresses to perform as Disney Characters, who greeted Myron and Mikayla at the entryway. A few minutes later, Shaniece's college friends also showed up with their little ones. Everyone pretty much knew the situation and accepted Tyler as if he was Shaniece's child.

Finally, after thirty minutes, Derek walked down with Tyler in his arms. When he reached the bottom step, he put him down, and little Tyler took off running towards the balloons. Shaniece jumped in front of him and picked him up.

"Don't you look handsome? Give me some kisses," she stated as she kissed all over his rosy red cheeks. She put him down, but Mrs. Reeler, Karina, and Ms. Brown swooped him up one at a time to love on him some more. By the time he got to Grandma Brown, he was ready to break loose and head to the playroom where he saw Mickey Mouse singing to the kids.

Derek entered the living room and listened to the multiple conversations going on in the room. He realized there was one person he didn't know and figured out who she was. "Hi, you must be Cassandra," he said as he walked over to her. "I'm Derek, Joe's youngest son."

"Hello, Derek. Nice to meet you," she replied while reaching her hand out for a handshake. Derek took her hand and shook it, nodding once to make her feel welcome. He then turned away and listened as Karina shared that she would be moving to New York in a few weeks and opening her own publishing company. Shaniece also talked about how she had gained over ten new clients for her business during the last three months. Everyone was excited about all of the good news; however, Cassandra just smiled and kept quiet. Mrs. Reeler saw behind her awkward smile and knew she was feeling out of place.

"Well, it's no longer a secret to everyone that Cassandra is now part of the family. She forgave me and let's just say that I'm one happy camper." Shaniece looked over at her mother-in-law because she didn't understand why she would bring up the subject now, especially at a kid's birthday party. Cassandra had the same look on her face. She met eyes with Shaniece, who looked at her apologetically and mouthed "I'm sorry."

Derek didn't want to get caught in the middle of another awkward moment, so he immediately left the room of women and walked into the play area to tend to the birthday boy. A few minutes later, the doorbell rang again. Derek walked to the door and greeted Melanie, her husband, their son, and Mrs. Nixon, Melanie's mother.

"Hey, Melanie. Hey, Aaron. Hiiiii Mrs. Nixon. Glad you guys were able to make it," Derek stated as he completely opened the door to let them in.

"You know we wouldn't miss this," Melanie stated. Shaniece walked into the foyer to greet them as well.

"Hey, Melanie. Thank you for coming." Shaniece always respected Melanie because she was a smart and educated woman. However, when she first started dating Derek, she wasn't too fond of her. Whenever Derek had a personal or business problem, he always called on Melanie. Shaniece finally shared her feelings with him one day and told him that she wanted to be the first one he called, not Melanie, whenever he needed help. After finding out about the way she felt, he respected her wishes and would call her first and when needed reached out to Melanie as a backup. Shaniece was okay with that as long as she was considered. After that, Shaniece grew to be more comfortable with her and didn't mind her being around.

Shaniece directed the family to the play area and little Nicholas ran in to join the other kids. An hour later, while prepping to cut the cake, Shaniece heard the doorbell ring once again. Shaniece walked to the door and saw a very light-skinned, heavyset, older woman standing on the other side. "Hello. I'm Ms. Sanders, Danita's mother," the woman mentioned.

Shaniece took the time to catch her breath because she was very surprised to see her. Three weeks prior, Derek had asked Shaniece how she would feel if he reached out to Danita's mother. He explained the situation and stated he wanted his son to know someone from his mother's bloodline too. Shaniece was initially hesitant but then agreed with his decision. When he called, she had no idea that her daughter passed or had a baby. She was heartbroken, and Derek wished he had the opportunity to break the news to her face to face. However, she lived in North Carolina, so it wasn't possible at the time. Still, even though he knew it was short notice, he offered her an invitation to Tyler's first birthday party. He offered to buy her a plane ticket, but she declined. She told him she would get back to him but never did.

190

"Well, thank you so much for coming. Please--come in," Shaniece stated as she began to open the door even more. Ms. Sanders stopped her.

"Well, my niece is parking the car. She'll be walking up soon. I just want to wait for her." Shaniece was even more surprised because she wasn't expecting Ms. Sanders, let alone someone else. She was used to doing things in order and being prepared ahead of time, but this time around she had to ad-lib as she went along.

"Oh, yes, no problem," Shaniece stated. Derek walked up to check on his wife because she was at the door longer than expected. Shaniece turned around and bumped into him.

"Honey, I was just about to come get you. This is Danita's mother, Ms. Sanders. She and...I'm sorry, what's your niece's name?" Shaniece looked at Ms. Sanders.

"Oh! Keisha," she advised. Shaniece went on to finish her sentence.

"Ms. Sanders and her niece, Keisha, decided to come to see Tyler for his birthday." Derek put on a fake smile because he didn't know what to do. He hadn't heard from her until she showed up at the door, so there was no warning about what to expect if she decided to come.

"Well, welcome, Ms. Sanders. We're glad that you could make it." She smiled and stuck out her hand to greet him.

"I know it's quite a surprise, but honestly I hustled up a ride last minute. I accidentally deleted your number from my phone so I couldn't call. I still had your address written down so when my niece agreed to drive me, I packed my suitcase, and here I am." By the time she finished her sentence, Keisha had finally walked up. Shaniece was caught off guard because she favored Danita. She didn't want to look at her in disgust and take out what her cousin did behind her back, but the resemblance was shocking.

"Hi, Keisha. I'm Shaniece, and this is my husband, Derek." Keisha smiled and shook both of their hands.

On the ride there, Ms. Sanders updated Keisha about all that she knew. They both wanted answers and closure from Derek, and he felt the same way. They all walked into the living room together, even though it was awkward to have walked into a house full of family and close friends. Derek decided to just put it out there. He really didn't have a choice at this point.

"Hello, everyone. This is Ms. Sanders, Tyler's other grandma, and this is Keisha, her niece." Derek tried not to look into the direction of his mother because he didn't want to see her face. Everyone in the room greeted them, and Derek offered them food and something to drink as he walked into the kitchen. While sitting at the table, Derek left and went to the playroom to get Tyler. He walked back in a few minutes later, and both Keisha and Ms. Sanders dropped their forks when they laid their eyes on him.

"Wow…he looks just like Jesse…except lighter," were the first words out of Ms. Sanders' mouth.

"He does, Aunt Cheryl. He looks just like Uncle Jesse." Derek was confused at this point. He just smiled as he watched Tyler's grandmother hold him on her lap.

"If you don't mind me asking, but is Uncle Jesse…Danita's father?" Derek asked. Ms. Sanders looked up at him.

"Yes, he is. Tyler looks just like him." Derek was glad that he could make sense of Tyler's looks. He finally got the answer he needed. Keisha and Ms. Sanders sat in the kitchen playing, kissing, cuddling, and taking pics with Tyler. Twenty minutes later, everyone surrounded the table to sing "Happy Birthday." Everyone watched and laughed as the birthday boy struggled to blow out his candles. Both Shaniece and Derek helped him out. Derek picked up a piece of cake and gently smashed it in his face, and everyone laughed except for Tyler. He cried and cried until he was all cleaned up. For the remainder of the party, everyone mingled, ate, took lots of pictures, and watched as the kids ran around.

* * * * * *

After close to three hours, guests started to leave. The only people who were left were family, Cassandra, her children, Ms. Sanders, and Keisha. Cassandra and Shaniece ended up talking for a long time. They exchanged numbers and agreed to do coffee in the upcoming days. Shaniece liked her vibe and saw a piece of the old her in Cassandra and wanted to help in any way possible if she let her.

Shaniece's mother, mother-in-law, and Ms. Sanders were in a corner of the family room, finally able to talk more privately.

"I'm sorry; I didn't get your first name," Mrs. Reeler asked as she leaned toward Ms. Sanders.

"Cheryl. My name is Cheryl." Mrs. Reeler nodded her head and straightened back up in her chair.

"Well, Cheryl, I'm sure I can speak for most of us that we were all surprised today, but I want to say that I'm glad that I'm able to meet you. Tyler has three grandmothers now. You can't tell me that baby not blessed." Ms. Sanders smiled and nodded her head in agreement.

"Yes, he is. I'm happy that I could see him. He's my one and only grandbaby."

"You know what? Tyler is the first grandchild for all three of us when you think about it." Mrs. Reeler went on to say.

"Well, not my first but the first baby in the family in over seventeen years," Shaniece's mom interjected. She knew Tyler didn't come from her bloodline but accepted the fact that he was now part of the family. Mrs. Reeler then thought about it and corrected herself.

"It's quite possible Mikayla and Myron could possibly be my first grandchildren...."

"Point taken," Ms. Brown stated and halted the conversation there. The three women changed the subject and talked about life and all that it had to offer.

* * * * * *

Once everything was cleaned up, Shaniece flopped down on the couch. Before she knew it, she woke up two hours later and found Derek on the other end of the couch holding Tyler, patting him on his back to keep him sleeping.

"Well, hey, sleepyhead," Derek whispered. Shaniece yawned and sat up, smiling at him.

"Hey…I didn't realize I was that tired. I guess it was that great of a birthday party." Derek laughed quietly and stood up.

"It was, babe. You pulled it off again," Derek stated as he walked toward the steps with Tyler sleeping on his chest. Shaniece got up too and stuck her hand out looking for a high-five as she walked beside him.

"Yes, *we* did. We pulled it off as usual."

SAY IT AIN'T SO

"Hey, Charlie. It's me, Joe. How you doing, man?" Mr. Reeler asked his long-time friend. He and Charlie Jones grew up together and had known each other for close to fifty years now.

"Hey, Joe. What's going on, man? I'm surprised to hear from you." Mr. Reeler had to admit that he wasn't good with staying in contact with his buddies. If they didn't live within the neighborhood, then he spoke to them maybe once or twice a year.

"I'm doing good. I can't complain…it's been a while." Mr. Reeler went on to say.

"I know, man; it has. Things are same-ole-same-ole on my end." Mr. Reeler knew something was up. If Charlie was having problems, he always used the same line.

"C'mon, man, spill it. It's me you talking to." Charlie kept denying that anything was wrong and told him that he was fine. Mr. Reeler didn't push the issue any further.

"Alright, whatever you say. Hey, I did have a question for you. Remember Gloria from back in the day? The one we met at the parties they used to have downtown?" He wanted to see if Charlie remembered any details that he may not have remembered from back then.

"Yeah, party-girl Gloria. How could I forget her? But why the heck you asking about her?"

"I just found out she passed."

"Oh, wow…I'm sorry to hear that…I just can't hear nothing else about another death. Too many to count lately."

"Yeah. It's just crazy. She was always around when we used to go those parties."

"Yeahhh I remember. Not to speak bad on the dead but heard she got around back then. I didn't believe it until she pulled that stunt like she did." Mr. Reeler pressed his phone closer to his ear.

"I wasn't the only one she had been with at the time?" he asked naively.

"Nah, man… I remember that you and Georgie both had her that night at William's house party but why you asking about that, though? Your wife found out or something? Let me guess she had a child and now you have to pay up?" Charlie laughed out loud at his own joke. Mr. Reeler's heart dropped because Charlie had almost guessed the situation correctly. To not show any suspicion, Mr. Reeler sucked his teeth.

"Man, none of the above. When I found out she passed, I couldn't help my mind from going back down memory lane. I just didn't know about Georgie though." Charlie laughed.

"Well, after you left from getting yours, an hour later, she was in the back having sex with Georgie. I rode with him that night, and he talked about her the entire ride home. I'll never forget it because he wouldn't shut up about her. He met up with her a few times after that too. She would ask Georgie about you, but you was afraid of your wife and ditched us and wouldn't party with us no more." That was all he wanted to hear. He didn't want to be reminded about that night anymore, so he cut the conversation short.

"Charlie, you something else, man. Listen, how about we meet up for drinks or something and include Georgie too, like old times?"

"Georgie might not join us...he's strung out on those drugs. Haven't seen him in over a year, but I heard through the grapevine that he still not doing good. Good luck with finding him, but I'm down for it." Mr. Reeler scratched his head trying to figure out what to do.

"You know where he be at?"

"The last I heard he lived in the projects in Green Lake. I'm not sure if he's there no more though, but then again where would he go?" Mr. Reeler got off the subject of Georgie and wanted to catch up with Charlie some more. They talked briefly about family, children, and grandchildren before hanging up, but Mr. Reeler didn't mention anything to Charlie about Cassandra.

* * * * * *

A week had passed, and Mr. Reeler couldn't help but to think about his conversation with Charlie. He knew he needed to get a paternity test to find out if Cassandra was his. He wanted and needed to know for sure. He didn't tell anyone about what Charlie told him, and he didn't want to plant any seeds into anyone's head. He called Cassandra up for small talk but really to talk about getting a test done.

"Hey, daughter," he greeted.

"Hey, Dad. What's up?" Cassandra responded. He could hear her smiling through the phone. He didn't want to crush her spirit, but if he didn't put out that he wanted to get the test done early on, he would never go through with it. Cassandra went on to tell him how she enjoyed meeting everyone at the party. She bragged about Shaniece, how she admired her, and how they had plans to meet up at the coffee shop. He heard her talking but could only respond "That's good" because he only heard every other word. After she finished speaking, he finally told her the reason for the call.

"Cassandra, I consider you my daughter and Mikayla and Myron my grandkids already, but don't you want to know for sure? I think we both need closure...it's owed to us." Cassandra was quiet on the other line because she was on cloud nine and felt like he had just knocked her down. She knew they would eventually need to discuss it but wasn't prepared to do so at the time.

"Well…I have a right to know and you have a right to know…so…when will we find out?" she asked directly.

"Well, I wanted to see what schedule worked best for you. We should go to a lab and get swabbed…I can call and set up an appointment."

"Just set up an appointment, let me know, and I'll be there." Her tone was totally different now; he wished he never asked or brought up getting the paternity test.

"Okay, I'll call you a little later or tomorrow and let you know." Mr. Reeler hung up the phone feeling worse than he did from when he hung up after talking to Charlie. The joy he felt the past few weeks was now starting to escape him.

* * * * * *

Mr. Reeler's thoughts were racing as he thought back to the day of the testing. Two weeks ago, he and Cassandra arrived at the lab to get swabbed. He trusted the lab more than swabbing himself. In his mind, the accuracy of the results would be more believable. Cassandra had no doubt in her mind that he was her father. She was ready to get the results and for everyone to be happy once and for all. Mr. Reeler wanted nothing more than for Cassandra to be his daughter, but according to Charlie, that could be untrue. He didn't know what other men her mother may have been with at the time besides Georgie and himself, so his doubts were starting to increase. After everything was done, they embraced then left the office praying that the results would come back in their favor.

A week later he and Mrs. Reeler were sitting on the couch staring at the envelope with the results that just arrived in the mail. Before opening the envelope, they prayed over it and asked God for the outcome to have been what they wanted.

"You ready to open it now?" Mrs. Reeler asked. Mr. Reeler looked down at the envelope and grabbed it off the living room table without saying a word. He opened it up, and they both read the results together.

"Noo, nooo, nooo! Please tell me this isn't so!" Mr. Reeler yelled out. He couldn't believe the results came back that Cassandra wasn't his daughter. He wished he never pursued it and left things how they were. Mrs. Reeler had her hand over her mouth, and for the first time she didn't know what to say. She didn't try holding back her tears and allowed them to fall down her cheeks and soak into her blouse. Mr. Reeler sat there repeating, "This can't, this can't be!" He decided to call Cassandra once he calmed down, but she answered on the first ring, bawling her eyes out as she saw the results just a few hours before.

"I'm sorry! I'm sorry! My mom…my mom told me you were my father. I didn't know!" Mr. Reeler tried to interject to tell her to stop apologizing, but he couldn't get past her screaming and sobbing. Mrs. Reeler could hear Cassandra freaking out over the phone, and the pain cut her like a knife. Mr. Reeler put his own emotions to the side for the moment. He knew he had to be strong for both women and tried his best to hold it together.

WHAT A DIFFERENCE A YEAR MAKES

Cassandra felt bad about how the results turned out. She thought hard and tried to figure out why her mom would tell her Joe was her father. She decided not to pursue her real father; she didn't have any real leads. She decided to shift her focus elsewhere and started pursuing a new career. Cassandra went back to nursing school after Shaniece motivated her to go. They had become close, hanging out at least once or twice a month. As they both shared their stories over time and realized they had much in common, the women agreed that it was time for Cassandra to do something for herself. She was happy with her life now and felt how things played out was part of God's plan.

After they found out the truth, Mrs. Reeler told her husband that Cassandra was a part of the family now, despite the fact that she was not his biological child. After all she went through, she just couldn't leave her out to dry. While Cassandra was in class, Mrs. Reeler kept an eye on Mikayla and Myron at least twice a week and would sometimes fix dinner for Cassandra and the children when Cassandra had long days. She felt like she owed her for shutting her out so many years ago, and she worked on building a relationship like the ones she shared with her daughters-in-law.

Mr. Reeler couldn't get himself to tell Cassandra that he had knowledge of who her real father could be. He drove through Green Lake looking for Georgie, and there was no sign of him. He finally met up with Charlie for beers and learned that Georgie had been doing good until he lost his wife a few years back. He didn't know how to cope without her and turned to drugs and alcohol. To him, Cassandra had been through enough and having a father who was strung out wasn't something she needed to deal with. He knew it was selfish to make that decision for her, but it was a risk he was willing to take. He thought how ironic it was that he was mad at his wife for keeping the same secret, and now he was in her shoes doing the same thing.

* * * * * *

"Melanie, I need you in my office for a moment," Derek requested. Derek's business finally took off and was recognized in the newspaper as one of the small businesses in the city that was on the horizon toward remarkable success. After the article was published, his client base increased tremendously. He had to hire a few more employees to keep up with the volume.

Melanie waddled into the room, barely able to walk, and sat in her usual chair.

"Sir, I'm ready," she told him with a pen and pad in her hand, propping it up on her belly.

"Melanie, I don't know why you're still working. You're eight months and about to pop. You don't have to work up until your due date." Melanie chuckled.

"I told you. I'm not letting no one else fill that seat. We both know what happened the last time." Derek looked at her, and they both laughed. Melanie looked so uncomfortable, but he couldn't make her stop working if her doctor didn't demand it. She even agreed to work from home as a virtual assistant once she was out on leave. Derek was happy to have Melanie in his life. Not only was she a good employee, she was a good friend too. She helped him out in his time of need, and he could never thank her enough for all that she'd done.

* * * * * *

"I can't believe it. I'm a married man. Who would've known?" Marcus stated with pride. Derek and Marcus met up at the bar once he and Natalie returned from Jamaica. Derek couldn't believe they eloped.

"Man, I'm still mad not even Shaniece and I were invited. You needed at least one witness to be there," Derek joked. Marcus didn't want to go through all the stress of having a big wedding. He wanted to go and get it over with. He knew he could've invited Shaniece and Derek, but he wanted to keep it simple and a personal intimate moment for him and his wife to enjoy. Derek and Marcus talked about the wedding and married life.

"So, what about kids? Tyler needs a play buddy," Derek asked. Marcus shook his head back and forth.

"Nooo, man we don't want no kids. We're okay with Tyler."

Derek remembered Marcus telling him that before but thought he would've changed his mind once he got married. He didn't understand how a couple didn't want to have at least one to carry on the family legacy. However, Derek respected his decision and realized that every couple is different when it comes to life goals. Besides, after what he had been through, he couldn't knock another couple's decision about anything.

Before the wedding, Marcus called and thanked Mr. Reeler for allowing him to see the changes he needed to make in his life. He loved Natalie but knew he was taking advantage of her and could possibly lose her forever. He didn't realize the blessing he had in his life until that day at the lake when Mr. Reeler let him have it. Instead of taking offense, he did something about it. He still respected Mr. Reeler's words even after he heard about what happened with Cassandra and the cheating. He didn't judge Mr. Reeler for his mistake because he had cheated on Natalie so much in their relationship early on that he understood temptation well. He didn't know the full story but figured Mr. Reeler was faced with temptation one night when things weren't going right in his marriage, and he caved in. He just didn't know the repercussions it would bring later down the line. Marcus ended up making a promise to himself that he would be completely faithful to his wife. After seeing the damage that infidelity caused in both Derek's and Mr. Reeler's lives, he decided to learn from all of the mistakes and be a one-woman man.

* * * * * *

"Jeffrey, I can't wait until you and Morgan come home next month. I'm counting down the days," Mrs. Reeler stated with excitement. Jeffrey and Morgan had been in Thailand for a little over a year now. Jeffrey was doing extremely well with work and picked up additional contracts. Morgan loved working for the private school she was stationed at too.

"Mom, we're excited too. We really miss you guys. We're happy here, but it's nothing like having family around, I tell you." Mrs. Reeler had never gotten used to the change. She loved her son so much, and only being able to see him once a year was not what she wanted. Her husband would catch her crying every now and then and when he asked what was wrong, she always mentioned Jeffrey and Morgan. He missed them too, but he also knew that Jeffrey was his own man and had to live his life on his own terms. If moving to another country was deemed fit for Jeffrey, then he had no choice but to accept it.

"How's Morgan coping? Did she make any friends?" Jeffrey laughed because his mom was doing her usual. She had to know about everyone and everything.

"Yes, Mom; she hangs out with some of the teachers down at the school. She really likes it here. I know her and Shaniece talk at least once a week. Sometimes they are on the phone for hours." Mrs. Reeler was glad to know that she was happy and didn't make the move just because her son wanted to. Jeffrey loved his mom dearly but knew by now she would never change.

* * * * * *

Karina moved to New York with her soon-to-be husband and opened her publishing company a few months back. Shaniece and Derek attended her grand opening then and were finally able to meet the love of her life. Derek and Lonnie hit it off right away. Shaniece wasn't completely head over heels about him, but if he was the man her best friend was going to marry, she had no choice but to be on board. Shaniece thought he was somewhat controlling. She felt Karina was making all the life changes, but he wasn't giving up anything. Shaniece knew how much Karina loved Atlanta and knew she didn't really want to leave. She lived there for years, and most of her fan base lived there too. When she revealed she was moving to New York, Shaniece was completely surprised.

"Shaniiieeeece, I don't know why I can't fit my dress. I bought it two months ago, and I could fit it then. My wedding is less than a month away, and I'm freaking out," Karina whined. Shaniece laughed as Karina vented to her about the smallest things. After what she had been through the last few years, she didn't make a big deal out of much of anything anymore. If it wasn't there to kill her, she just let it go and didn't worry about it.

"Girl, you still have time to hit the treadmill. If all else fails, just put on some Spanx and call it a day. Stop stressing about it." Karina wished she was face-to-face with Shaniece so she could throw a shoe at her head.

"Okay, Mrs. 'I Have a Killer Body.' Not everyone has time to hit the gym every day like you." The last thing Shaniece wanted to do was offend her.

"Oh, Karina, stop it. We both know you have the better body," Shaniece lied. Karina knew Shaniece was trying to make her feel better but accepted the compliment.

Shaniece was the matron of honor and was all ready for the wedding. She hadn't been to a wedding since her own or out dancing since her honeymoon. She was ready to let her hair down and enjoy herself. She couldn't wait to spend a weekend away in New York in just a few more weeks.

* * * * * *

"Would you guys stop crying? I'm going to be okay," Justin promised. Shaniece, Derek, and Tyler were all standing outside of Justin's dorm with him. He had decided to attend Penn State; he received multiple scholarships but felt Penn State was his best choice. A few of his buddies were accepted there too, so Shaniece was for sure that was his determining factor.

"Justin, I can't believe you are leaving me! You don't understand how hard this is," Shaniece told him in and out of tears. Justin looked at his mom, and at that moment he knew he had to make her proud. Within a few moments, he thought back about their journey over the years and knew he had to keep the success torch rolling. His mom put in so much effort and sacrificed so much for him that he had no choice but to be great. He looked at Derek tearing up and hugged him.

"Take care of my mom," Justin told him as he hugged him goodbye. Derek respected Justin and knew he disappointed him in the past but was going to be the best role model for him moving forward. Justin could have held a grudge against Derek and never welcomed him back into his life. That was mainly because he knew half of the story about Shaniece and Derek's relationship and judged from his own point of view. Justin didn't know about his mother cheating too, but Derek was willing to be the scapegoat for it all. He would never jeopardize Shaniece's reputation in the eyes of her son no matter what. His intent was to always protect her through every situation even though the actions involved were wrong.

Justin squatted down, looked at Tyler, and patted his head.

"I'm going to miss you, little guy." Tyler looked up at Justin with his big, bright eyes and quickly pinched his nose.

"Ouch! What you do that for?" Tyler started giggling nonstop. Shaniece and Derek laughed too.

"Look what you taught him -- now he doing it to you," Shaniece mentioned as she grabbed Tyler by his hand. Justin stood up holding his nose.

"I taught him well. That's my little homie." They all laughed as they headed toward the car. Justin hugged everyone goodbye again before heading back to his dorm. Shaniece sat idle with the window down until she no longer could see him in sight.

* * * * * *

"Who would've ever thought that all the hurt and pain we've experienced these last few years would lead us here?" Shaniece said as she sat at the kitchen island, watching Derek cook dinner for the evening. Considering everything that had gone on with her, Derek, and their relationship, she learned her lesson and would never cheat again. She would walk away from him before she would allow that to happen. She knew Derek was her soulmate, and it was meant for them to be together.

"I know. I was thinking about it myself. What I learned is that no matter what you do behind closed doors, it will always come to light sooner or later. At some point, everyone's exposed," he responded. Derek didn't only learn his lesson from his failures but from his father's as well. He made a vow to himself and to Shaniece that he would never cheat again. He loved his son and considered him a blessing, but if he had a chance to make the same choices again, he wouldn't have allowed temptation and sex to control him. Every day, he woke up still upset with himself for hurting Shaniece the way he did. He thought that he was protecting her by not telling her about Danita, but in reality, it made things worse. He knew a woman of her caliber deserved the best, and he had to put in more effort to make her happy. He tried his best to become a better man and father daily.

After dinner, they sat in the living room lounging around before heading up to bed. Shaniece looked at Tyler nodding off on the couch barely watching his cartoons. She picked him up and walked him upstairs to his room. He was two years old now, and he definitely kept them on their toes, but Shaniece loved him so much. She was finally able to admit to herself that she was happy Tyler was in her life. She closed his door, leaving it open slightly so she and Derek could hear him whenever he woke up.

"What movie do you want to watch?" Derek asked after Shaniece entered the bedroom. Shaniece climbed up on the bed, picking up the bowl of popcorn that Derek had sat on the bed for her.

"It doesn't matter. Whatever you want to watch," she stated with a mouthful. Derek flicked through the channels to see if anything good was on.

"What's wrong with this stupid remote? It's always getting stuck." Derek flipped it over and took the batteries out trying to get it to work. Shaniece looked up at the TV and noticed that it had stopped on the Baby Channel. She started laughing hysterically. Derek looked over at her, confused.

"What's so funny?" he asked.

Shaniece shook her head and continued laughing holding her chest. Derek didn't get it. He thought, *Oh no, she's losing it.* He finally got the batteries in and attempted to change the channel, but it still wouldn't work. Shaniece finally stopped laughing and asked for him to hand her the remote. He gave it up without a problem because he was losing his patience and ready to throw it across the room. He looked up at the TV and saw a very pregnant woman on the screen. He looked over at Shaniece.

"Babe, seriously what's going on?" he asked. Shaniece turned and looked him in the eyes.

"We're pregnant." Derek sat there for a few seconds in shock.

"Are you serious? Stop playing!" he yelled out excitedly. He looked at her face and saw that she wasn't joking around. He jumped out the bed and started dancing around the room like a madman. He went from doing the Carlton to doing the Michael Jackson moonwalk. Shaniece couldn't stop laughing at his reaction; she couldn't have been any happier.

* * * * * *

Shaniece thought about how everything happened like a chain reaction; from every mistake came a blessing. When she lost Junior, she couldn't imagine life getting any better for her; she was ready to hibernate and shut love out forever. She experienced so much joy because of what God did for her and witnessed through her own story of how he was the master of taking a mess and working it together for her good. God gave her everything she wanted and needed even if she didn't realize it at the time. She was living quite the fairytale -- not the one she dreamed of, but the one that was meant and written just for her.

Let's Stay Connected!

 Dismantled Hearts
@authoressj.henrybooks

www.ingramcontent.com/pod-product-compliance
Lightning Source LLC
Chambersburg PA
CBHW051824020726
47502CB00005B/1611